Published by the

Walmsley Society

www.walmsleysoc.org

Leo Walmsley

FOREIGNERS

LEO WALMSLEY

Walmsley Society

First published in 1935 by Jonathan Cape

Published in 2008 by
The Walmsley Society
www.walmsleysoc.org

This edition published 2020

ISBN 978-0-9534449-5-3

British Library Cataloguing-in-Publication Data:
A catalogue record is available for this book
from the British Library.

Printed and bound by
Catford Print Centre
London

For
Jerry, Ann and
Henrietta

BOOK ONE

I

MOTHER WOKE ME up, shouting from the foot of the attic stairs that it was nearly half-past eight, that breakfast was cooking, that I mustn't be late for school; that she wasn't going downstairs until she heard me moving about (there was another flight of stairs to the living-room), and that if she didn't hear me soon she'd have to come up and pull the covers off the bed. I shouted back "all right," I was up, and I reached out of bed for a stick I kept handy, thrust the end of it into one of my boots, and made a shuffling noise with it on the bare floor boards, so that she'd think it was me moving. She shouted that I must on no account go back to bed again, and that I must wash the back of my neck and not leave a tidemark, and then she went down to the living-room. I pulled the covers over my head, for the skylight was open, and the morning was very cold, and I started thinking.

I thought first of Grab Fosdyck, and his brother Len, and the thrashing I'd given Len on the shore yesterday afternoon. Grab, who carried out for Thompson, the grocer, after school hours, had been away with his mother to Sunderland to see his father "on board ship". He would be back at school this morning. Yesterday afternoon, from a hiding place in the South Cliff, I had watched Len (acting for his brother) on his way to Garry Mill with a basket of groceries. The other village lads were playing football on a patch of sand near the coastguard's wall, Kid Fosdyck, Len's twin brother, among them. But I took no risks. I shadowed Len, hiding among the clumps of whin and bramble that grew almost to the shore, and I waited for him at Garry Nab while he went to the mill on his errand. The Nab jutted out from the cliff, hiding the beck and the cove and the mill from the north. Soon I heard Len whistling, and then his footsteps on the hard scaur, and I stepped out and met him face to face.

I had a score to settle. Twice in a week I had been forced to fight the Fosdyck twins, with Grab himself looking on, ready to join in if I'd shown any sign of winning. Last time, Kid, by Grab's orders, had got behind me and held my arms, while Len had rained blow after blow on my unprotected face. My nose and lips were bleeding. I was blind with tears, choking with rage and shame, but I had shouted at Len, "Wait till I get you by yourself and I'll kill you." And Grab had said, "Give him another for that, Len, he's nowt but a bloody foreigner. I'll kill *him* if he ever touches *you*." And Len had given me another.

I could still feel the smart of those blows as I faced Len; and that was nothing to the memory of the shame I had felt at the taunts of the other lads, egged on by Grab and the twins.

"Eh! Look at him blubbing!"

"Look at his nose bleeding!"

"That'll larn him!"

"Look at his starched collar! Look at his velvet trousers. Bloody foreigner!"

"Look at him blubbing like a lass!"

Len looked frightened. He had stopped, tightly hugging the basket under his arm. We were a mile from the village. The shore was deserted. He knew I was going to hide him. He said, blustering.

"If you touch me I'll tell our Tom. He'll be back from Sunderland tomorrow. I'll tell Mr Thompson too. This is his basket, remember. I'll tell him you've interfered with me on an errand. If you lay hands on me our Tom will kill you."

Tom was Grab, but Grab was in Sunderland. I asked Len if he would fight.

"I don't want to fight," he answered. "I'm on an errand for Mr Thompson, and you'll get into a row if you touch me. He told me to hurry back. I've got to go up to the Station Hotel with something important."

I didn't wait any longer. I took the basket from him because I didn't want to get into trouble with Mr Thompson, then I gave Len a light touch with my hand on one ear, and then on his cheek, saying as I did so the rhyme that Bramblewick boys always said when they were starting a fight,

"Here's yan on thy lug, here's yan on thy mug ..."

And then, with a light blow on his chest,

"And here's yan to start with."

The fight began. It was soon over, for Len was so used to having Kid to help him, and Grab to egg him on, he wasn't much use without them. Besides he must have known that he deserved to be beaten, while I knew that I had right on my side, even if I was disobeying Mother's rule that I must never fight except to protect myself or a weaker boy. I made his nose bleed, and slightly blacked one of his eyes. I picked up his basket for him, and he walked blubbing along the shore, blubbing and shouting:

"I'll tell our Tom, I'll tell our Tom."

I'd been so pleased with having paid him back that I'd shouted after him:

"Tell your Tom. I'm not afraid of him. Tell your Tom."

I thought of Grab Fosdyck as I huddled shivering under the covers, and I wished that I had left his brother alone. I felt very miserable. I wished that I wasn't a foreigner in Bramblewick; that my father, instead of painting pictures, was a fisherman, or better still a ship's captain like Grab's; that he talked like Bramblewick men talked, and swore, and drank beer, and joined in the fights outside the Mariner's, or the Fisherman's Arms on Saturday nights. I wished I could wear a blue fisherman's guernsey and corduroy breeches like the other village boys instead of velvet trousers, and a Norfolk jacket, and a starched collar and a bow. I wished that suddenly God would make me twice as big and twice as strong as Grab, that I could walk up to the school door this morning and smack him in the face, and have all the other boys shouting:

"Go on, Worms! Hit him! Sole him! Pay him

back... He's blubbing. His nose is bleeding. You've won! You've won!"

And that after this I might step straight into Grab's shoes, be the boss of his gang, thrash any boy that cheeked me; be the one to set other boys on fighting (only see that they fought fair); be the one to say what games should be the craze, and above everything be the boss of the Guy Fawkes bonfire, and, on the soon-coming Fifth of November, be the one to light it. Then, knowing that God never did anything like this, no matter how religious you were, I wished that I might be taken ill, say with measles or scarlet fever, something infectious that would keep me away from school for weeks. I wondered whether it would be any good if I pretended to have a headache, or a pain in my stomach. That at least would be an excuse for not going to school today. But I'd no sooner thought of this than I remembered that the tide would just be leaving the cliff at dinnertime, and that with luck I might be "first on" along the shore. And then I thought of Chicken, and the two other "foreigners", Fatty Welford and Joss Hall, and the secret Guy Fawkes bonfire we were building among the whins close to Garry Nab. I could trust Chicken, although I didn't like him very much, but I felt I couldn't trust Fatty or Joss at all, and that if they went to it without me they might easily set fire to it. If I was poorly enough to stay away from school Mother would certainly keep me in the house all day, perhaps in bed, and anyway Grab would be at school tomorrow. The sooner I got it over with Grab the better. Mother suddenly shouted from the living-room.

"I can't hear you moving about! You haven't gone back to bed, have you? It's nearly twenty minutes to nine!"

I shouted that I would be downstairs in a minute, and I got out of bed, put on my shirt and the breeches I hated so, quickly pulled on my stockings, and got into my boots, and without stopping to lace them, walked noisily to the wash-stand. There was ice on the water, and I washed very quickly. Then I hurried down to the living-room.

I liked this room on a cold morning. It was dark, for the window was small, and you could see no sky through it, only the stone walls of the cottages on the opposite side of the narrow, cobbled road which was called Cliff Street. But it was warm and cosy. I loved the firelight. It shone on the oilcloth, yet it didn't show the worn places where the pattern was gone. It shone on the sideboard, but it didn't show, unless you looked hard, the cracks, and the place where Dad had mended one of the doors with a piece of cigar-box wood, which he said was the same as mahogany, although really it looked quite different when the light was good. You could see in one corner of the room the cupboard Dad had made out of a packing-case, and it looked almost like a real one that had been bought in a shop. You couldn't see the patches of damp on the wall nearest the sea where the paper was peeling off, and had to be stuck with drawing-pins. And I loved Mother in the firelight, fussing about with the frying-pan, and the teapot and the shining plates she kept hot on the kerb. Her cheeks were plump and red, and she looked warm and kind, and it wasn't until she turned on me, and with a stern expression looked at the back of my neck, that I felt vexed and thought of all the trouble she got me into through making me wear such silly clothes, and making me different to the other boys, and forbidding me to talk "Bramblewick", or say rude words, or fight, or buy a "surprise packet" with my Saturday ha'penny (she said "surprise packets" were a form of gambling), or spit on my school slate instead of using the bottle of water, which I saw she had put by my slate on the table. I don't know how many hidings I had got because of that bottle alone. The other boys thought it was stuck-up not to use spit.

"You do worry me, Sonny," she said. "You haven't as much as touched the back of your neck. There's a tide-mark to show."

I had touched it, but I knew it was no use saying I had, and while I ate my breakfast she washed it again, and then made me keep still while she fastened on a clean, stiff collar round my neck, and tied the bow. Then she sat down, opposite me, not eating or drinking; just looking first out of the window, then at me. I knew, by the way she looked at me, that she knew I had something preying on my mind. I hoped that she would not ask me what it was, for I could not tell her about Len and Grab.

It would only get me into deeper trouble if I did. If I told her Grab had set his brothers on to me and was going to hide me this morning, she would think nothing of putting on her hat and coat and marching up to school with me, and making a scene in front of all the other boys. She would think nothing of going for Slogger himself, or of taking me round to Mrs Fosdyck and having a row with her. She wasn't afraid of anything or anyone when she was angry. But she didn't speak at all. When I had finished she looked anxiously at the clock, and gave me my slate and bottle, and suddenly put her arms round me and hugged me and kissed me, and I saw tears in her eyes, and I didn't feel vexed with her any more. I felt sorry for the trick I had played her with the stick and boot, and for not getting up when she called me, and not washing properly. I knew that I did worry her, that in nearly every way I wasn't the nice boy she wanted me to be. I did talk Bramblewick when I was outside the house, I did say rude words and swear, I did fight, and I had once bought a surprise packet, although there was nothing in it but a whistle I didn't want, and some sweets I didn't like. And I had done worse things I didn't even like to think about. I nearly started to cry myself as I moved towards the door, and opened it, and felt the cold air in the stairway. I wished that after all I had pretended I had a headache, or a pain, and that I was staying in by the fire, while Mother looked after me. Then, thinking of Grab, and of how I wouldn't have been in trouble with him if it hadn't been for Mother, I felt vexed again, and a bit braver, and I went down the ten steps that led to the shop and the street, the door to which was open, for Dad had just come in, and was in the shop, tying up a parcel.

Dad was not a big man, but he was quite strong and healthy. He had reddish hair, and a beard, and although he didn't speak the same way as Mike Regan did, Mother often said that he had quite an Irish brogue, for he was born in Ireland, and his mother was Irish. I loved him because he was my father. I was proud of him for some things too. He could paint lovely pictures. He was painting a picture of Mike Regan. Mike was Irish, of course. He was a labourer and the parish grave-digger, but he was a fisherman in summer, as soon as the salmon season began. He had been living in Bramblewick a long time when we came to it, but he was still called a foreigner, and was hated by the other fishermen. The picture Dad was painting of Mike was to be sent to the Royal Academy when it was finished, and Dad thought it would make him famous. But at present he couldn't earn much money painting so that he had to take photographs, too, and this often made him very bad-tempered, because he thought it was lowering for an artist. He seemed to be in a bad temper this morning. He didn't look at me. He just said, grumpily:

"You'll be late for school if you don't hurry. Shut the door after you."

I shut the door, and slammed it on purpose so that it would make him jump. I hurried up Cliff Street, feeling as vexed with Dad as I had been with

Mother. I did love him, I knew. He was very clever at making things like model windmills that worked, and cranes, and drawbridges, and clockwork engines. But he didn't very often make things for me, and when he did, and they worked very well, he put them away for fear I should break them. And while he was more religious even than Mother, and terribly strict about swearing, and not doing anything you wanted to do on a Sunday, he didn't bother a bit about the clothes I wore, or whether my neck was washed, or my boots clean, or whether I had anything preying on my mind. Mother worried too much. Dad didn't worry at all. If he took me for a walk, he'd go ahead and then stop and look round and seem quite surprised to find I was there. I didn't want to have *him* interfering with what went on between me and Grab and the other boys. But it did make me feel angry that he didn't seem to care. I wondered what he would say if Grab really *injured* me, and I was brought home unconscious, and he had to run for the doctor to save my life. I almost wished something like that *would* happen. It would serve him right.

The school was not more than a hundred yards in a straight line from our cottage, for it formed part of the old Wesleyan Chapel, and the chapel itself, like our cottage, was on the edge of the sea-cliff that made one side of the valley in which most of Bramblewick was built. At one time Cliff Street led to the seaward front of the chapel. But there had been a landslide, and three cottages had fallen over the cliff, and there was a wood barrier at the top of the street, so that to get to the chapel you turned in to a short alley on your left (called Chapel Street) that led to the chapel back. Here was a kind of open yard formed by the chapel and a high brick wall fending a steep precipice into Bramblewick Beck. Here, for a few minutes before school-time, the boys played until Slogger, the master, appeared along the other end of Chapel Street, when all playing and shouting stopped, and there was silence while the school door was unlocked, and Slogger stood aside, and gave the sign that school was open.

I didn't quite know what the time was when I reached the top of Cliff Street, but I could tell by the shouting that Slogger hadn't arrived. I stopped at the cliff barrier, screwing up my courage for what was to happen when Grab saw me. Through the chinks in the boards I could look down at the sea. The tide was flowing. The sea was rough. The wind was north-east. It was just the weather for things to be washed up on the shore, and at dinnertime the tide would be exactly right for getting down the south cliff, and finding things. I had best get it over with Grab now, before school-time; then there would be nothing to delay me when school came out. He would hide me, of course; but if I didn't lose my temper and try to hit him back, or cheek him, it wouldn't be so bad, and it would be off my mind anyhow. I turned into Chapel Street, and started whistling. The alley twisted. It was not until I had turned the last corner that I had a fair view of the yard, of the boys who were there, and Grab himself.

I had always been afraid of Grab. It wasn't that he was so big and strong. There were several boys bigger and stronger, and I didn't fear them half as much. Really he wasn't big for his age. But he had big, knuckly hands, and when he hit you, it was as though he was hitting you with a stone. He had an ugly, sneering face, with very bright eyes, and I think it was his eyes that frightened me most, for they always looked so proud and sneering and cruel. Usually when I arrived in the school yard, even when he had nothing special against me, Grab would smile in his sneering way, and say something to make all the others laugh. But this time he didn't seem to notice me at all. He was too busy.

He was leaning with his backside against the chapel wall, with most of the other boys crowding round him, and as I drew near, I saw that he was holding up one of his feet for them to look at, and that his feet were shod in a pair of brand-new leather seaboots, reaching to his knees.

There would be nearly forty boys altogether. With their backs towards me, facing Grab, were Len and Kid, and the rest of Grab's gang were close about him. Fatty Welford and Joss Hall stood farther away, and soon I saw Chicken, and he saw me, and came and stood near to where I was, hoping I would speak to him and be friendly. But I didn't take much notice of him. I just looked at Grab, and the new boots he was showing off, holding up first one foot, and then the other, showing the wood-pegged soles, the welts, the little tags for pulling them on, and even my fear of him was overcome by envy. They were wonderful boots. I could not have imagined anything I would have liked better for myself, not even a sheath knife, or a real revolver. And it wasn't enough that Grab should own such lovely things: he had to boast about them.

"Aye," he was saying. "They're real ones, all right. They're real sailor's boots. Father says they cost him nearly a pound, but it was foreign money of course. He bought them in Amsterdam. That's in Holland. He says that you can't get them this size in England. They don't make them so small ... See, they haven't got any nails in them. Nails rust in salt water. Wood pegs swell up, and they last forever. Of course he wouldn't have got them for me if he wasn't going to take me for a long voyage next summer holidays, out foreign. But anyway they'll be useful here in rainy weather, and for going down the scaurs. They'll be champion, I reckon, champion, and they're easy as carpet slippers to walk in."

"Aye. And Tom brought home a great box of crackers for us, from Father," Len Fosdyck put in. "There's squibs and roman candles, and pinwheels, and a whole packet of boxes of Bengal lights – *all* colours. But we've got to keep them for Guy Fawkes night, Mother says."

"He let me go halfway up the main mast," Grab went on. "He wanted to see if I'd get dizzy. But I didn't. I *liked* it. I wanted to go up again! I'm going as cabin boy on the *Sarah* as soon as I leave school. I expect I'll be captain of her when Father gets too old, and he retires."

It was just as though Grab must have felt how I was hating him, for suddenly he looked at me with a sneering smile, and said mockingly, to the others:

"Hey – there's Worms ... *What* was it you said he said about me, Len?"

The whole crowd of boys turned, and those standing between me and Grab moved to one side, leaving a clear passage with Grab at the end of it, and Len and Kid standing one on each hand. Len's eye was still black, but in the quick look he gave me I saw he wasn't frightened now that he had Grab to stick up for him.

"He said he wasn't afraid of *you,* Tom, and he called you Grab. He had a stone in his hand when he hit me, too."

It was a lie, but I didn't say anything. I tried to keep my temper. Grab had thrust his hands in his breeches pockets, and was leaning against the wall, and he was still smiling.

"Oh," he said, slowly and mockingly, just as though he wasn't angry at all. "So you said you weren't afraid of me – eh? ... Well, are you – or aren't you? Would you like to give Len another black eye? Now that I'm watching? Or maybe you'd like to try and give me one ... Are you afraid of me?"

He suddenly took his hands from his pockets, and took a step towards me. "Are you afraid of me?" he said again.

I was horribly afraid of him. He was older and bigger and stronger than I was. I had never seen him beaten in a fight with anyone. Besides he had almost every other boy in the crowd to back him up. I knew quite well that although Fatty and Joss were foreigners, they would have been with him if he had let them. And while I knew that Chicken would do anything for me, he was too small to be any use. I thought of dinnertime, and the shore, and how much better it would be for me if I said "yes". But just as I tried to say it, something burst inside me, and I clenched my fists and put my face right up to his, and shouted out loud:

"No – I'm bloody well not."

I saw Grab clench his fists. I thought he'd kill me with one blow, and instead of trying to fight I put my arms to my face to protect it, and shut my eyes. But Grab did not strike. Just then there was a low shout of "Look out, there's Slogger," and the next moment Grab was back at the wall, quiet and respectful, and the other boys were standing back, leaving a clear way across the yard to the school door. Slogger was already abreast of the chapel wall.

I was more afraid of Slogger than of any person I knew. I feared him almost as much as I feared God. But I don't think it was just because of the way he punished you. His nickname was certainly well earned. He would box your ears, or thrash you with his cane, for the slightest offence against the strict rules of the school. You were slogged if you talked, if you dropped your slate pencil, or didn't pay attention, or if you were late, or if you got your sums wrong. This did make you fear him of course. But there was something else about him that was terrifying quite apart from what he did. He wasn't like an ordinary man at all. For one thing you felt he knew just everything, that he could never make a mistake about the answer to a sum, or the spelling of a word, or the length of any river, or the date of any battle, or when the kings and queens of England had been born, and came to the throne, and died. He knew the names and boundaries of all the countries and states of the world, their capitals, populations, longest rivers, highest mountains, most prominent capes, chief exports and imports. He knew how things like coal were made, and what was made out of them, and everything else about the members of the Animal and Vegetable and Mineral kingdoms ...

And then he *looked* different from any other man I knew. He wasn't young, but he wasn't very old. He was tall and straight and thin, although he wasn't weak. His hair was reddish, and he had a big moustache, with bushy side whiskers that left only the upper parts of his cheeks showing, and his eyes were light blue, and piercing, and fierce as a hawk's when he was angry. And I never knew anyone who looked so clean. From his shiny black boots to the hard black hat he wore in wintertime, you never saw a speck of dust or dirt on him. He wore a dark overcoat, and under this a suit of fine blue serge, with a very low waistcoat showing his shirt, that must have been clean on every day, because it was so white and stiff. He wore two gold studs in it. He had a gold watch and a heavy gold chain, hung in two loops across his waistcoat. He wore a stiff collar with a black bow, and stiff cuffs with gold links in them. There was never a mark on his cuffs, or a speck of chalk, or a wisp of cotton on his serge suit. His bow was never out of place, like mine always was. His hands, when he took off his gloves, were clean and almost as white as the trotters of a scalded pig, and his face was always as clean and fresh as though it was scrubbed with hot water and soap every few minutes. You felt that dirt couldn't touch Slogger. You felt it was just the same with sin; that if anyone swore, or said a rude word in his presence, he wouldn't really hear it inside him, and that he never could do anything sinful himself, any more than God could, although he had to know all about sin so as to stop others doing it. I didn't fear Slogger quite so much as I feared God, of course, because God could punish you with eternal fire, and Slogger only boxed your ears, or caned you, or kept you in. But I feared him in the same way, and just as you couldn't hate God, because he was so powerful, you couldn't hate Slogger, no matter how he punished you. You just felt that he was right, and that you deserved it, and that you couldn't get your own back even if you wanted to, so it was no good trying.

There was a silence, while Slogger took the key from his pocket, and unlocked the door, and then stood to one side, and gave the sign that school was open. On a cold morning there was always a competition for the first to be in, for there was only one fire, and the last in had to sit at the ends of the desks farthest from it, in a draught strong enough to turn over the leaves of a book, and keep the wall maps always shaking. But Grab, early or late, could always take his choice, and he purposely loitered now, so that he could pass in abreast of me, and whisper fiercely in my ear:

"All right. I'll be seeing you at playtime."

II

AT THE BEST of times I hated school. The room itself, which was under the chapel gallery, was small and dark, and its windows were heavily barred, for the narrow playground that separated it from the edge of the cliff was actually above the level of the floor, so that really we were half underground, and it was gloomy as a prison. Through the bars you could see patches of sky, so that you always knew whether the sun was shining or not, but the sun itself, even in summer, never entered the room, and while you could hear the sea breaking on the cliff foot, or on the scaur ends if the tide was down, it was not visible. I could always think of a hundred places where I'd rather be than in this gloomy room. I hated having to sit still. I hated writing, and doing sums, and learning poetry off by heart, and learning about nouns and pronouns, and history. I liked looking at maps, and imagining I was seeing the places marked on them, but I hated having to learn off by heart the names of capes and rivers and mountains. I liked reading, but you only got one reader a year for the standard you were in, and you could read it through by yourself in one lesson (skipping the poetry) so that even the interesting bits became dull when you had to go through them word by word, spelling the difficult words out aloud, or writing them on your slate. And while you sat in school you heard all the time the sound of the sea, and the cries of the gulls which often would alight on the playground railings, and stay there, making a queer laughing sound, just as though they were laughing at you, and mocking you because you had to stay in. No matter what time of the year, there was always something exciting to do at Bramblewick. In spring there was bird-nesting. Even if there had been no school, or bounds made by Mother, the days wouldn't have been long enough to explore the woods and fields and cliffs within an hour's walk from the village. There were trout in Garry Beck and Browe Beck. There were some monster trout in the miller's dam in Garry Wood, and real salmon in the pool below, but because of school, and having to dodge the miller and the squire, who owned the fishing, there was never time to fish there properly. In summer there was sea-fishing. Mike Regan's coble the *Shannon Rose* was launched down, and he would actually let me go off with him, but I couldn't do this while I went to school, only in the holidays, and they were very short. And there was always the shore, and finding things that had been washed up, and the scaurs that were bared across the whole stretch of Bramblewick Bay when the tide was down, with pools where you could catch flatfish, and holes where you got lobsters and crabs, and weedy places where you found queer animals like urchins and brittle stars and sea-slugs which were just as pretty as flowers. When the tide was up, the cliff whins, where we were building our secret bonfire, was quite an exciting place to play in. When the weather was too bad to go out, it wasn't so bad being at home, if Mother would let me have a fire in the attic or Dad lent me his tools to make things, and his saw to saw wood.

I hated school, because it stopped me doing so many things I liked, and I had never hated it so much as I did this morning. I took the cold end of one of the two desks belonging to Standard VI. When we were all in, Slogger, having taken off his hat and overcoat and gloves, closed the door. Then, while we stood in silence, he walked to his desk, took a tuning-fork from it, rapped it sharply, and sounded the key note, which he repeated himself, singing the word DOH. We had to do this next, but with some boys being so little and others big and having different sorts of voices, it didn't sound very nice. Then, following Slogger, but never quite catching up to him, we sang the morning hymn. We had two morning hymns, *A Charge to Keep I Have,* and *Captain of Israel's Host and Guide,* and they were sung in turn, throughout the year. Slogger never forgot which one it was. The hymn finished, we repeated the Lord's Prayer. Then we sat down with our hands clasped behind our backs while he marked the register, after which school began. The first lesson was always arithmetic for the whole school. Slogger would say, "Give out the sum books," and the boy who was at the warm end of the front desk of each standard would go to the cupboard near Slogger's desk, get his batch of books and start giving them out. At the same time one of the Seventh Standard boys would walk down to the north end of the school to Standards I and II, and take charge of them. It was a nice job this, and it was given to a boy who had been good at his lessons, and had behaved himself in other ways. At present it was held by a boy called Jim Hessle, only he was nicknamed Putty because his father was a painter, and because his face was almost as white as putty, too, because he had consumption.

When the sum books were out, Slogger would begin at Standard VII and say the page and the numbers of the sums to be done, and would walk down towards the north end of the school, setting the tasks for each standard. Then he would take a glance at Putty to see that he had got the little boys at work, walk back to the fire, pick up from his stool The *Yorkshire Post* (which had been laid there by the woman who cleaned the school), sit down with his feet on the fender and begin to read. Then for a long time there would be no sound in the school itself but pencils scratching on slates, the hoarse whispering of Putty among the little boys, the rustle of Slogger's paper, and the steady *click-clock* of the big clock on the south wall. But the newspaper made no difference to the way Slogger knew what was going on. If a boy dare as much as whisper to his desk mate, Slogger would be up and to him in a second, rap him across the ears, and be round again to box the ears of any other boy who had dared to stop work. The first to be punished this morning was Grab. It was for taking his attention from his slate to look at his new boots.

But I didn't feel happy about it for long, for Slogger caught me smiling, and gave me such a slap across the side of my face, that for a minute I could scarcely see the figures on my slate, and I thought I was going to be sick. Two other boys, however, were punished for grinning at me, and as Slogger returned to his paper, he gave Grab a warning that for his next offence he would be caned and kept in at playtime.

I recovered from my punishment, but I felt very miserable. I worked at the sums, but all the time I was thinking about playtime, and what Grab was going to do to me. I hadn't much hope that he would be kept in, and anyway there was dinnertime. As he was in Standard VII, and nearer the door, he would be out before I was, and could wait for me in the yard. I wished again that I had pretended I was ill, and that I was at home with Mother. I wished that I had told her everything, about my fights, about my swearing, and my lying and the other bad things I had done. It wasn't too nice confessing things to Mother. It was just like wanting to be sick, and not being able to, but once you had done it, and said you were sorry, she would be lovely. I just longed for her to look after me. Then I was vexed with her again, and vexed with myself for having been such a fool as to swear at Grab and tell him I wasn't frightened of him when I was. I stole a glance at Grab's boots and my fear turned again to envy. If only my father was a sea captain, and I could go on board a real ship, and climb the rigging, and be taken on a real voyage – out foreign! If only Dad was *rich!* I made up a picture of Dad as a rich man. We would be living in one of the new houses up Bramblewick Bank, and have servants, so that Mother wouldn't have to do any washing or other housework, and would always be able to wear her Sunday clothes. The house would have a bathroom and real furniture, and carpets, and fires in every room. I would have a pair of boots just as good as Grab's; and a real oilskin coat too and a sou'wester, and at least half-a-crown a week as pocket money. It would go a long way to make up for being a foreigner, if, for instance, you had a real leather football, or a proper cricket bat to show the other boys, and let them play with you. And I could have a great box of fireworks, too, to set off on the Fifth, a hundred times bigger than the packet Grab's father had sent home, and everyone would want to see them. Every boy in the village would want to be friends with me then. I shouldn't need to feel worried about Fatty and Joss being faithful. I had never liked either of them. They only came with me because they were foreigners, and because Grab wouldn't have them. But Chicken wasn't so bad, and while I felt I could never have him as a real friend, I would remember how he had stuck to me when times were bad.

I wasn't getting on with my sums of course. Suddenly I knew that Slogger was striding between the desks towards me. I put my hands to my face, and protected the part that was already sore, but he got me on the other side, and this time I cried a bit, but only because he had startled me out of my thoughts, and I soon stopped, and got on with my sums, and finished them.

When you had finished you had to turn your slate over, sit back from the desk and fold your arms until Slogger was ready to do the marking, which he did by standards, beginning at Standard VII. I did this, except that I didn't turn my slate over. Fatty and Joss were sitting in the desk just behind me. They were both fools at sums, and I had an agreement with them that I should let them look at my answers as soon as Slogger started marking, and had his back turned. I wanted to go to the lavatory, but I daren't put my hand up yet, and I kept very still, wondering whether I should be able to last out till playtime, and whether I'd have a chance to go then before Grab got me. Soon Slogger folded his paper, got up, stroked his moustache, and walked to the first desk of Standard VII. As soon as he was looking at the first slate, I looked slyly round, and saw that Fatty and Joss were trying to see my answers. It made me feel a bit happy. I didn't like either of them. Fatty, whose father was a signalman on the railway, was ugly as well as fat. He wore corduroy breeches that stank, and he was lazy, and had scarcely helped at all with the bonfire. Joss, who had no father, and whose mother had come as cook to an old woman who lived up the Bank, also was ugly, but thin, and his eyebrows met in the middle, and he had shifty eyes. I couldn't trust either of them like I could trust Chicken. But Chicken, who was only in

Standard IV, was so small. He was dirty, too, and his clothes were ragged, for his father was a drunkard, and he annoyed me by following me when I didn't want him, and offering me sticky sweets or bad apples or bits of pie out of his pocket, and he always looked so sad when I wouldn't take them. Yet it was something to feel that I had *any* sort of friends at present. It was something to feel that there were three other boys who hated Grab, even if they couldn't do anything to help me. Slogger had finished with Standard VII. Grab had got all his sums wrong, of course, and Slogger had boxed his ears, but hadn't told him he had to stay in. The marking went on, and now he had reached my desk. I wasn't worried, except about going to the lavatory. I was certain all my sums were right. But as soon as he had reached me, and I had turned my slate the right way up, I knew without looking up at him that something was wrong. There was a deadly silence. Then he said:

"Were you listening when I set the sums for Standard VI?"

"Yes, sir," I said.

"But you thought that it would be easier to do the sums you did yesterday, instead, eh? Particularly if you remembered the answers?"

I saw at once that I had made a mistake, although I hadn't remembered the answers, and I hadn't meant to do anything dishonest. But I knew it was no good saying anything. I just put my hands to my ears and waited for him to hit me, but to my surprise he gave me back my slate and said:

"Stay in at playtime and do the sums I set, and one extra." Slogger moved to the desk behind. I daren't look at him or at Joss and Fatty. Again there was silence. Then Slogger laughed, in a queer dry way.

"Very clever, Welford," he said. "Very clever indeed. Today's sums but yesterday's answers... And Hall has been just as clever – eh? You couldn't have copied from anyone of course, could you, Welford? Could you, Hall? ... Stay in at playtime, both of you, and do the right sums, and two extra... And *this* is for dishonesty."

Fatty cried with the hiding he got. I daren't look round to see how Joss had taken it. I felt more miserable than ever, and there was no real comfort in the thought that I was to stay in at playtime. It only meant putting it off with Grab till later, and I *did* want to go to the lavatory worse than ever. As Slogger got back to the fireplace, I put my hand up. Sometimes he would let you go, sometimes he wouldn't. But he must have seen how anxious I was, for without asking me what I wanted, he said:

"Very well. And don't loiter, or I'll box your ears."

I had never known a morning drag like that one. Playtime seemed as though it would never end. Once, when I dared to look up from my slate, I saw Grab smiling at me through the window, and holding his clenched hand to his face, which was the usual way of showing another boy that you were going to give him a good hiding. And again I saw Chicken munching an apple, which he had probably found in one of the grocer's refuse boxes, and trying to make friendly signs to me, which I didn't take any notice of. I didn't look at Fatty and Joss. Slogger had made them sit apart, and several desks behind me. They didn't get any of their sums right, and Slogger boxed their ears again. But I was right with two out of four, and I did not get punished for the ones I had wrong.

There was spelling and grammar and reading after playtime. I tried my best to do well and avoid further punishment. I was afraid of being kept in. I could hear by the sound of the sea that the tide was leaving the cliff. I made up my mind that I would let Grab do what he liked with me, and not try and stop him no matter how much he hurt. If he asked me again if I was frightened of him I would say I was; and I would even say I was sorry that I had sworn at him, and that I had touched Len. The only thing I hoped for was that he wouldn't make my nose bleed, and that Mother wouldn't find out, and make a fuss about it.

I escaped punishment, although twice Slogger nearly caught me looking at the clock, whose minute hand seemed to move slower and slower as it rose towards twelve. But Slogger was always punctual. At exactly three minutes to twelve, he gave the order to the whole school, "Arms folded", the signal that lessons were done, and he walked towards his desk. The whole school waited attentively, all of us sitting back with our arms folded.

"Hands behind," he ordered.

We clasped our hands behind.

"Arms folded."

We folded them again.

"Stand."

We stood.

"Eyes closed."

We closed our eyes.

"Silence."

There was a deadly silence, then the rap of the tuning-fork, the sound of it, and Slogger's DOH, which we repeated. Then a little quicker than the morning hymn, we sang:

"Be present at our table, Lord.
Be here and everywhere adored.
Thy creatures bless, and grant that we
May feast in Paradise with Thee."

Again there was silence; then Slogger's, "Eyes open", and we waited for the final "Dismiss". But between the giving of these two commands, Slogger was always specially strict. I was looking at Grab. There was no harm in this for he really was in front of me. But Grab himself was fool enough to look round, and to smile, too, in his sneering way, and as much as to say:

"Only another minute before I get you!"

And Slogger must have seen that smile, for he snapped:

"Stay in, Fosdyck, and write the word 'Attention' a hundred times ... The others, dismiss."

I did not dare to look at Grab again, for I knew I would not be able to resist smiling. But I looked at Len and Kid, and saw what distance we all were from the door. I forgot how anxious I had been to get it over with Grab. I didn't think that now he must be feeling even angrier with me. I thought that Len and Kid might try to hold me outside until he got out. I had to beat them, and I did so, and to my relief none of the other boys of Grab's gang thought of stopping me when I got to the yard. And once there I had a clear way for home. I ran, and for the time being all my worries went. I forgot Grab, forgot Slogger, forgot the soreness of my ears and face, in the exciting prospect of being "first on" along the shore. I had to go home first to leave my slate, but we didn't have dinner until one, which was a good thing, for the village boys had dinner as soon as they got home. It meant nearly an hour during which they could not bother me. There was, however, the danger that Mother might have some errand for me to go. She might want me to fetch a pail of water from the tap at the top of the street, which would take me back into the path of the boys who lived down our way, including Chicken; so I opened the street door quietly, put my slate at the foot of the stairs, and, glad that Dad wasn't in the shop, shouted up the stairs that I had come back, and shut the door again before Mother had a chance to answer. I ran down past Thompson's shop, past the Dolphin Hotel, to the Dock.

The Dock was an open space where the main street of Bramblewick (called The Road) joined Cliff

Street and several other alleys close to the shore. A steep slipway led from it between the breakwater and the old coastguard's station, to the shore itself. The lifeboat house, standing well back, faced the Slipway. The rest of the Dock was used for the fishermen's cobles, and today, with the weather too bad for fishing, or for the cobles to be moored in the fishermen's landing, there was scarcely room for a cart to pass between them from the road to the slipway top. There were no fishermen about. My fear was that someone might have gone along the shore already. But this was not very likely, just at dinnertime, and with the tide still too high for anyone to go down the slipway and under the coastguard's wall. And the other way was slippery and dirty, and awkward. Mother thought it was dangerous, too, and I was strictly forbidden ever to use it; but I didn't think about that, and anyway, it wasn't dangerous if you knew where the slippery places were and avoided them. I crossed the Dock and ran up an alley at the back of the coastguard's station. There were terraces of cottages on my right, and the highest of them made the south end of the village, for here the shale on which they were built gave way to the tumbling clay which formed the whole of the South Cliff as far as Garry Nab. At the end of this highest terrace a short alley turned to the cliff edge. There was a gap, and through it you had a view to the south; of the clay cliff, and the shore as far as the real cliff of High Batts, which made the south end of the Bay.

I paused at the gap, and one look was enough

to tell me I was not too late. The cliff, whose bottom edge was always falling, made the shore irregular. Here and there masses of clay which had fallen lately stuck out and were being washed by the breaking waves. But between them were little coves, strewn with weed the tide had left, and with space enough for you to stand unless some extra big wave came in. It was in these coves, in among the weed (or by scratching among the gravel), that treasures were found, and for the whole distance between the village and Garry Nab there was no sign of a human being.

The way down was not very steep. It was because it was used as a rubbish shoot by the people living near that it was so awkward. Wherever the slope of the clay allowed there were thick heaps of ashes, and mussel shells, and tin cans; and wherever water had collected the clay had turned to bog in which you could sink up to your knees. But I had learnt how to tell these places; where to tread lightly, and the spots to which I could jump and keep my balance, and then jump again before my feet sank in; and soon I had reached the first of the bared coves.

It was terribly exciting. You never knew what you were going to find. In a tin box that I kept under a loose plank in the attic (out of Dad's way), I had, among many other treasures, a gold ring (stamped with a lion and 12 ct.), a gold tie-pin also stamped but with the jewel missing, a piece of real mail from a suit of armour, a silver horseshoe brooch (with only its hinge missing), a big lump of amber, a coin like a spade guinea, (only it wasn't pure gold), a George II two-shilling piece, three silver groats, and dozens of Georgian pennies and ha'pennies and foreign coins; and I had found them all at one time or another on the shore between the village and Garry Nab. I had found plenty of modern coins, too; a crown piece, several half crowns and florins, and shillings and sixpences, and coppers. One day after a very rough sea I had found nearly ten shillings' worth of English coins. But I had always given these to Mother, because I knew we were poor, and modern coins really weren't so exciting as old ones. No one knew how all these coins came to be on the shore. Some people said they were just lost by the summer visitors, but visitors didn't carry Georgian and William and Mary coins, and coats of mail; and I believed they were washed out of the cliff, and that somewhere in the clay there was a great trove of them, which some old Bramblewick smuggler had hid, and whenever there had been a big fall of cliff I kept a sharp look out for anything like the iron-bound corners of a treasure box.

The waves were very big, and they made an awful sound as they broke on the scaur a few feet away from the cliff, and then rushed up, chewing at the shingle and sand. They sounded worse when I turned my back on them, as though they were going to break right on top of me, and wash me away. But I had learnt to tell exactly, without looking at it, how far a wave would come; and if it was a big one I would rush for the cliff and jump out of harm's way until it was spent and going back.

I always searched the stranded weed first, for here were things that floated, like buoys, sometimes with bits of tangled net or line to them, pieces of wood and bottles. I always looked at bottles to see if they had secret messages inside them, for once I had found a message, only it was just a note from a Bramblewick sailor to his mother, dropped overboard as his ship was passing the Bay at night, and not saying anything very interesting. But I took it to his mother, and she was very pleased, and gave me a jam tart. After I had searched the weed I would start on the patches of shingle and sand. The best places were where you saw bits of old iron and nails. Sometimes there were coins actually showing, but usually you had to "scrat" for them with a bit of bent iron. Brass buttons often misled you into thinking you had found a gold coin, especially if they were lying with their eyes downwards. And when you did find a coin it might be so covered with verdigris and a hard cement of rust and sand that you couldn't tell what it was until it was cleaned. But I didn't mind this. It was more exciting still. I put such coins in my pocket, and kept them for when I got home, then scraped them carefully with a knife, and soaked them in vinegar. If they were silver they would clean up just as though they were new, and the greatest excitement of all was when you saw the name of the king and queen on it, and the date. I had once cleaned a silver coin like this, and got part of the king's face showing and part of the date, and then Mother had thrown away the old tin I was soaking it in, and I had never seen it again. It might have been a very valuable coin, and I often thought about it.

I didn't find anything in the first cove except a few copper nails and some jet. Once a month an old rag-and-bone man came over from Burnharbour, and he paid a penny a pound for old copper and brass, and threepence a pound for jet if it was in pieces big enough to carve; so they were well worth keeping. I climbed up over the wet, greasy clay into the next cove and started work there. But I knew that I could not search any of the coves properly. It was always the same with anything exciting I found to do. There wasn't time. There were plenty of other boys just as keen on finding things as I was. As soon as they had had their dinners they would be rushing down, and while few of them dare come down the rubbish shoot the tide would soon be low enough for them to get round the slipway. If you were "first on" it meant that you had the pick of anything that was *showing*. But some of my best finds had been made long after the tide had gone down, and close to the village, by "scratting". I had to choose between spending a long time in one place or making a quick search of the whole shore before someone got ahead of me. After the second cove had yielded nothing but some more nails, and a button which had looked exactly like a spade guinea, I decided to hurry on. I could get to the Nab easily in twenty minutes; and I might do some scratting on the way back if there was time, and Grab wasn't in the way. Every time I left the shore and climbed over the clay I thought of Grab, but as soon as I was down looking for things I forgot him because of being so excited. It wasn't long, too, before I found a coin which looked like a George II penny. I wondered whether, if I didn't clean it too much and I went in at dark, I could pass it as a real penny in Thompson's shop and get some crackers. I had only saved about sixpence for crackers so far, and it didn't look as though Mother was going to give me any more, for I had heard her saying to Dad only a day or two ago that she wondered where the next week's grocery money was coming from. That made me think of Grab in another way. *He* would have plenty of crackers, quite apart from the parcel his father had sent, for he earned three shillings a week carrying out for Mr Thompson. And with the rest of the boys in his gang each having some, it looked as though his bonfire would be a great success, while ours, with Chicken and Joss poorer than I was, and Fatty's father very stingy, wasn't going to be much more than a fire and a few crackers. There wouldn't be any squibs or roman candles. I wished I hadn't been such a fool as to give Mother all the money I had found on the shore. I could easily have kept back half a crown, and she wouldn't have known anything about it. I thought if I found some real money today I *would* keep it. It was Dad's fault we were so poor. He ought to have been a sea captain instead of an artist.

I went on. Gradually the waves were breaking farther and farther away from the cliff, so that I hadn't to leave the shore at all. I began to feel a bit worried about the time. I was now nearly halfway on to the Nab, and when I glanced back I saw that a man and one or two boys had got round the slipway and were scratting in the first cove.

I did not "scrat" any more. I stuck to the cliff foot and the weed, and suddenly I noticed something bright between a piece of weed and a rather large stone. I thought at first it was the edge of a large silver coin, jammed under the stone, but when I moved the weed I saw that it was only the wire frame of a lady's bag purse, with two little knobs on it for snapping the two halves of it together. I had often found old purses like this, with only the frame left. I kept them because they were brass and went to make up weight for the rag-and-bone man, but I was disappointed, for I had been almost certain it was a coin. It wasn't until I started tugging at it and found that at least part of the bag was still attached to the frame that I began to feel a bit excited. Yet even when I lifted the stone and saw that the whole bag had been buried beneath it, I didn't really think that I might have found something very valuable. It was quite rotten, and it seemed to be filled with wet sand. I laid it on the stone and began scraping the sand out. With it came a bundle of hair-pins, cemented together with rust, and a small bottle of what I knew was smelling salts, for Mother had a bottle, and always let me sniff at it if I had a headache. I knew at once that it could not be an old bag that someone had thrown away. I pulled out what looked like the remains of a handkerchief, and then I saw the catch of an inner pocket. The hinges were rusted and stiff. I prised them apart. And then I saw coins inside, silver coins, and one yellow coin, too bright to be a farthing. It was a sovereign! For a while I dared not pick it out, for fear it might slip out of my fingers and be lost in the sand. I just poked at it, made certain by the George and Dragon that it *was* a sovereign. Then I counted the silver coins. There were half crowns, shillings, and sixpences, nineteen shillings altogether, nearly another sovereign. I was trembling with excitement. Then suddenly I had an awful fear that someone had seen me, that someone would make me give them up.

I looked quickly along the shore. Some more boys had come round the slipway, but there was no one near. I took the money out with my right hand, put that hand into my breeches pocket and kept it there. I looked at the bag again, made certain there was nothing else in it, then with my left hand, I scratched a hole in the sand, buried it, and the bottle, and the handkerchief, and the hair-pins and put the stone over the spot. I looked along the shore again. Then I started for home, running, with my hand still in my pocket, tightly clutching the coins. I had never felt so excited. I had never had so much money all at once. And it was mine, every bit of it was mine. A pound, and nineteen shillings. What couldn't I buy with such a sum of money? Grab's boots had only cost a pound. The packet of fireworks only half a crown. How many fireworks could I buy, say for ten shillings? Very likely there wouldn't be ten shillings' worth all together in Thompson's shop. I could buy the lot, and still have some for something else, for a football, a cricket bat, a fishing rod, an airgun, almost anything I liked out of Gamage's Christmas catalogue, a copy of which someone had sent Dad last year.

Then I thought of Mother. She was always worried about money. She had actually cried when I had taken her that big sum I had found. She had said that God had sent it in answer to her special prayers. Was this money also an answer to her special prayers for the week's groceries? Had God guided my eyes to the very place? I felt frightened. God I knew was everywhere, always watching you. He could see the coins in my pocket, just as clear as if they were on the shore. He could see inside my mind too ... Yet this money was four times as much as I had taken her before. If I gave her the sovereign, surely it would be all right if I kept the rest, and spent some of it on fireworks. I prayed, too, every night. I had prayed that God would help me against Grab. Why shouldn't it be an answer to my prayers too? And anyway, if it was wrong He could stop me. He could stop me thinking such a thought.

I hurried on, and as I drew near the village, I saw Chicken coming towards me. It was no use trying to avoid him. For once I didn't want to so very much, although I thought I wouldn't tell him what I had found. As he drew near, he shouted:

"Eh! I've been looking everywhere for you!"

As he usually said that, I didn't answer, but I listened anxiously to what he said next, as he turned to join me.

"I heard Fatty and Joss talking when we came out of school. Fatty said it was your fault Slogger hit them and made them stay in all playtime. Fatty said that he wasn't going to our bonfire, on bonfire night, and miss all the fireworks Len Fosdyck had to set off. Joss said he wouldn't either ... I heard Grab say that he was going to flatten your nose, and black both your eyes when he caught you ... Would you like a bit of toffee? I found it in a tin Mr Thompson had chucked on to the shore. There was only a little bit, but it's champion."

He had it in his hand, all sticky, and the look of it made me feel sick, but I knew he meant to be kind, and I just told him that I didn't want to eat anything just now, before dinner. I asked him if he knew where Grab was. He said he didn't know, but that he thought he'd be on an errand for Mr Thompson. I believed Chicken, of course. I knew that he would never lie to me, and that he *didn't* know that Grab was now actually on the shore, hiding, waiting for me. We were getting near the clay bluff which formed the first cove I had searched when the tide had been up, right under the rubbish shoot. Several boys were scratting there now, but none I was afraid of. I thought I would risk going round by the slipway, and that once in Dock, I'd make a rush for home. But as we rounded the bluff I saw Grab, standing there, waiting, still in his seaboots, smoking a fag, and smiling. There was no chance of escape. I stopped, clutching my money tightly. He came towards me, still smiling, and the other boys, as though they'd been waiting too, stopped scratting and followed him.

"Hello, Worms," he said quietly. "You didn't expect to see me waiting here, did you? I've just been having a fag while I waited for you to come along. I just wanted to have a talk with you. Have you got time now, or are you in a hurry to get home to your mammy?"

I said nothing, but I clutched my money tighter. He moved nearer to me, and reached out his hand, and took hold of my left arm. His fingers were like teeth, biting me. He took a deep breath at his fag, and blew the smoke into my face. I trembled, but I still said nothing. Then, still holding me, he put his face close up to mine, and said, mockingly:

"Come on – now's your chance. Give me one. Give me a good 'un, hard as you like."

It was a terrible temptation. No matter what he had done to me after, I could have given him one blow that would have made up for a lot that he had done to me. But my right hand was still in my pocket, clutching the coins. I kept cool. I tried to be humble.

"I don't want to hit you," I said. "You're older and bigger than I am."

"Oh! Then you *are* afraid of me after all, are you?"

"Yes," I said, and then, thinking it might please

him, I said, "Everybody is. You can fight anyone in school. Everyone knows that."

He drew back his face, but gripped my arm tighter. I watched his other hand, and I got ready to shield my face from the expected blow. But he didn't hit me. He pointed to his feet.

"See these new seaboots of mine, Worms?" he said.

"Aye," I answered quickly. "They're champion, *aren't* they! They've got wood pegs, haven't they? Didn't your father buy them out foreign? I bet they cost a lot of money. They're champion."

"They'd be champion for kicking your backside," Grab said. "And I've a mind to try them, too ... Are you going to touch our Len anymore?"

"No," I said.

"Are you afraid of me?"

"Yes."

He let go my arm.

"Go on," he said. "Get away home to your mammy, and think yourself lucky she'll be able to know who you are. You're not worth mucking my boots on, you're not, you bloody foreigner..." He turned to the other boys who had now been joined by Len and Kid. "Come. Let's see how far I can wade into the sea with them. I bet they don't leak. I bet they're tight as a bell."

The boys followed Grab to where the seas were running in. The way to the Dock was clear. I ran; and Chicken ran alongside me.

"*By!*" he said. "That was lucky, wasn't it. I

thought he was going to hit you as hard as he could. But I bet if you did have a fight, you'd give him summat. I bet you could beat Grab if only you were his age ... Shall we be leading for the bonfire tonight, if it doesn't rain? We don't need to have Fatty or Joss."

"All right," I answered. "After tea. But you can tell Fatty and Joss, if you see them, that I'm getting some fireworks to let off. They can come if they like ... I don't believe in saving everything up for bonfire night," I added as we reached the bottom of the Cliff Street. "It might be raining."

I left him, staring, and I ran up Cliff Street. I looked into Thompson's window as I passed. He had a special show of fireworks in it. I felt terribly excited thinking what I would buy, and what the other boys would think of me when they saw what I had got; not only Chicken and Fatty and Joss, but Grab's gang too. It was just as though the very thing I had been dreaming about had come true. It was wonderful ... I was nearly home. I made certain there was no hole in my pocket. Then, without taking my hand out, I separated the coins, clutching the sovereign, ready to give it to Mother. I thought I had better not mention the purse at all. I would tell her that I had found the sovereign scratting.

III

WHEN I GOT home to tea that afternoon, Mother was still full of excitement about the sovereign. She kept saying how wonderful I was and what sharp eyes I had, and what a load off her mind it was now that she could pay Mr Thompson's bill on Saturday. She was sure that it was in answer to her prayers to Almighty God. I enjoyed being made a fuss of like this, although she worried me a bit by talking about God. Even Dad was not so bad-tempered as he had been lately. He said it was a blessing some money had come, for he had run short of paints and hadn't dared to get any because he owed for the last lot, and now he could get some and get on with his picture of Mike Regan. He said I must have very sharp eyes, and he asked me to tell him exactly where I had found the sovereign, and if I had looked to see if there were any more. He said he might go with me along the shore tomorrow as two pairs of eyes were better than one. I did not tell him the exact place for fear he would find the purse, but I described the place where I had found the button that had looked like a spade guinea, and told the rest of the story as though the button *had* been the sovereign. All the time we were having tea, however, I kept putting my hand into my pocket to feel the other coins, and as soon as I could I rushed for my coat and made for the door, not looking at the empty bucket that stood near it for fear I should be sent to fill it, and so waste more time.

"You mustn't be a minute later than seven o'clock," Mother said. "I'm going to make a special treat for supper. And don't go farther along the shore than Garry Nab."

She got up, and hugged me, and said again how clever I was, and what a help to her, so that I half-wished I had given her all the money. I thought no more of this as soon as I closed the street door, and looked down Cliff Street to Thompson's shop.

Mr Thompson himself was an old man, but quite active. He was big, and rather fat. He suffered from some sort of skin disease, and his face was always red as butcher's meat, with funny little patches on his cheeks and nose. He had practically no hair, and no teeth, and he made little sucking noises when he talked, so that it wasn't easy to make out what he said. He was a Wesleyan, like Mother. Every other week he conducted the Sunday School, and in chapel he took round one of the collecting boxes, and in summer helped to show visitors to pews. He was also head of the Bramblewick Band of Hope and like Dad (who was a staunch teetotaller) always wore a bit of blue ribbon in his buttonhole. I was afraid of him, but not in the same way as I was afraid of Slogger. He was very rich. He was mean, but he had been kind to Mother once when she was ill, and he had been a good customer of Dad's, giving many orders for photographs and also getting him to paint a picture of his son who had been drowned at sea, for which he had paid three pounds. And I had often heard Dad say that Mr Thompson was very influential, and that he owed a lot of other orders to him, so that we must never do anything to offend him like getting into debt. Several times, when I had gone into his shop and both he and his assistant had been in the warehouse, or down in the cellar where the oil and vinegar were kept, I had helped myself to things like apples, and nuts, and jelly squares, and while I had never been found out, whenever I looked at him I thought about it, and wished I hadn't stolen them, especially if he was in a good temper, and gave me an orange or a banana with only part of it bad.

But Mr Thompson himself was still at tea when I went in. I was served by the assistant, Stan Thompson, who was Mr Thompson's nephew. Stan had served his time in a Burnharbour grocery shop, and he rather fancied himself. He had yellowish hair, and a thin yellow moustache, and wore very high stiff collars with fancy ties. He was always stuck-up when he had the shop to himself, and he didn't take the slightest notice of me when I went in, until I said loudly that I wanted some fireworks. There were two sorts of ordinary crackers – chinese and ladies. They were like each other only chinese were big, and ladies very small. Their wicks were plaited together in a string and you got twenty chinese or forty ladies for a penny. They weren't so exciting as squibs and jumping crackers, but they went further, being so cheap.

Stan, taking his time, and not looking at me at

all, pulled out a drawer behind the counter and said:

"Chinese or ladies?"

"I want *all* sorts," I answered. "But I'll have three penn'orth each of chinese and ladies."

I thought this would have startled Stan, but it didn't. Without saying a word he took out the whole drawer, and tilted it on the counter so that I could see into it. I felt bewildered. I had decided to get half a crown's worth now, and some more later, but it wasn't easy to make up my mind whether to get a lot of the cheaper ones, or just a few dear ones like roman candles and rockets. The rockets were three pence and sixpence each. Even on bonfire night there were very few rockets set off, because they were so dear. But I said I would have two sixpenny ones, and decided that these would be extra to the half crown, because I wanted the other things just as badly. I made a selection of squibs, jumpers, wheels, and fountains. Stan put them to one side. Then he said, quite coolly, just as though I was buying ordinary groceries:

"And the *next*, please?"

I looked towards the back door of the shop to make sure Mr Thompson wasn't in sight, and then I said, as coolly as I could, as though to make out I was getting them for someone else:

"Oh – and a packet of Woodbines, please."

Even this did not seem to startle Stan. He handed the packet to me, and made the fireworks all into one parcel. I put two half crowns on the counter. They were still a bit dirty, but he didn't seem to notice this, and he put them in the till and was just handing me the change when the back door opened, and Mr Thompson came in, wiping his mouth with his handkerchief, as though he'd just had a last drink of tea. He looked at me, and at the drawer of fireworks, still on the counter, but I had got the fags in my pocket, and the parcel under my coat, and he just smiled, and made one of his funny sucking noises, and I took my change, and got out and ran down to the Dock as fast as I could go, for I was afraid that Dad might have finished his tea, and be coming out of the house to get the water.

There were two ways to the south cliff. You could either go along the shore, or go up the alley past the rubbish shoot, above the last row of cottages to a path that led up to the cliff top. I took the second way, for I had arranged to meet Chicken where the cliff path began. He was there, and so were Fatty and Joss. I thought again as soon as I saw them that I didn't like any of them. Chicken wouldn't have been so bad, if he had been bigger, and not so ragged and dirty. I felt anyway that he liked me. But I couldn't feel that about Fatty or Joss. They only came with me because they were lonely. They were only here now because Chicken had given them my message, and because I had dropped a few hints myself at afternoon playtime. And the first thing Fatty said was:

"Eh – have you *got* some crackers? ... I bet you haven't."

"All right, then," I said sarcastically, "I haven't.

This parcel's full of nothing."

I took out the parcel, and opened one end, showing a little of what was in it. Fatty made a greedy noise. So did Joss. But they weren't so cheeky now, and Fatty said:

"God! That's a rocket, isn't it? Are those things squibs or roman candles?"

"Both," I said. "*And* jumpers, *and* pinwheels, *and* sixpenn'orth of chinese and ladies. There's more than three bobs' worth altogether."

"*By!*" said Joss; and then in his cunning way, "Where did you get all that money from? Did your father give it to you?"

I wasn't quite ready for this, but I soon made up a lie.

"No," I said. "It was from my Uncle Fred, in Liverpool. He sent it to me, and a lot more, just for a present."

"Is he rich?" asked Chicken.

"He's got any amount of money. He's richer than anyone in Bramblewick. He's a hundred times as rich as old Mr Thompson."

"Does he keep a shop?" Chicken asked again.

"Not likely," I answered, after I'd thought a moment, "he's a shipowner."

I don't think I'd ever told quite such a big lie. I had an Uncle Fred in Liverpool. He was my Aunt Emma's husband. He was a little wizened man with white hair and beard, and he wore black clothes and a hat just like a clergyman, only he didn't wear a round collar. I didn't know how he earned his living, but it was something to do with an office. He was more religious than either Dad or Mother. Mother had taken me to stay with him once. I had been very excited about going, for Dad had told me I should see the docks, and the landing-stage, and hundreds of big ships, and a museum full of all sorts of curios. I didn't see any of these things, as it happened. Uncle Fred's house was a long way from the town itself. He made everyone get up early, and join in prayers before breakfast, and he said long prayers at every meal instead of an ordinary blessing, and read the Bible and prayed for nearly an hour before bed, and if he thought that anyone had anything preying on their mind, he would ask them to join in a special private prayer, and even Mother had got a bit sick of it on Sunday, when, on top of everything else, he had taken us to chapel three times. It certainly was a big lie saying that Uncle Fred was a shipowner. He wasn't a bit rich, and he had never given me as much as a ha'penny; but I had to say something, and I could have gone on telling lots of lies about him, only Fatty said:

"I've got a box of matches. Let's set a squib off."

I fastened the parcel up.

"We're going to lead for the bonfire first," I said. "We're not going to set off anything until it's dark."

"No," Chicken agreed. "It's twice as good for crackers when it's dark. They show up better. Let's get on."

We climbed the cliff path. It was nearly dusk, but there was just time, I thought, to get a few more whins for the bonfire before dark came. From the top of the path you could look down and see the whole of Bramblewick in the valley behind the cliff on which our cottage stood. At the north end of the village the cliff rose higher and jutted out seawards to a point called Gunny Nab, and north of this was an uneven stretch of ground called the Slack, used as a drying ground for nets and washing. It was here that Grab was building his bonfire. It was already very big, many times bigger than ours. But then he had almost every boy in the school helping him, and if any of their parents had any rubbish that would burn, like old mattresses, or piles of paper, it was taken there instead of to the midden, and it was no wonder that Fatty and Joss had said they'd rather see it burn than ours.

I thought suddenly, as we hurried along out of sight of the village, that I hated Fatty and Joss almost as much as I hated Grab. I had fought Fatty once and beaten him, and I thought I would like to start on him now and give him a good hiding, although I didn't know why. Joss wasn't worth fighting. He always started to cry when anyone just threatened him, but I thought I would like seeing him and Chicken have a fight, and Chicken win. I began to feel a bit miserable, and started to think about Mother all over again, and to wish that I hadn't kept back the nineteen shillings, and spent more than three shillings on fireworks. I remembered how I had once found a parcel of new knitting wool in the street, and taken it home to her, thinking how excited she would be; and how she had promptly put on her hat and coat, and taken it to the police station; and I remembered how thankful she had been when she heard that it had been claimed by an old woman who was very poor; and how she had told me that I must never keep things I found, if there was anything to show they belonged to someone. It was just as bad as stealing. But there had been nothing in the purse to tell who it had belonged to. The hairpins and the bottle didn't tell anything. I hadn't seen any name or initials on the handkerchief. It was too rotten. It must have been lost by a summer visitor, and no one could ever find out who. I tried to stop thinking about Mother, and to think only of the fireworks. One minute I was miserable, and the next I was excited. Suddenly I remembered the fags. We were now near a place in the cliff where you could get down into the whins, and where we had the bonfire. I took out the packet and helped myself, and asked Fatty and Joss if they would have one. I didn't offer one to Chicken for fear he would be sick. We stopped and lit them, and went on, and soon we had reached the bonfire deep in among the whins and brambles, halfway between the cliff top and the shore. It wasn't a very big bonfire. Chicken and I had done most of the leading for it, and even then we had only worked a few evenings in each week, and Saturdays, for there were always so many other things to do; yet what there was of it was good; dead whins, and grass and bracken, and some lengths of tarry rope and old net, all of it built on a foundation of thorn branches (so as to let in plenty of air); and what was more important still, protected from rain by some old sheets of corrugated iron Chicken and I had dragged from the shore. It was all beautifully dry.

We set to, collecting more whins from the thicket around. Joss worked well, but he wasn't so good at finding the branches you could break as Chicken and I. Fatty soon got a prick into one of his fingers, and sat down to try and get it out. He turned sulky. Then suddenly he said he was going to be sick, and he was sick, and again I was tempted to pick a quarrel with him and have a fight; but I was feeling a bit sick myself, and as it was getting dark very quickly, I soon decided that we had done enough, and after we had put what we had gathered on top of the bonfire, and put back the sheets of iron, I said we would go down to the shore and have some fun. The tide was not up yet.

I wasn't feeling so excited about the fireworks now. I had thrown away my fag. I knew I wasn't going to be sick for I'd got over the worst, but I was angry with Fatty, and I didn't see why he should share in the fun, when he had done nothing but sulk and nurse his finger and be sick. I decided I would let off only one roman candle, and one squib and perhaps a pinwheel, and a few ladies, and save the rest for when Chicken and I were by ourselves. But as we reached the shore we saw a flash, and heard the noise of a cracker, along by the coastguard's wall. It was too far away, and too dark for us to see who it was. It couldn't be Grab, for evening was his busiest time carrying out, and Thompson's didn't close till seven. I knew that it must be some of Grab's gang, and I suddenly felt excited again, and reckless. I didn't take any notice of Fatty saying we were in a good spot to begin. I led on towards the village, until we got within hearing distance of the boys who were still letting off chinese and ladies under the coastguard's wall. Then I stopped, close up to the cliff, so that for the present they could not see us, and undid my parcel. Grab wasn't there I knew, for his voice was always the loudest in his gang. I heard Len, however, and Kid, but I didn't worry. I took out a sixpenny rocket, fastened the stick in some clay, and asked Fatty if he dare light it. He daren't. Neither dared Joss, and I couldn't ask Chicken. I thought for a moment that I'd better leave it and set off something instead; then I got over my fear, struck a match, put it to the fuse and jumped back. There was a long wait. Then with an awful hiss it went off, shooting as high as the coastguard's roof, and falling almost to the ground before it went out. And, before I had got over the excitement of it, there was a shout from the boys who were there, the sound of them running towards us.

"Hey! They're all coming," Chicken shouted. "Shall we run up the cliff?"

I didn't stir. I didn't want to run away. I *wanted* them all to come. I took a squib out and quickly lit it. I had once seen Grab hold a squib in his hand until it burst, and I felt I could do anything after the rocket. I held it in my right hand, holding it out. It started to hiss and pour out a rain of sparks, by the light of which I saw the lads crowding round. It hissed harder. I knew the bang was coming soon. I nipped the end tight with my fingers, held my breath, closed my eyes, and felt for a moment that my fingers had been blown off. But the burst case with its end smouldering red remained in my hand, and as I dropped it I heard one of Grab's gang say in a way that thrilled me, and made me forget the pain:

"By God – it's Worms! Let a squib off in his bare hand!"

And while I felt for another squib, I greedily listened to the talk around me.

"Was it him fired off that bloody rocket?"

"*By!* Fancy holding a squib until it banged!"

"Has he got any more?"

"I bet that was a sixpenny rocket. It went twice as high as a threepenny one. He's going to let off another squib!"

"He's got his pockets full of squibs and things," I heard Chicken say. "He's got more than three bobs' worth. He's got another rocket, and roman candles, and pinwheels and jumpers!".

I let off another squib. It hurt more than the first but I didn't mind. I offered to let any other boy hold one. No one would. But Kid Fosdyck said:

"I bet our Tom would, if he was here. He'd hold one in each hand."

I didn't take any notice of this. I took out a fag, and lit it on the smouldering end of the second squib, and went on to light a roman candle. It was like a squib, but instead of banging, it shot out little fiery balls, which was just as exciting, because they looked as though they *would* bang. I didn't know how many boys there were watching me, but there must have been at least half of Grab's gang, and there wasn't one, apart from Len and Kid, who didn't seem friendly, and full of admiration. I felt that if I went on like this, I should have no more trouble because I was a foreigner. I felt that I might easily persuade them to give up Grab and make me their leader. With the help, say, of one of the biggest of them and the egging on of the rest, I might even fight Grab, and finish him forever. The thought of this made me still more excited. Instead of lighting something else, I took out the strings of chinese and ladies, and shouted, proudly:

"Hey! I've got a lot of these. Share them out among yourselves!"

I didn't offer any to Fatty and Joss, but I gave a whole string of ladies to Chicken. I took out some jumpers and some more squibs and handed them round, shouting as I did so:

"Let them off now! No keeping them!"

I was almost out of my senses with excitement. I didn't risk two squibs (I was certain Grab had never done so), but I dared to hold a jumper in each hand while someone set them off, and, thrilled by the wild shouts and swears of the boys, hung on to one of them almost to the last crack. I did not try to give further proof of my bravery. For the time being I was content to be the giver, to hear the merry cracking of chinese and ladies, to see the bright flashes, and the golden rain of squibs and fountains and wheels, to smell gunpowder and the reek of smouldering cases, to hear the swears and the delighted shouts around me, in which I felt was such a gratitude and admiration for myself. I stood in the middle of the crowd, smoking my third fag, not caring that it made me feel sick. I gave advice about the setting off of another roman candle, putting in a swear between each word I said. Every firework was a bloody firework, every boy a bloody boy, every bang a bloody bang, I had emptied the parcel of everything except the second rocket. This, I thought, I would keep until all the other things had been set off, and then I would say, just quietly, that I was going to buy a lot more fireworks before the fifth, and that anyone who wanted to come with me in future could. A boy had just lit a squib. It had started to hiss, and he had dropped it to the ground close to my feet. Holding the fag in my mouth, I picked the squib up, and held it out, shouting at the top of my voice:

"That's the bloody way to let the bloody thing off!"

It spluttered and hissed. It banged. There was a shout from the boys, which stopped very suddenly, leaving a dead silence in which I was horrified to hear Mother's voice calling my name. I could not for the moment see her, but I knew that she must have seen me; and I knew that she must have heard me, too. She called me again. I spat the fag from my mouth. The boys in front of me moved to one side, and then I did see her, against the lights in the windows of the old coastguard's station, and I moved between the silent boys towards her. She didn't say anything. She just took my hand and held it tightly, and led me towards the slipway. And it was not until we turned up past the coastguard's that someone let off a jumper – one of my jumpers – and threw it after us. And a boy shouted!

"Eh! Worms is going to get his backside slapped!"

And this was followed by shrieks of mocking laughter.

IV

DAD WAS OUT. Mother told me to take my coat off, and sit down at the table, which was laid for supper. I daren't look at her. She was taking off her things, but I could hear her breath going very quickly, and I knew that she was angrier than I had ever known her be. She frightened me more when she didn't speak, like this. It always made me think she had found out something specially bad, like my stealing from Thompson's shop. What *had* she found out? I knew she must have seen me with the fag in my mouth. She must have heard me say bloody. That was bad enough; but had she found out about the money? Did she know about the fireworks; had Mr Thompson told her anything?

I felt horribly sick. My head was aching. The smell of supper, the heat of the room, made me feel worse. I wished she would start and get it over, that she would punish me by sending me to bed. Suddenly she sat down at the table opposite me, and said in a dreadfully quiet, religious voice:

"I want you to look me straight in the face."

I tried to do so, but I couldn't really look at her eyes. They were like two bright lights shining right through me. I could only look at her breast and a little silver brooch she wore, and this seemed like another eye, although not so fierce. I waited, listening to her breath. Then she said:

"To think that all day I have been so proud of

you, Sonny, so *proud* of you; and that I should see you standing among all those rude boys, smoking, swearing, using that shameful, *horrible* word. To think that you could do anything so *low*, and shameful."

She stopped, and I had a sudden hope that she was going to tell me to go straight to bed. But she went on in a voice more dreadful than ever.

"Now you've got to tell me the truth, the real truth. Whose were those fireworks the boys were setting off? Look at me straight in the face."

I looked her straight in the face, but only for a second, and I said, looking at the brooch:

"Mine."

"Where did you get them from?"

"I bought them at Thompson's shop."

There was another pause. Then:

"Did you buy some cigarettes there, too?"

"Yes," I answered; and already I knew what the next awful question would be. But I thought I mustn't, I *mustn't* tell her. No matter what she said and did, I mustn't tell her about the purse: for her sake I mustn't, because of Thompson's bill and Dad's paints which perhaps he had already bought out of the sovereign.

"Where did you get the money from?"

I stared at the brooch, and inside me, as though I had two voices. I kept saying:

"I won't tell her about the purse I won't – I won't." But aloud I said, "I found it. I found it on the shore."

"When? Today?"

"No. A long time ago. I've been saving it up. There were two half crowns."

"And you didn't say a word to me about them?"

"No. I wanted to save them up."

"And don't you think, Sonny, if you had asked me to, that I would have done that for you? Couldn't you have trusted me? Couldn't you guess that I have been saving up some money so that you could have some fireworks on the Fifth, like the other boys? ... I've got one and sixpence I've been keeping for you..."

I did dare to look at her face then. There were tears in her eyes, and I don't know how I managed not to cry myself, at the thought of her love and kindness in saving up for me. But I knew that if I once gave way I should have to tell her everything. I felt sick in my mind as well as in my stomach. I'd start confessing. I'd tell her about the purse, and she'd be sure to say we mustn't keep the money, that it must be taken to the police station. I just said nothing, and looked down at her brooch again, while she went on in a low voice now more religious than ever.

"Oh, Sonny, don't you know how low and disgusting and wicked it is to smoke and swear? Don't you know that these are the things that lead to worse evils, like drinking and gambling, and even stealing? Don't you want to be a nice, clean, good boy, and grow up to be a good man? Don't you want to be different from those coarse, vulgar boys you were playing with? Don't you understand what pain you give me by doing things like this, when I want to be proud of you? Don't you understand how deeply it hurts me to have to talk to you like this, and punish you? Haven't you any love for me?"

When she said the word "love" I knew I couldn't stand it any longer. I started to cry, but I went on saying inside me, "I won't tell her. I won't tell her." She suddenly got up, and put her hands on my head, and stroked my hair. I felt worse and worse.

"Sonny," she said, very solemnly, "You've been good to tell me the truth about it. I knew that you had bought those cigarettes and fireworks because Mr Thompson told me, when I went in to get something. But I'm going to punish you. I'm going to send you to bed the minute you've had supper. And I want you, before you go to sleep, to think of what a wicked thing you have done, smoking and swearing like that, and to think of God, and to ask Him to forgive you, and ask Him to help you to go His way, and not yield to Satan's temptations. God is always watching, remember. He sees everything. He *knows* everything. But God is Love, and He forgives us our sins when we are sorry for them ... Take your boots off by the fire. They look quite wet. Then have your supper. There's tripe stew I specially made for you as a surprise, because I was so proud of you finding that sovereign, and because you brought it home, when we needed the money so much. Just think how happy we would all have been. Dad has gone to Mr Fenwick for some colours, and he'll be able to get on with the painting again. And I was going to ask him to lend you his saw after supper ... You make me very, *very* sad."

I don't think it would have been possible for anyone to feel sadder than I did, at this new proof of Mother's love for me. I could scarcely see to untie the knots of my bootlaces for tears. I knew I couldn't eat any supper either, although I like tripe stew better than anything. I would be sick for certain if I did, but if I didn't eat anything, I might just get over it by lying very still in bed. I told Mother I didn't want any, although I didn't say why. But she must have guessed, for she gave me a quick look and said:

"Very well. I'll keep it for tomorrow. You'd better tell me if you feel sick. I'll give you some medicine."

But just then there was the sound of Dad at the street door, and Mother said, very quickly:

"Hurry up. I don't want Dad to hear a single word about this. It will upset him too much."

Dad came in. I stopped myself crying, and kept my head turned so that he couldn't see my eyes were wet; but I took a sly glance at him, as he took off his coat and hung it behind the door. He had a loose brown-paper parcel which he had put down on a chair. He looked rather cross, and I was afraid that he had found out something too, although I wasn't afraid that he would punish me, for Mother would never let him do that. She did all the punishing herself, but if I did get into trouble Dad blamed her and said it was her fault, because she didn't bring me up the right way. He didn't look at me, however. He only looked at Mother, and he made a sound of disgust as he pointed to the parcel.

"Another of those nasty jobs," he said. "Another coffin plate to be lettered, and a rush job too, got to be done tonight. I went round to Fenwick to pay his bill and get the colours, and he was there making a coffin, and he asked me to do it ... Why can't he employ a proper sign-writer to do his lettering for him? He seems to think there's no difference at all between an ordinary painter and an artist. But he's got influence in the place, and he lets me have the colours at cost price, so I daren't refuse."

Mother always looked sad and spoke in a hushed voice when she was speaking about dead people.

"Who is it?" she asked.

"Oh – it's no one we know," Dad answered. "An old woman from one of the farms, who's been an invalid a long time. It's all down on the piece of paper he gave me, and a verse of poetry that's got to be lettered too. I'll have to start it as soon as we've had supper if I'm to finish it tonight ... I've just passed Captain Lingdale in the street. He must have only got home from sea this morning, yet he's already drunk. He was outside the King's Head shouting and swearing at the top of his voice. I shouldn't be surprised if there's fighting tonight, when the public-houses close. I only hope Mike Regan doesn't start on the spree again now that I can get on with the portrait."

It didn't make me feel any better to hear about Captain Lingdale, or to see the quick look Mother gave me when she said:

"Oh – that dreadful, *dreadful* man. His poor wife!"

Captain Lingdale was called "Boozer". He was the worst character in Bramblewick. It wasn't that he was just a drunkard, and fought, and used terrible language. He was an atheist, and actually boasted about not believing in God. He had once done a terrible thing. In the middle of a thunderstorm, he had stood on the very edge of Gunny Nab holding his hands upwards just like a preacher, and shouting at the top of his voice:

"God strike me dead! God strike me dead!"

And he still boasted about it, saying if there was a God he would have struck him dead with a thunderbolt. I felt that Mother must be thinking of what I had done, and that I might turn out just as bad a character as Boozer, after what she had seen and heard tonight. I kept my face hidden, hoping that Dad would not notice me at all. But suddenly he did, and he said:

"Has that boy been getting into trouble again? Why is he crying?"

But Mother was taking a piece of iron out of the oven and wrapping it in a piece of blanket. And when she had done this and got it under her arm, she lit a candle and all she said was:

"Yes. He's been naughty. But he's told the truth about it and he's got to go to bed as a punishment. Are you ready, Sonny?"

She opened the upstairs door, and I followed her, not looking at Dad, although I could hear him unfastening the coffin plate. I followed her to the attic. She went to the bed, put in the warm iron, and smoothed the pillow as she always did; and she lit a night-light, and I saw that she was going to take the candle away, as part of my punishment, so that I couldn't read or play. She put the night-light inside the washing bowl. Then she put her arms round me, and said again how it hurt her to punish me; but that I was to be sure and say my prayers, and that I was to do all that she had told me to do about asking God's forgiveness, before I went to sleep. She kissed me, but didn't say good night. She said she would come up later, and do this, and take the light away. Then, still looking very solemn and religious, she took the candle, and went downstairs; there was just enough light in the attic for me to move about.

For a moment or two, while I took off my clothes, I felt better. Although my head ached, I didn't feel so sick in my stomach. I hadn't told her about the purse; and she had believed what I had said about finding the half crowns; and perhaps she wouldn't ask me again, and everything would be all right. But when I took my trousers off, and heard the rest of the money chinking, I started to feel anxious again. I took it out, and it weighed like lead in my hand. I put it in my treasure-box. under the loose plank, but I couldn't stop thinking about it, and when I knelt down to say my prayers I was too frightened to start and I got up quickly, and got into bed, without even saying "Gentle Jesus".

I was glad to put my feet on the warm iron, for they had got very cold, and I was just as glad to put my head on the cool pillow, for my head was hot. But I daren't close my eyes, and I daren't start thinking about what I had done and about God. I wished Mother hadn't taken the candle away. The night-light spluttered and flickered, and, because of it being in the bowl, all the light from it went upwards, leaving everything else in shadow. I got more and more frightened. There was just one window, a skylight, and it was in the side of the roof that faced the street. I could hear people passing up and down; and now and again the shouting of boys in the Dock, where they'd be playing, now that they'd let off all the fireworks I'd given them. I thought about that and the way they'd shown their gratitude to me, and then, when Mother had taken me away, thrown that jumper and shouted. I wasn't quite certain, but I thought that I'd heard Fatty's voice among them. Anyway, Chicken would tell me in the morning, and if he had, I would give him the worst hiding he'd ever had in his life. But I soon stopped thinking about that.

My headache got worse, through my staring up at the slanting ceiling, with its bare rafters. I doubled my pillow and sat up a bit, so that I could see across the room to the fireplace. There was a dark recess on one side of it, and on the other side another recess where the stairs began, and this was even darker, except near the ceiling where a rafter caught the light, and stuck out like a hangman's scaffold I had seen in a picture in a history book. I stared at this rafter, and I knew I must start thinking of my sins, and then ask God to forgive me. I thought I'd best begin by saying my prayers properly, so I began, but without closing my eyes, to say "Gentle Jesus, meek and mild" – then there was a sudden sound of shouting from the street outside; men's voices quarrelling; and then, quite distinctly, I heard Captain Lingdale walking past, shouting the most dreadful swears, and the name of God, and Jesus Christ. I was staring at the rafter, but in the darkness below it, I could almost see the face of Boozer himself, as I had often seen it look when he was drunk, only bigger, like the face of the giant in "Jack the Giant Killer", with his hair and beard wild and tousled, and his mouth slobbering, and his eyes not looking at anything straight, yet bright and fierce like the eyes of a savage animal. I tried not to look, but I couldn't help myself. It was as though he was *ordering* me to do so. And as I looked the face of Boozer changed. His hair and beard became white and long, and flowing, his face became dreadfully stern, his eyes got brighter and stared straight at me. And I knew it was *God Himself!*

I shouted at the top of my voice:

"Mother – Mother!"

I heard her voice and Dad's and the door of the living room being quickly opened, and Mother's hurried footsteps on the stairs. I tried to shut my eyes, but I couldn't. I still saw God, and as the light from the candle Mother was carrying moved up the dark stairway, and then lit up the attic rafters, His face seemed to move towards me, and His mouth opened wide, gnashing with anger, and I thought I saw two enormous hands, with claws reaching down on me from the ceiling. I screamed at the top of my voice. I couldn't stop screaming even when the face seemed to change to Mother's face, and the dreadful hands became Mother's hands, holding me tightly. She kept asking me what was the matter, and her own voice was terrified.

"It was God. It was God," I screamed. "I saw Him."

I could feel her trembling. I knew she was frightened as she looked to where I pointed.

"I saw Him. I saw Him ... He came to get me for being wicked."

She waited quite a long time before she said anything, and although I could feel her comforting me, I knew she was still frightened herself. Her voice was shaking when she said at last:

"Hush – hush, Sonny. No one ever *saw* God. You mustn't say such a dreadful thing. God doesn't show Himself like that."

" But I did – I did," I cried. "I was trying to think of all that I'd done wicked, and to say my prayers, and He came to punish me."

Dad shouted from the foot of the stairs:

"What's the matter? Is he ill? Shall I come up?"

"No. I think he must have woken up from a nightmare," Mother shouted back. The door slammed again, then Mother said, not quite so terrified, but very religiously:

"Come, come, Sonny. It was only your imagination. God doesn't come like that for little boys. If you had said your prayers properly, God would have forgiven you. It was your conscience that made you think you saw Him. Look – there's no one in the room except just you and me. Is there anything else wicked you have done, that you didn't tell me about? Don't be afraid to tell me – to tell me everything."

She put her arms right round me, and I could feel words like little lumps, pressing inside me, and I felt they would kill me unless I spat them out; but I still thought I mustn't tell her about the purse for her own sake. I told her that I had often used words like that before, and even worse words, and that I had often smoked. I confessed that I had told her lots of lies, and that I had disobeyed her by going past Garry Nab, and to the Mill Dam. I confessed about my fight with Len. Then I said how I had stolen things out of Thompson's shop, including the jelly square which I'd stolen not more than a month ago.

She didn't say anything even when I told her that. She just stayed with her arms about me, and it was worse than if she had been angry; and suddenly, before I could stop myself, the last word pressing inside me came rushing up. It was a lie about the two half crowns, I said. I had told her a lie about the sovereign. I had found the sovereign in an old purse near Garry Nab, and there were nineteen shillings too. I had spent three of them on fireworks. I cried then. I cried, and cried, and cried. Mother cried a bit, too, but she got up, and soon she stopped crying and became very quiet. Then she said:

"Sonny. To keep something that you find is stealing, and it's almost worse than stealing to tell me a lie about it, for you have made Dad and me steal. I gave some of that money to Dad to pay for his colours, and that's gone, and I've paid Mr Thompson something, too. But I don't believe that you thought of this, that you could have done such a wicked thing deliberately ... Now you must tell me everything else. Where is the purse?"

"I buried it in the sand. It was all torn."

"Was there anything in it to tell who it might belong to?"

"There was only a rotten handkerchief, and a bottle of smelling salts, and some rusty hairpins."

"Where is the rest of the money?"

"It's in a box under the loose plank by the wash-stand."

"You must show me where."

I had to get out of bed, and Mother held the candle while I lifted the plank and took out my box. I gave her the money and got back to bed, still crying. Mother came back to me, but she didn't put her arms round me. She said:

"Sonny, darling. I know you've told me the truth now. You needn't feel frightened any more about God. You must just close your eyes and say your prayers, and ask Him to forgive you, and help you never to do a wicked thing like this again. I'm going downstairs now, and I'm going to ask Dad to go round to the police station, and tell the sergeant everything; and take all the money that is left, and say that if it is claimed by the person who lost it, we'll make up all that has been spent."

She put her arms round me again, and hugged me, and kissed me.

"Oh, Sonny," she said. "I don't want to punish you anymore. I don't think you meant to be wicked. I know it's because you have to mix with these low, vulgar village boys, and I pray so hard that soon Dad will earn enough money for us to leave this wicked place, and go somewhere where you can go to a *nice* school, and have nice boys to play with. I know you wanted to please me by bringing me that money. But the Bible says, 'What shall it profit a man, if he gain the whole world, and lose his own soul?' It would be better for us all to starve rather than take money that isn't ours. It makes me far happier to know that you have spoken the truth about these wicked things, and that you are sorry, than if someone had given us a hundred pounds, and Dad and I hadn't to worry about money any more. Now you're not to be frightened again. God will forgive you, just as I have forgiven you, and Mr Thompson will forgive you, when you go and tell him and say that you are sorry, and pay for what you stole out of the money I was saving for your crackers ... I'll leave the candle for you this time. You *are* sorry, aren't you, Sonny?"

I could scarcely get my breath to say yes, I was

crying so hard; but I did say it; and I promised that I would never again swear, or tell lies, or be disobedient, or fight, unless another boy hit me first, or was cruel to a smaller boy who had no one to protect him. She kissed me again, and I listened to her going downstairs, and then talking to Dad, and Dad shouting a bit, as though he was vexed, and then the sound of him going out and banging the street door. But I didn't feel frightened, any more than I'd feel sick when I'd been sick, and after I'd said my prayers, and asked God to forgive me, I didn't think any more about Him, or the fireworks, or Grab or Mr Thompson. I just thought of Chicken, and wished I hadn't been unkind to him so often, and then I imagined Fatty hitting Chicken, or twisting his arm, and my going for Fatty – after I'd warned him – and giving him a good hiding. I must have gone to sleep very soon, for I didn't hear Dad come back, and I didn't remember Mother coming up last thing, to tuck me in, and kiss me good night.

V

THE POLICE SERGEANT told Dad that he hadn't heard of anyone losing a lady's purse, with all that money in it, and a bottle and a handkerchief and a lot of hairpins; but that he'd put up a notice saying a purse had been found, and that if anyone claimed it and proved it was theirs, they would have to have the money; but that if no one did so in a month, then Dad had better just keep it. Dad told Mother that it would be all right if she used some of it for paying Thompson's next bill, and he used some for paying Mike to sit for him again, so that he could get on with the Academy picture. The sergeant didn't think that there was any chance of it being claimed, and anyway someone was bound to give an order for some photos or perhaps a portrait before long, and it would be a pity if he had to stop work just because of that. Mother stuck out for not using any of it; but at last she agreed to let Dad have some, and regard it as a loan. She wouldn't let me have any more of it for fireworks though, and she said I mustn't have the one and sixpence she had saved, seeing that any moment she might have to give up the whole amount I had found. But she didn't go for me anymore, and she was very kind about Mr Thompson and the jelly, and she said she would pay for this herself, and not make me go and confess to him, and I don't think she ever did tell him I'd stolen it.

Yet, while I was relieved about this, and felt better with having no sins preying on my mind, I was not happy next day, which was the day before the Fifth. The only exciting thing I could think of was the bonfire, for the sea had become smooth again, and anyway the tide would be too late for me to get along the shore at dinnertime and be "first on"; and by tea-time all the best places would have been "scratted". And while the bonfire *was* an exciting thing to think about, I couldn't do so without thinking of the fireworks I had let off and of how more thrilling it would have been if I had saved them.

School that day was worse than ever. The boys mocked me about last night, asking me if Mother had smacked my backside, and imitating her voice as she had called me. I had to tell Grab twice, in front of all the others, that I *was* afraid of him. I had no chance to talk to Chicken alone, and didn't wish to anyway. And whenever I looked at Fatty and Joss, I knew that they disliked me, and that I disliked them even more, and it was all I could do to ask them if they were going to help with the bonfire after tea. I remembered later how Fatty had grinned when he had said "Aye", and how Joss had given Fatty a shifty look; but I didn't suspect then what they were thinking and planning.

I had to call at the studio on my way to our meeting-place, at the foot of the cliff path. It was at the west end of the last row of cottages, not far from where the cliff path fell to the back end of the village. It had been a fisherman's warehouse, but

Dad had got Mr Fenwick to take off one side of the tiled roof and replace it with glass, so as to have what he called a north light. Dad didn't very often let me go inside the studio, for fear I might touch any of his things, like his camera or his paints or his treasures. Mother said that most of his treasures were just rubbish, but I didn't think so. Some of them had been bought in auction sales. Others had just been given to him, by the wives of local sailors, who, Dad said, didn't realise their true value. He had, for example, a Zulu war shield, and a real bow and a quiver full of real arrows. He had a harpoon which had belonged to a Bramblewick whaler more than a hundred years ago. He had a bottle containing a snake which a sailor had brought from South Africa, and the sword of a sword-fish, and a shark's tail, and a lot of queer-shaped pots that had come from all over the world. And one of his most wonderful treasures, and the one I longed for most, because really it had been given to me by an old captain, only Dad had claimed it, was a model of a South Sea Islander's war canoe, with a sail and paddles. He said it was much too valuable a thing to play with and that I'd only lose it or smash it up, and it was hung up on one of the walls, quite thick with dust.

Dad had been painting Mike Regan all afternoon, and I had to tell him that tea was ready. I always had to knock at the door, and I did so, and to my surprise, Dad asked me to come straight in, so that I knew he was in a very good temper.

"Now, Sonny," he said, very cheerfully. "Would

you like to look at the picture of Mr Regan?"

I didn't look at the picture first but at Mike himself who was standing with his back to the fire, just lighting his clay pipe. I don't think there was anyone, apart from Mother, that I really loved as I loved Mike. He was bigger than any man in Bramblewick, and he never stretched himself to his full height, but always kept his shoulders bent, and his head leaning forward, as though he felt that ordinary people wouldn't be able to hear what he said when he spoke to them, although his voice was deep and strong, and terrible when he was angry. There was no man in Bramblewick who talked to me like Mike did. Often he talked to me just as though I was grown up, and in summer, when his coble was launched for the salmon fishing, he would let me sit inside her with him for hours while he mended his nets, and unless he was in one of his sad moods when he was thinking of his brother Tom, he'd be talking all the time. I knew all about how he had come to Bramblewick. He had come (with his elder brother Tom), as a navvy, when they were building the railway line. Tom was bigger than himself and a great fighter. The navvies had lodgings in the village, among the fishermen, and every Saturday afternoon there were prize fights on the shore, with everyone free to join in; but no one had ever stood for long against Tom, and one day he and Mike had taken on four Bramblewick fishermen, and nearly killed them. But Tom, whose job was to light the fuses when they were blasting the rock in the railway cuttings, got very drunk one day, and forgot to run to shelter after he had lit a fuse, and he was struck by a piece of rock and killed. When the railway was finished, Mike, who had learnt all about salmon fishing when he was a boy in Ireland, decided to stay in Bramblewick where he'd be near the grave of his dear brother, so he took a cottage, and sent to Ireland for his sister to come and look after him. He bought a coble in Burnharbour, and re-named her *Shannon Rose,* and started salmon fishing in the summer months, although he worked as a labourer in winter, and was now grave-digger in the very churchyard where Tom was buried. Mike's hair was turning grey, but he was still himself the strongest man in Bramblewick, and the best fighter (although some of the boys said Boozer Lingdale was). Yet he only fought when he was drunk, and this was rare, for the death of Tom had been a great lesson to him, and he'd go for months and not touch a drop at all. Once he started, he'd go on until he had spent all the money he had earned for weeks before, and he'd go from pub to pub in Bramblewick, asking every man to fight with him, so that the publicans had to complain he was driving their trade away.

The first thing he did was to get hold of me with his great rough hands, and swing me high above his head, and hold me there as though I weighed no more than a cardboard box. Then he let me down, and pointing his pipe to the picture, he said:

"Look at the likeness your father is painting.

Can you tell me why he'd want to paint a picture of a rough fellow with a mug like mine, and think he's going to make a great fortune out of it? Don't you think he'd have done better if he'd let me wear the clothes I wear for the church, and a decent hat, and a clean silk scarf round my neck, instead of the old shirt I work in, and the hat I wear in summer for the coble, and the dirty pipe in my mouth!"

The picture was fixed on an easel in front of the platform where Mike must have been standing before I came in. There was a screen behind this platform, with a woodland scene painted on it, including a rustic seat, and it was against this people had to stand when they were having their photos taken. The woodland scene came out in each photo, but the trees and the seat didn't look real, and I was glad Dad hadn't tried painting them into Mike's picture. It showed Mike as he always looked on a hot summer's day when he was in the *Shannon Rose,* wearing a cotton shirt without a collar, and his sleeves rolled up, and an old cotton hat on his head; and, tied by the sleeve ends in front of his chest, a blue fisherman's guernsey. It wasn't finished yet, but no one who knew Mike could have any doubt as to who it was meant to be, and I *did* like it, and I was very proud of Dad having done it. But I couldn't say anything to Mike because of Dad, and I couldn't say anything to Dad because of Mike; but Dad himself said very quickly, as he looked at the picture:

"Oh – you don't understand, Mr Regan. This isn't like the portraits I've got to paint of the

Bramblewick people, of their fathers and mothers, and other relations, to hang up, in their houses, whether they're picturesque or not. It wouldn't look anything at all if I had you in your best clothes. I'd lose all the character of the subject. You wouldn't look like a fisherman. You wouldn't be picturesque. People who go to the Royal Academy don't bother so much as to whether a portrait is a good likeness of the sitter unless it's someone like the King or the royal family. They judge the thing as a *picture*, and if it's a character picture, it's character they want. I'm very pleased with the way I've got on this afternoon. If only the weather was fine enough I'd like to have you outside for an hour, leaning against the coble, so that I could get some of that in. Then a bit of sea in the background, and perhaps the point of High Batts, but all very subdued, so as not to take away from the chief point of interest..." He suddenly picked up a paint brush, and moved towards the picture. "Now, just give me a few more minutes, Mr Regan, while there's light. I don't think I've got the shadows under the nose as deep as they should be." He turned on me sharply. "What did you come for, Sonny?"

"Mother said tea was ready," I told him.

"Well, run back and tell her I'm nearly finished, and I won't be long ... Hurry up, now."

I turned to go, but Mike suddenly put his hand in his pocket and took out a penny, and gave it to me.

"Here's a copper to buy crackers for the fifth of November," he said.

I looked at Dad, and I saw him give me a sharp glance, and I wondered if he had told Mike anything about the purse, and what had happened last night; but I thought he must have forgotten all about it, for all he said was:

"Now, you shouldn't do that, Mr Regan. You shouldn't give the boy money."

But he didn't stop me taking it; and as I went out I couldn't help thinking how queer it was that he should have said that at all, seeing that he wouldn't have been able to have Mike stand for him, if it hadn't been for me finding the money; and I didn't see why I should go back and give Mother his message, if he was going home himself so soon. I hurried straight on to the cliff path, and there was Chicken waiting for me, but no sign of Fatty or Joss. The first thing Chicken said was that he'd been wanting to talk to me all day, but that I'd never given him a chance. Then he said that he'd heard Fatty and Joss saying that they were not coming tonight, and that while he wasn't quite sure, he was almost sure that Fatty had shouted after me last night, and that he had certainly laughed when the others had, and that it was Kid Fosdyck who had thrown the jumper.

"Did your mother give you a hiding?" Chicken asked as we hurried up the steps. "Your mother was vexed, wasn't she, seeing you with a fag in your mouth, and hearing you swear? I'd have told you if I'd seen her coming, but I was looking at the squib you were letting off. Did she give you a good hiding?"

I never answered all of Chicken's questions – he asked so many – and I didn't want to be reminded of the nasty part of what had happened. But I was quite pleased when he reminded me of how I had held the squibs, and the jumpers, and how none of the others dared; and I almost forgot about the nasty part when he said:

"*By!* It was a treat, those squibs, and roman candles, and that rocket, and everyone letting off chinese and ladies at the same time. I bet the others won't have a better go tomorrow night. I bet Grab, and Len, and Kid won't have such a lot of different things to set off. And our bonfire will be better than theirs even if it isn't so big. It's twice as dry ... Are you going to buy any more fireworks?"

This made me feel sad again. I had got the money I had saved before I had found the purse, and now the penny Mike had given me, but this wouldn't buy much more than a few squibs or some strings of chinese and ladies, and that wouldn't look much after last night. But I didn't tell Chicken I was sad. I just told him that I'd be getting some more tomorrow. and he went on:

"I wish I had an uncle with a lot of brass. Father came home tight again last night, and he *did* make a row. He started swearing at Mother, and Mother went for him with the frying-pan. He didn't go to bed. He slept on the kitchen floor, and he's got a great lump on his brow, where Mother hit him with the frying-pan. It was Captain Lingdale set him on drinking, Mother said. Boozer nearly got locked up last night. He went for Mr Wright, at the

Dolphin, because Mr Wright wouldn't give him any more to drink, and it took all the chaps who were there to chuck him out, and he's on the booze again today. Mother hasn't had any money to buy real meat for over a week, and we've had nowt but a rabbit that someone picked up dead at the bottom of Low Batts cliff and gave to Father."

I remembered that Mother had given me a piece of cake to put in my pocket, because I had wanted to get tea over quickly, and I gave this to Chicken. I always felt sad when I thought of Chicken's home. I'd often heard Dad and Mother saying how sorry they were for Mrs Burton, and when she was ill, Mother had made Dad go round and leave a parcel of food, with a shilling in it, on the doorstep; but Mother wouldn't have anything to do with Mrs Burton herself, because she sometimes went on the spree, too, and she used filthy language, even in front of her own children. Mr Burton was a pedlar, and I had heard that he was nothing better than a tramp when he first came to Bramblewick. There were four other children younger than Chicken, one of them only a baby. They lived in a broken-down cottage, up a dark alley, and as Mr Burton had no regular work, and spent nearly all the money he did earn on drink, Mrs Burton had to keep the family out of what she earned by washing clothes.

But Chicken didn't talk any more about this. As we walked along the cliff he munched at the cake, and he said it was champion, and he went on praising me about last night, so that I soon felt quite happy, and, forgetting the promise I had made to Mother, I told him a lot of lies about Uncle Fred, and my holiday at Liverpool, and I boasted about Dad and the picture he was painting, and said he was certain to get a hundred pounds for it, when it was sent to the Royal Academy. And Chicken listened to me in such a way that I forgot he was so ragged and dirty, and that I was really ashamed to be seen with him, and I quite liked him. I didn't once think about Fatty or Joss, or Grab.

We went down into the whins, and came to the bonfire. We took off the sheets of iron, and it was all beautifully dry. It wasn't going to be so bad tomorrow night after all, I thought. We'd have plenty of chinese and ladies to set off, and I said to Chicken that I'd bring some potatoes with me so that we could roast them in the embers when the bonfire burnt low, and eat them.

"*By!*" he cried, "that will be champion. I only wish we'd got some now. I like taties almost better than anything. I'm glad Fatty and Joss aren't with us. They don't help much, and they only argue. I believe we're better without them."

We set to work. There wasn't much daylight left. We had already collected all the dry whins and grass close to the bonfire, and we had to work upwards through the thicket, towards the cliff top. I agreed with Chicken that we were better without Fatty and Joss. We worked twice as hard, and Chicken and I couldn't quarrel, for Chicken always did exactly what I said. We found a big clump of whins, and almost every branch was withered and dry. We broke off as much as we could drag, and started down towards the bonfire. Then we were startled by the sound of voices on the cliff path above.

We stopped where we were, listening.

The cliff path led to Garry Beck, but was never used in wintertime, except when the tide was up. The tide was down and anyway there were no boys who lived at Garry Beck, or at the farms to the south. And the voices *were* boys' voices, moving quickly our way.

"It's Grab," said Chicken. "It's Grab."

I knew it was, before he spoke. I pinched his arm, and whispered:

"Shut up. Keep still!"

We waited. The voices came nearer. And now distinctly I heard Grab say:

"Aye. I reckon this is it. Fatty said it's about halfway down the cliff, and they've got it hid under some old iron. I'll go first, and then we'll all spread out."

I knew, from the direction of Grab's voice, that he had found the path that led almost straight down to the bonfire. Between us and him and the other boys, the thicket was dense, and we might have stayed hidden. But before I had time to think of this, or of the consequences, I ran down and I reached the bonfire just as Grab appeared between the bushes above, and discovered it. Chicken had followed close behind. I was nearly crying, but it was more with the thought of Fatty's treachery than fear. I looked Grab straight in the face, and he looked almost frightened himself until the other lads appeared behind him; and then he laughed. and said, sarcastically:

"Eh – lads. What the hell's this? Here's Worms! What's that heap of grass and whins? Damn it – it looks almost like a bonfire!"

The other boys, among them Len and Kid, but neither Fatty nor Joss, laughed and came closer. Grab laughed again, and he suddenly took a handful of grass from the top of the bonfire, and showed it to the others.

"*By!*" he said. "That's nice and dry, drier than anything we've got on our bonfire. Look at those iron sheets. It's a good idea, you know, keeping it covered up every night. We ought to have summat like that. When are you going to set fire to it, Worms?"

I knew that he was only playing with me; that Fatty had told him about the bonfire, that he had come either to light it or steal it. I didn't say anything, but I still looked him in the face, and I was too angry to be afraid, even of him. Len suddenly cried:

"Set it alight, Tom. You ought to have heard him last night boasting about holding a squib in his hand, and smoking a fag, before his mammy came to smack his backside. Set it alight. Let's see it burn. There's only Chicken with him. and he's another bloody foreigner."

The other boys joined in a shout of:

"Go on, Tom. Set it alight. Set it alight!"

But Grab. turning to them, only grinned. and

said sarcastically:

"Garn. Don't talk so daft, set it alight – set it alight. Don't be so cruel. You want to think of all the trouble Worms and Chicken have had, leading all this and keeping it dry. None of you would like to have someone come and set fire to your bonfire. You ought to have more thought for another kid's feelings. I bet Worms and Chicken have been looking forward for weeks to setting it alight tomorrow. Just as we have for ours. Haven't you, Worms?"

I didn't answer. I knew he was playing with me. And the others did, too, for they laughed, and one of them said mockingly:

"Aye. Tom's right. We mustn't be cruel."

"Nay," Grab went on. "We mustn't. All I'm thinking of is that a bonfire like this is going to be wasted, along here with only Worms and Chicken to see it burning. So I reckon we ought to take it, and put it on ours. Each of us can carry a bit down to the shore. Then we can tie it up and drag it. Now what do you all say to that? That wouldn't be cruel, would it? Worms and Chicken could come and see it burn, same as anyone else."

There were shouts of laughter, and of "Aye. Aye. Come on!" from the rest of the boys, who moved closer. Grab took a coil of rope from under his jacket; and grinned at me. I could have killed him at that moment, I hated him so; but I tried to keep cool, and I tried to get a box of matches out of my pocket, without him noticing it. I thought I would stop him stealing it, at any rate. I waited until he reached forward over the bonfire to get hold of an armful; then, with my eye already on a good place close down to the foundations, I quietly struck a match, and held it against some dry grass.

I might have known that Grab would stop me. He swung round, kicked at my hand, and stamped at the burning grass until it was out. He got hold of me by the shoulder and snatched at the matchbox, and suddenly I saw his face as close to mine as it had been yesterday, when he had caught me on the shore. And this time I could not stop myself. I struck him with my clenched fist as hard as I could, on his nose.

It wasn't a fight that followed. I was on my knees when I struck. Before I could get up, he gave me a stinging slap across the face, that blinded me, and set me rolling over on to my back. He gave me another. Then he kicked me, and gave me still another slap on my face; and I could see nothing of what was going on, because of the pain, and my tears. Everything was mixed up. Everyone was shouting and swearing, and I couldn't make out anything except that they were tearing the bonfire to pieces, and that some of them were already starting down the cliff to the shore. But I knew when the last of them had gone, and I sat up, and saw Chicken standing beside me. He was crying, too.

"Are you better? – are you better?" he was saying. "Hurry up and tell your mother. Tell her to go and get the policeman to them. They're thieves, that's what they are, they're thieves. I wish I was bigger. I'd *kill* Grab Fosdyck. You hit him, anyway. I bet you made his nose bleed. Come on. Let's go and tell your mother. Let's run along the cliff top. We can get there before they reach the Dock. They've taken everything except the bottom bushes. Even the iron sheets."

I got up, wiping the tears away with my coat sleeve. I was still nearly mad with pain, but I was madder with rage. I thought of God, and I prayed to Him inside me to punish Grab, to stop him and the others stealing the bonfire. Then I thought of Mike Regan, and with just one look at the empty place where the bonfire had been, I shouted madly to Chicken:

"Come on!"

It was nearly dark, but we knew every inch of the way up the cliff, and we could run when we reached the level path at the top. We *did* run. We could hear the other boys on the shore. They were laden with what they had stolen, and we gained on them, and by the time they had reached the coastguard's wall, we had reached the top of the cliff steps, and I thought that if Mike was at home I could get him to cut them off before they reached the edge of the Slack. I didn't think of what we should do then, but I just felt that Mike could do anything he wanted to, because he was so brave and strong. But he lived on the opposite side of the Dock, down an alley leading from Cliff Street, and when we had run down past the rubbish chute, and by the end of the coastguard's cottages we saw Grab and his gang just coming up into the Dock itself, dragging the bonfire, and I touched Chicken's arm, and we stopped by the wall of one of the cottages, so that we could see, yet not be seen. The street lamps were lit. A group of fishermen stood by the lifeboat house, smoking and talking. Grab stopped, quite close to them, for the rope of the bonfire had worked loose. Among the fishermen were Luke and Tindal Fosdyck, and Tom and Reub Stainforth and Zach Graham, who belonged to the three cobles which fished all winter. I didn't like any of them. They were all big men and very brave, but they were gruff, and mean and never friendly; and they would never let me go near their cobles, and they hated foreigners just like the boys did. The only thing I had ever heard Mother say in their favour was that they went to chapel or church regularly, and didn't drink like Bramblewick sailors did.

They all looked at the boys and the bonfire; and Zach Graham, whom I disliked more than any of them, because he had once caught me sitting on his coble, and hit me, shouted at Grab:

"Now then. Where have you got all those whins from?"

One of the boys, not Grab, shouted back:

"It's Worms' bonfire. We're taking it to put on ours. He had it hidden in the cliff."

All the fishermen laughed, just as though it was a joke, and Zach shouted:

"Eh! You'd best not let his mammy know about it. She'll come and bray all your backsides with her umbrella."

"We're not afraid of *her,*" Len Fosdyck shouted back, "Nor his daft father."

The fishermen all laughed at this, as though it was an even better joke; and I felt angrier than ever. But I knew that we must wait for the gang to move on up the road, leaving the way to Cliff Street clear before we could dash across it. Grab gave a shout to the others to get hold of the rope again. But they had no sooner started to haul than Captain Lingdale came round the corner of Cliff Street into the Dock. He was drunk, and singing a song at the top of his voice, and he was carrying his hat in his hand, and waving it. He saw the bonfire. He walked, rolling from side to side, towards it, and gave a great shout.

"Ahoy! Ahoy!"

All the boys except Grab let go of the rope, and ran back out of his way; and he shouted at Grab, in his deep, rough voice:

"What *is* it? What is it? A Guy Fawkes bonfire?" Grab didn't seem a bit afraid of him. He just said, cheekily:

"Aye, Captain Lingdale. Are you going to give us summat to buy crackers?"

I thought Boozer was going to hit Grab for that. I thought he would kill him; but instead, he put his hands in his pocket, and pulled out a handful of coins, and threw them in the air, and shouted:

"Come on – come on. Haul away, lads. Haul away!"

And he got hold of the rope close up to the bonfire and started to drag it up the Road, while the fishermen laughed, and the boys scrambled for the coins, and then followed him, shouting and cheering. I nudged Chicken, and we rushed down and across the Dock, and up Cliff Street. I looked anxiously towards home, but the alley where Mike lived was only halfway up, and I turned into it, Chicken following close. I knocked at Mike's door. It was opened by Miss Regan. She was a little woman, with grey hair, and a wrinkled face, and weak eyes, and she always looked as though she had just stopped crying. She spent all her time in the house, and never seemed to have anything to do with Bramblewick folk. I tried not to show her that I had been crying, and I just asked her if Mr Regan was in. But she must have noticed I was very troubled, for she said, anxiously:

"No. He's not. Is it the Vicar who wants him? Has he got a grave to dig in the morning?"

I said no, I only wanted to see him, and she answered:

"Well, maybe you'll have a hard job finding him; for he's started drinking again, and there's no telling in which of the publics he'll be. Is it your father wants him?"

I was so disappointed I nearly started crying again; but I said no, I only wanted to ask him something, and she shut the door, and we hurried back along the alley. There were seven pubs in Bramblewick, and I'd no more dare to walk into one of them than I'd dare to walk in the graveyard at night; but Chicken often had to go to them, looking for his father when someone wanted him, and as soon as we got into the street, he said he'd go into the Dolphin, and ask if Mr Regan was there. The Dolphin was almost in the Dock, separated from Thompson's shop by another alley, which led to Mr Thompson's house. I waited while Chicken went in, but he was quickly back, saying Mike had been there, but that he wasn't there now. There was the Mariner's Tavern in the Dock itself, just beyond the lifeboat house. We had to pass the fishermen to reach it. We ran, and I didn't look at them, but I heard them laughing, and I felt I would like to see a thunderbolt fall and kill them all. Chicken popped into the Mariner's. Mike wasn't there. On the opposite side of the road was the Brig, and almost next door to it, The Fishermen's Arms. Mike had been in both, Chicken found out, but he had gone, and no one knew where. We hurried up the road, past the fried-fish shop, to the Bridge over Bramblewick Beck, where several other alleys left the road, and twisted among the cottages to the cliff edge. The first of these led to a narrow grassy ledge that overlooked Gunny Nab and the Slack, and I could see, by the marks on the cobblestones, and stray bits of whin and grass, that the bonfire had been dragged up it.

I began to lose hope of ever finding Mike. It was clear he had started on one of his sprees, and that it was the money Dad had paid him (which had come from the money I had found) that had tempted him to his first drink. He always began by having just one drink at each pub in Bramblewick; but sometimes he would go up the Bank then to the

Station Hotel, and make the round of the country pubs before coming back to the village. By this time the boys must have reached the Slack. I didn't think Boozer would have gone far with them, but they wouldn't need his help to put my bonfire on to theirs; and I thought that if this happened it wouldn't be easy for Mike to make them take it all back. But there were two other pubs between us and the cliff, and we soon reached the first of them, which was called the Ship. It was a little crooked building with funny bottle-glass window-panes, and a sign with a sailing ship on it; and Dad said it was one of the most picturesque subjects in Bramblewick, and he had done several pictures of it. Chicken went straight in; but before he was out again I heard heavy footsteps coming up the alley, and there was Mike himself. He was wearing a reefer coat over his guernsey, and he was walking with his hands in the pockets of it, with his head leaning forward, and he was singing a Catholic prayer to himself, as he often did when he was drunk. Mother had told me that I must never go near Mike when he had been drinking; and I don't think she liked him very much when he was sober, or that she'd have had anything to do with him at all if he'd been a Bramblewick man. But I could only think of our bonfire and getting even with Grab, and I walked straight up to Mike, and I told him as quickly as I could what had happened. He bent right down to me, so that I could smell the drink in his breath. He didn't seem to understand very well, for he kept asking me to say what I had said over again, and I began to think that, after all, it was no good and that he was too drunk to help me. But when I told him about Captain Lingdale, he suddenly stiffened himself, and took his hands out of his pockets, and made a funny rumbling sound in his throat.

"Och – it's that man Lingdale has stolen your bonfire, is it? Why didn't you tell me that before, and I'd have understood. Do you mean he has taken it to put it with the bonfire the other boys have down the Slack by the Nab?"

I wasn't thinking about Boozer; only about Grab and the others; but I just said, "Yes," and he answered:

"Come on, then, and I'll see about it."

Chicken had joined us. We followed Mike up the alley, that was lit by flickering gas lamps, fixed to the cottage walls wherever the alley gave a twist. But we hadn't reached the grassy space, where the alley ended, when we heard a noise of voices, and three boys rushed past us, shouting:

"Boozer's set t'bonfire alight."

I ran past Mike, who was walking very unsteadily. As I turned the last cottage, I saw a red glare, and, looking down at the Slack, saw Boozer with a torch of paper in his hand moving round Grab's bonfire, which was already well alight, and setting fire to it in other places, and shouting as he did so.

"Hurray! Hurray!"

I didn't think just then about it being our bonfire, too, that was burning before its proper time, nor of how the stealing of it had been avenged. I was fascinated by the flames, and the showers of sparks, and the crackle and the roar and the smell of burning; by the sight of Boozer with no hat on his head, and his hair wild, and his face red in the light of the fire, careering round with the torch in his hand, shouting. I scarcely noticed the boys, although most of them were standing quite near the fire, with Grab; and Grab himself nearly screaming at Boozer with rage. I even forgot about Mike, until he strode past me, down the Slack, taking off his reefer coat as he went, and shouting dreadful swears.

Boozer didn't see him until he was quite close. Then he turned, and Mike shouted at him, and knocked the torch out of his hand, and gave him a push that sent him stumbling back, well out of the way of the fire. And then, as Boozer got his balance, Mike threw his coat on the ground, and shouted at Boozer:

"Come on with you, let us fight!" and he reached forward and gave him a slap across the face; and Boozer came for him, and they began to fight. I knew it was wicked for grown men to fight; I knew that it was wicked to watch them, but I couldn't help watching them and hearing them shout and swear; and I couldn't help shouting myself:

"Go on, Mike! Go on, Mike!"

Everyone must have forgotten the bonfire, which was burning fiercely, lighting up the whole of the Slack to the cliff edge. Everyone was shouting. I didn't know whether the other boys were cheering Mike on because of Boozer having lit their bonfire, or cheering on Boozer, because Mike was a foreigner and they wanted him to lose. But Chicken got hold of my arm, and kept jerking at it, and shouting for Mike, and I kept shouting, too, although we couldn't tell who was winning. They just went on hitting each other, and swearing at each other, until suddenly Boozer stumbled and fell flat on his stomach, and rolled over and lay there panting and coughing, while Mike stood over him, shouting:

"Och – you dirty beast – you dirty beast! Would you steal the children's bonfire and then set fire to the thing itself! You dirty beast! You dirty beast!"

And then I knew Mike had won, and I was mad with joy and excitement, just as though I had been fighting myself with Grab, and beaten him. I got hold of Chicken's arm, and we shouted together, and I felt I would like to go down and start a fight with Grab, while Mike was there to see fair play; and it was a strange thing that I should look round just at that moment and see Fatty Welford, standing by himself behind us, staring at Mike and Boozer and the fire, and not knowing I was near him. Mike was putting his coat on again. Boozer had sat up, but he was coughing and spitting and there was no fight in him. Grab and the boys were crowding round the fire, and I heard a boy shout:

"It's no use. We can't put it out now. Let's go and get our crackers, and set 'em off. Let's pretend it's Plot night."

I turned on Fatty. I didn't ask him anything. I knew he had told Grab about our bonfire, just to get in with him, but I knew he would say he hadn't. I didn't bother saying the Bramblewick rhyme either, in case he ran away. I just said "Sneak," and I hit him, and went on hitting him, while Chicken egged me on. He gave me several good hits, once on the place where Grab had hit me, and it was a real fight. But in the end he put his head between his arms and began to cry. I didn't hit him anymore. I let him go. I looked down at the Slack again. The fire was burning fiercely. Mike was still swearing at Boozer, and was trying to get him to stand up and go on with the fight, but Boozer wouldn't. I should have liked to have stayed to see what happened; but Grab and the others were now coming up towards us, and as I knew it must be nearly seven o'clock, and that Mother might be out looking for me; and as I didn't want to see the Fosdycks letting off their fireworks, while we hadn't any, I thought I'd better go home. I felt very happy as we turned down the alley. I didn't feel sorry that we'd lost our bonfire, or for anything I'd done although I knew I'd been wicked, and that I'd already broken quite a lot of the promises I'd made to Mother last night. I remembered that there was last night's tripe stew for supper. That made me feel sad a bit, for I thought of what Chicken had told me about having nothing but one rabbit for a week. It was awful to think of him feeling hungry, when I had such a nice supper to look forward to. But I thought next that I could easily make up a story to tell Mother about him; and get her to give me some of the stew in a mug. I'd ask him to wait outside the house, and not tell him why. It would be a surprise for him.

VI

DAD NEVER TALKED much about his past. But I knew that he had lived in Ireland, and that he had a rich uncle who had paid for him to go to an art school in Liverpool; and that he would have stayed at his school a long time, and then gone to an art school in Paris, if his uncle hadn't died, leaving Dad without any money at all; so that he had to take a job with another man, painting the faces and robes of the images of saints for Catholic churches in Ireland. I think it was this that had made him religious. I didn't know much about Mother's past either, except that she had lived in a proper house in Liverpool, and that her parents had been religious, although, of course, they hadn't been Catholics. They had been dead a long time, and I had never seen them.

I couldn't remember coming to Bramblewick. I was only three then. We had come because a friend of Dad's (another artist) had been to the place for his summer holidays, and he had raved about it so much that Dad thought he would come and have a look at it. He thought it was the most beautiful place he had ever seen, and that if we could live in it for just a year or two, he'd be able to make a name for himself and paint and sell enough pictures for me to have a good education, and for him and Mother to go to Paris, and Italy, and other places where he could paint and earn even more fame and money. The rent of our cottage was only half a crown a week. It hadn't any water laid on, and there was no sink or drains. It was damp. The fire smoked whenever the wind blew a certain way; and at first it swarmed with rats and mice and beetles. But the great thing in its favour, Dad had said, apart from its being so cheap, was the shop and the shop window, which had just the right light for showing pictures, and he thought it would be a mistake to spend money on drains or water, or having the walls mended, seeing the place wasn't his and that we'd be out of it very soon, and when there was so much to be done making the studio.

Dad earned money in summer, selling watercolour sketches to the visitors. He didn't like painting these pictures, because the most popular subjects were those showing as much of the place as possible, for people to remember it by when they had gone away, while the subjects which he called really picturesque, like the Ship Inn, no one seemed to want. But he didn't hate this like he did having to take photos; although Mother often said that if it hadn't been for this we should have all gone to the workhouse. There was no other photographer in Bramblewick, so that he got all the trade. Whenever there was a wedding Dad had to take the wedding party, at the house or church if it was fine weather, or in the studio if it wasn't; and he had to take the bride and bridegroom by themselves. He took ordinary photos, too: family groups, children, babies. He hated it because, he said, it was bad for his name as an artist for him to have anything to do with photography, and because it took up so much of his time that ought to have been spent painting. Yet all he had to do was to take the photos and develop the negatives. Mother had to do the printing, and the toning and fixing and washing; and then the mounting and burnishing of every photo that was sold; and all this in the living-room between meals, using the bedroom washing bowls for the washing of the prints. Every drop of water had to be fetched from the tap at the top of Cliff Street, and the waste had to be carried downstairs and tipped into the street gutter. Dad, of course, had to fetch the water, but he didn't like it, and he had long ago said that I was strong enough to do it, and I *did* do it, too, when he was busy, or when he forgot.

Dad still liked Bramblewick. He got on well with almost everybody. He didn't like drinking and swearing, but that didn't stop him from being quite polite to the men who did drink and swear. He got vexed when the boys called after him in the street, or disturbed him when he was painting outside. But he didn't mind people watching him when he was at work, and he liked it when they admired what he was painting. Even Captain Lingdale had pleased him once when he said that a picture he had done of one of his relations was "the very spit of the chap". But Mother had always hated Bramblewick. She hated the well-to-do people who lived in the new villas Up Bank as much as she hated those who lived in the village itself. They nearly all had something to do with the sea.

Bramblewick once had been the biggest fishing village on the coast; but there wasn't so much money in fishing as in shipping, and most Bramblewick men were now sailors, and most of these captains or officers earning plenty of money. This was good for business, of course. Many of them had retired from sea with large fortunes, and if they were close with their money, they were very proud of living in their new houses, and they liked to have pictures done of themselves, and their parents or children, both painted pictures and photos. But Mother hated even having to do business with them. Although they were nearly all religious, good chapel- or church-goers, she thought they were vulgar. They were broad in their speech. I had heard her say that you never knew when the most genteel of the women was going to come out with some coarse expression. I had overheard her telling Dad how one woman, whose husband, Captain Haines, was a trustee of the Wesleyan Chapel, had asked her to come inside her living-room, and she had pointed jokingly at something on the mantelpiece, which her husband had brought from abroad. It was something *disgusting*. Mother had at once walked out, and felt she could never speak to Mrs Haines again, although she had been a very good customer. She hadn't said what it was, but, passing that house one day when the door of the living-room was open, I had peeped in and seen it. It was a working model of a baby sitting on a chamber-pot, and it stood right in the middle of the mantelpiece like an ornament; and I thought it was disgusting myself, and always when I saw Captain Haines and his wife in chapel I wondered how they could go on pretending they were religious. Mother had scarcely any friends in the place. All she wanted was to earn enough money to get out of it. Yet I think she wanted to do this more for my sake than her own and Dad's. She thought that Bramblewick had an evil influence on me. More than once I had overheard her telling Dad that she hoped we would soon have enough money for me to go to a nice school at Liverpool, and that, if we hadn't enough for us all to move there, it might be all right for me to stay with Uncle Fred. I didn't think she really meant that. In spite of Grab, and school and the other things I hated about Bramblewick, I hoped it would never happen. I thought I would rather we all went to the workhouse than that I should ever have to live with Uncle Fred, and listen to nothing but prayers and Bible readings from getting up till bedtime.

Doing sins was just like eating sweets or very ripe bananas, or anything else that was nice but disagreed with you: you could eat quite a lot and *feel* sick, and yet not *be* sick, if you didn't go on. I knew I had committed several sins that day of the bonfire. I had lied and boasted to Chicken about Uncle Fred, I had spoken to Mike Regan when he was drunk, and while I hadn't entered a pub myself, I had let Chicken do so for me, which was even worse. I had watched the fight between Mike and Boozer and egged them on. I had fought with Fatty, I had deceived Mother by not telling her all that had happened, when I got home, and I had told her still another lie about Chicken, for I said I had found him crying in the Dock, because he had nothing to eat since breakfast, which had nearly made her cry while she was putting some of the stew into a mug for me to take to him.

These sins stayed on my mind, but they didn't make me want to confess like the purse business had done; and I didn't feel so frightened about God as I had done before Mother told me He never appeared to people, even sinners, so that you couldn't see Him as I thought I had done. I realised that I must have imagined Him, just as I could imagine I saw Mother or Dad, or Mike, or anyone else I knew, if I shut my eyes. And I discovered, too, that if I had a sin on my mind, and I did something which I knew was good, the sin became much lighter; and also that if I did several good things, then, when I did do something bad, it didn't seem anything like so sinful. For example, if I got up in the morning the moment Mother called me, and washed properly, and cleaned my boots, it didn't seem to matter so much if I disobeyed her by going farther along the shore than Garry Nab. And if, without being asked, I fetched a pail of water, it almost made up for pretending I didn't hear her when she asked me to do something else; only when I did do something without being asked, she spoilt it by praising me so much that I felt I was doing something wrong.

Anyway, for a long time following the bonfire night I tried as hard as I could to be good and make Mother happy. I did get up when she called me. I didn't try to avoid running errands for her, or getting the coal up from the cellar at the back of the shop, or fetching water when she asked me. I smoked a fag-end I found in the street, but I didn't buy any more fags, although I found several pennies scratting. I told a few lies, but they weren't big ones, and as much as anything I told them to save making her unhappy, as, for example, that I hadn't been punished at school one day when Slogger had boxed my ears at least six times. And I scarcely swore once, and I never said "bloody", or used a dirty word.

Mike Regan kept on the spree for more than two weeks following that night. Dad was very vexed about it, for it meant that he couldn't get on with the picture; but Mother didn't mind, for a lot of orders for photos came in, and also an order for a picture, from someone Up Bank, of their father who was dead, which of course had to be copied from a photograph. Nothing more was said by the police sergeant about the purse, and Dad said it looked very much as though it was going to be all right, and that we should never have to pay back the money. Mother didn't say anything about it one way or the other, and I daren't ask her for fear of reminding her about the other things that had happened. She never mentioned that night again.

I was much happier being good like this, but I didn't get on any better with Grab. He gave me another good hiding for having hit him that night, and he set Len and Kid on to me again, and arranged one or two other fights with other boys of his gang, and took care to join in whenever there were signs of me winning. Fatty hadn't gained anything by telling Grab about our bonfire. The boys teased him about being fat as much as ever; but it wasn't long before he left Bramblewick, as his father had been sent to another station. Joss tried to be friendly again when he had gone. I wouldn't let him. I didn't want Chicken really, and at first I only let him come with me because I was sorry for him. One day he told me there was a lot of old floor canvas lying near the midden by the gas house. I went with him to have a look at it after school, and it gave me the idea of making an Indian wigwam close to where we had made the bonfire, only deeper in the bushes, where no one could see it. Once we had started it, it was more exciting than the bonfire.

First we carried the canvas to the cliff and hid it. Then we made a tunnel through the bushes, until we came to the thickest part, where we found a little hollow made by an old landslide. We were "first on" one afternoon and near Garry Nab we found a lot of bamboos that must have been washed from a ship. We carried them up, and they were just right for making the framework of the wigwam, although we had a lot of trouble tying them so that they didn't wobble. We put the canvas on the roof, and as there were several holes in it, we gathered grass and laid this on top; and we built up the walls with some more sheets of iron we found in the midden, and used another piece for the door. When we closed the door it was almost so dark inside that we couldn't see each other, and the first time we went into it when it was raining, scarcely a drop of water came through the roof. We pretended we were Indians, and I called myself Deerslayer, and Chicken, Little Warrior. I found an old carving knife when I was scratting, and I made a handle for it out of a piece of bamboo and called it my "bowie" and Chicken had a table-knife blade but it didn't look so good because it hadn't a curve to it, and there was nothing to fix a handle to. We had bows and arrows but they wouldn't shoot very far. We imagined lying in ambush for Grab and his gang, and shooting them down mercilessly, and we hung some tufts of grass and seagull feathers round the hut walls to represent their scalps.

One bitterly cold day Chicken said that all we wanted was a fire, so that we could sit by it and keep ourselves warm, and roast potatoes and eat them. I was afraid of this because of setting the whole place on fire; but we got some stones and built a proper fireplace; and although we were nearly suffocated the first time we lit it, it was all right when we made a hole in the wall for the smoke to get out, and whenever we went to the wigwam I took some potatoes with me and we roasted them and ate them. One Saturday afternoon we found a rabbit that had been killed by a weasel. There was a hole at the back of the neck where the blood had been sucked out, but it smelt quite fresh. Chicken said we ought to skin it, and put it in an old tin we had used to boil winkles in, with some water and potatoes, and make a rabbit stew. But I had read in an adventure book that the way savages cooked small animals was to leave the fur on and cover the whole body with clay and roast it, so that all the gravy stayed in. When it was done you could knock the clay off, and the fur came with it, leaving the meat just right for eating. There was plenty of clay, but it took us a long time to get it covered because the head and paws kept popping out, just as though it was alive, and in the end we had to tie it all up with string. The wet clay nearly put the fire out at first; so we raked the embers out of the way, pushed the rabbit right into the middle of the fireplace, and built the fire round it. Soon it was so hot we had to open the door and stand outside. It wasn't a success, though. When the clay got hot it began to crack, and jets of steam came out, and there was an awful smell of singeing fur. I don't think we waited long enough, either. The fur certainly came off when we broke the clay, and the flesh looked cooked on the outside, but it tasted of smoke and tarry string and singed fur, and even Chicken, after he had tried a mouthful, said it made him feel sick, and that he didn't want any more, and that it was a pity we hadn't made an ordinary stew of it.

I never told Mother about our wigwam; and I was certain that none of the other boys knew of it. We had a bush we always pulled across the entrance to the "tunnel" when we left it. We were always careful to make sure there were no boys on the shore when we went to it; and now that Fatty had gone, and I had finished with Joss, I knew Grab wouldn't find it, for he and the other boys always played in the street or on the shore, except at Gunpowder Plot time, or in spring when bird-nesting began. I don't think anyone would have ever heard about it, if it hadn't been for me trying to do a kind action.

Whenever a tramp came to Bramblewick, singing or selling bootlaces, or just begging, the boys shouted at him or pelted him with bits of clay or seaweed, or even stones if he tried to go for them. One afternoon, soon after we had cooked the rabbit, Chicken told me, when I met him at the usual place, that there was a queer-looking tramp up by the Bridge, and that the boys were all shouting and laughing at him because he hadn't any stockings on, and his trousers were split so that you could see his bare backside when he walked. I thought I would like to see him, so we ran down by the back of the gas house, and followed an alley which brought us to some railings at the edge of a wall that rose up from the Road, where we had a clear view of the Road itself. We were just in time to see the tramp walking down towards the Dock with the boys following him, and laughing and calling names. He was a queer-looking man and no mistake. He wasn't very old, but his hair was long and untidy, and he wasn't shaved, and I had never seen anyone with such ragged clothes. He hadn't any stockings, and you could see flesh through the holes in his boots, and also bits of straw sticking out round his ankles. He walked slowly and with a limp; and when he turned his head round to look at the boys, I saw that his face was blue with cold, and he looked terribly frightened, just as if the boys were wild dogs coming to kill him. But although it looked as though he was going to say something to them, his mouth only twitched and his eyes blinked, and he went on limping towards the Dock.

I felt very sorry for him. I would have liked to have run down and stopped the boys from teasing him, but although Grab was not there, they would have set on to me for certain and very likely shouted at the tramp all the more. We watched them out of sight. Then, knowing that the tide was down, and that the tramp would very likely go along the shore, we hurried back to the cliff path and climbed up a bit, so that we had a clear view of the slipway. Sure enough the tramp was already on the shore, the boys still following him, but throwing things at him, and shouting worse than ever. I wonder he didn't turn round and rush at them and half kill some of them. I wished he would. But he just limped on towards Garry Nab, and at last the boys stopped and began to turn back. I knew we could catch him up long before he reached the Nab; but we kept to the cliff top in case the boys should see us. We climbed down past where we had made the bonfire, and I saw that the bush hiding the tunnel was all right. We reached the shore and for a moment I thought he must have got round the Nab, for I couldn't see him. Then I saw him sitting on a stone at the foot of the cliff quite close, with one of his boots off, rubbing his foot with his hand, and groaning as though it hurt him very much. I didn't feel a bit afraid of him, although he gave a jump and almost stood up when he saw us. We went right up to him, and I said:

"It's all right. *We* weren't shouting at you. Those boys shout at everybody they don't know. *We're* different. *We're* sorry for you. Does your foot hurt very much?"

He got hold of his foot again. It was very dirty and covered with blood. He looked at us. His mouth twitched and his eyes blinked, but he couldn't say anything, and he just looked down at his foot again, and groaned, and all his body was trembling.

"He's a dumb man," whispered Chicken. "Ask him where he's going to. But maybe he's deaf, too."

I asked him where he was going to. He wasn't deaf, for he tried to speak, and then he shook his head and looked very miserably towards the village, and then towards High Batts Moor, and then shook his head again. I could tell he was only a poor tramp, with no home of his own, and nowhere to spend the night, unless he found a barn, and a farmer who'd let him sleep in it, and that wasn't likely because the farmers hated tramps, because they were supposed to be as bad as gipsies for stealing. His feet must have hurt him terribly. He was cold and you could see he was hungry. It was nearly dark, and the wind was cold, blowing off the sea. I thought of our hut and how cosy it was when the fire was lit, and the door was closed, and I remembered that the last time we had roasted potatoes we hadn't eaten them all, but left some of them in a tin box. If we got him to come up we could light the fire and get plenty of wood for him before dark. He could start on the potatoes, then we'd go home and I'd ask Mother to make some cocoa, and pack up something to eat, which I could say was for Chicken. I knew where there were some old sacks, and an old coat that would do quite well for blankets, and he could make a pillow out of a heap of grass, so that it wouldn't be anything like so bad as sleeping in a barn.

Although he couldn't speak a word he seemed to understand everything I said. I told him about the wigwam and the fire and potatoes, and he kept nodding his head, and when I pointed to where the wigwam was he quickly put his boots on, and got up, and followed us up the cliff. It was very steep in places and it must have been very bad for his poor feet, for he groaned all the time, and once he stopped and started coughing, but as soon as he had finished he came on, and soon we had reached the bush hiding the tunnel. He had to go down on his hands and knees then. Chicken went first, and I came next, and, as it was much darker here, I did feel a bit afraid of him, for he was still groaning, and it felt like a savage animal coming behind me. He went for the potatoes like a savage animal, too. He didn't stop to take their skins off. He'd eaten them all by the time we'd got the fire lit, and I remembered the rabbit which we had thrown into the bushes below the wigwam, and I wondered whether he would like to have a go at that, seeing that he still seemed hungry. But I thought that perhaps it would poison him, so I didn't say anything about it. He was very glad to feel the heat from the fire. He took off his boots again, and put his feet right up to it, and held his hands almost in the flames. I asked him if he would like to have some hot cocoa, and something else to eat, and some sacks to keep him warm. He tried to speak again and this time made a stuttering sound that was like "Yes," but he nodded his head to make sure that we knew what he meant. We got together all the sticks near the hut, and told him to keep the fire going, and that we'd very soon be back.

I felt a bit relieved when we got outside the tunnel again, and I think Chicken must have been frightened. for he said:

"*By!* He's a queer-looking chap. isn't he? Didn't he look queer eating those taties! *Are* we going to come back? It'll be dark."

I thought we would. because we'd promised, but that we'd just leave what we'd brought for him outside the tunnel, then shout to him and run away before he came out. I remembered that I'd left my "bowie" knife in the wigwam, and that I'd be really frightened if I saw him with that in his hand.

There was no need for us to go along the cliff path, for it was now dark. We hurried down to the shore, and we started running. But we hadn't got more than halfway to the slipway when we saw a man walking quickly towards us and, close behind him, Grab and several boys. I knew at once it was the police sergeant. I was always afraid of him, of course, because he was a policeman, and although I had nothing on my mind, I tried to steer up to the cliff, so as not to pass him close. But as soon as he saw me he stopped, and shouted, and then came right up. He had a very deep, stern voice, and he said, looking down at me:

"Now where have you lads been?"

I was so terrified that I hadn't a chance to say anything before he said:

"Have you seen anything of a tramp walking along the shore?"

I knew it was no use trying to tell a lie. I knew if I did he would find out and that I would get into terrible trouble. I told him yes, and he asked me some questions, and I told him everything and where the tramp was now. He looked at me very sternly, and he said:

"Come on, show me where the spot is."

I was too frightened now to be sorry for the tramp, for it was clear he had done something wrong for the sergeant to want him. Perhaps he was a thief, perhaps even a murderer. Yet I couldn't help thinking of him sitting by the fire, warming his poor feet and hands, and thinking about the cocoa I had promised him, and hearing us coming and thinking it was us fetching it when it was only the policeman coming to take him to prison. I nearly began to cry as I led the way, and Chicken got hold of my hand, and I didn't make him leave go as I usually did. I didn't notice the other boys following until the sergeant suddenly turned and told them sternly to run away home.

He followed us up the cliff, and it made him puff a bit for he was big and fat, and once he slipped and I heard him swear. We came to the tunnel, and there was the light of the fire shining from the wigwam, so there was no need for me to show the sergeant any more. He didn't try to get through the tunnel, however. He just forced his way through the bushes, and Chicken and I stood quite still, waiting. Then we heard the sound of the iron door being pulled away, and the sergeant saying gruffly:

"Hey – hey. Get up there!"

The tramp groaned, and the sergeant said, more gruffly:

"Come on, now. Get your boots on. I believe you're the man who was seen taking some turnips out of a field at Staintondale this morning. I'm going to take you in charge, and don't let's have any trouble with you. Get a move on. I don't want to be here all night ... Hey – you lads!" he suddenly shouted to us. "Did you put this fire on, or did he?"

I shouted back that we did.

"Do your parents know about this spot? And your having a fire in it? It's a wonder you haven't burnt yourselves to death. Let's have no more of it. And you'd better be running away home now, quick, or you'll feel my stick across your backsides ... Come on, now." he said again to the tramp.

There was a sound as though the sergeant was

trampling the fire out, and then both of them coming through the bushes.

We started down the cliff. I felt awful. Of course, if the tramp had been a murderer, or if he had broken into someone's house, it was only right that the sergeant should take him, and that he should be punished. But it was awful if he was going to be sent to prison just for stealing turnips, for he could have only done that because he was hungry, and I'd very often done it myself and it wasn't like real stealing. I didn't want to see him being led away by the sergeant. I didn't want him to see us, either, for he'd think we had just led him into a trap, and that it was our fault the sergeant had come. I felt even more miserable. when I thought that the sergeant had seen the wigwam, and of what he had said, and that most likely he'd tell Dad or Mother about it.

We hurried down the cliff, but we hadn't got halfway than we ran right into Grab and the other boys, who must have watched us come up, and were waiting to see what had happened. For once Grab wasn't a bit quarrelsome or sneering. He and the others crowded round us asking questions. They wanted to know if the tramp had done anything very bad, and if the sergeant had put handcuffs on him. This made me feel very important for a while, and I couldn't stop myself telling a lie, and making out that he had done something very bad, and that it was through us the sergeant had been able to capture him. It would have been a wonderful thing if it had been so, particularly if he had been a murderer, or a noted thief, and hadn't just stolen a few turnips. Chicken and I would have had our names in the papers, and we might have been given medals, or a very large reward of money. That would have been a score over Grab and his mates! I got so carried away by the thought of this, and the respectful way they all listened, I told them about the wigwam, and boasted that we *had* led the man into it as a trap, and that we were on our way to find the sergeant when we had met him: and it wasn't until the sergeant and the man got near that I saw how silly I had been, and that Grab would take the first chance of finding the wigwam, and smashing it up. It would be easy to find now that all the bushes had been trampled down.

We hurried on ahead of the other boys, towards home, and for the time being I forgot about Grab, trying to think out what I should say to Mother, in case the sergeant *did* tell her about it. I hadn't disobeyed her about having the wigwam, but I knew she would be vexed if the sergeant told her about the fire, and there was a lot about the wigwam that had been wicked really, and she would know this because I had never said a word to her about it. I had never told her that I had taken the potatoes, for example, which was stealing, and then it was wicked in a way to pretend that we had killed other boys, and scalped them, and I knew she wouldn't have liked me to be friendly with a tramp, although she was kind to tramps herself, and always gave them something when they came begging to the door.

But perhaps the sergeant wouldn't say anything about it, I thought. Perhaps she wouldn't find out anything at all. And after all, we had done something religious in trying to help the poor tramp. We had been like the Good Samaritan in the Bible, and if we hadn't been able to take him the cocoa, we had meant to. He'd had the potatoes, and got warmed up, and surely this would make up for anything wicked I had done. I felt that if I told Mother this, and mentioned about the Good Samaritan, she *might* be very pleased, but I wasn't quite certain. It would be best, I thought, if I didn't say anything so long as the sergeant didn't; but if he did, then it would be so much better if I *had* told her, so that it wouldn't come as a surprise.

As it happened, I didn't tell her, and the sergeant didn't, either; and she never found out at all; although it was actually in the *Burnharbour Gazette* next week about the man being brought up at the police court for stealing turnips, and being sent to prison with hard labour for a month. But it stayed on my mind for a long time, and several times I nearly *did* tell her, because I thought it might please her, and I only stopped because I thought it might vex her more. Of course, the next time we went to the wigwam we found that Grab had been there, and stolen all the bamboos, and torn the canvas to pieces. And I never saw my bowie knife again.

VII

NOTHING UPSET MOTHER so much as the drunkenness that went on in Bramblewick. Apart from Captain Lingdale and Mr Burton, there were at least six regular drunkards who lived in the place, and were never quite sober; and there were many other sailors who, when they came home from a voyage, always went on the spree and spent all their money buying drink for themselves or treating others. The pubs were open all day and until ten at night. Twice a week the brewer's four-horse dray from Burnharbour came down the Bank. Barrels of beer and cases of spirits and other drink were off-loaded at the ends of the alleys which led to the Ship and the King's Head. The dray would stop at the Bank bottom for the Laurel; then come down the Road to the Dock for the four other pubs; and when everything had been off-loaded, the men with it would start loading the empties, which would be waiting outside each pub.

I felt myself that drinking was about the worst of all sins, because of the other things it led to; and I often was worried about Mike for this reason. I worried more because Mike himself knew that it was wicked to go on the spree and was sorry for it when he was sober. He usually ended up by getting so drunk that he fell down unconscious, it might be in a pub, or in a country lane, or even in the graveyard, and he'd have to be carried home, and stay in bed, sometimes for several days. When he did get up and out again, he looked pale and very ill, with his eyes swollen and bloodshot, and his body shaky. He couldn't work and he'd go and sit on the cliff, or if the tide was down, on the scaur, as far out from the shore as possible; and if I went and spoke to him, he'd look at me in the most gloomy way, and start talking about his dear brother, and he'd cry just like a baby, with the tears streaming down his face.

He'd say that drink was a curse, and that he wished he'd never learnt the taste of it. It had destroyed his dear brother, and it would destroy himself in the end. If it wasn't for drink his brother Tom would be alive to this day; for there never was a stronger, healthier man; and there was not more than two years' difference to their age. He'd have been a fine partner for the salmon fishing. He'd have been a fine companion for any sort of trade where a man had to be strong. And there he was lying in the grave all these years, his fine body rotted away, and all because of the drink. And if it wasn't for the drink, Mike himself might have been married, and he might have had sons and daughters, to be company for him in his old age; instead of his poor dear sister, whose heart he'd broken, because of the drink again. In a day or two Mike would get quite well, and start work, and he wouldn't go inside a pub for months. Then, as he told me, a great thirst would take him, and he'd have just one drink, and then start on another spree.

I didn't worry about Chicken's father in the same way, because I didn't like him; but it upset me when Chicken told me about the rows he and his mother had. Sometimes he went for Chicken and the other children. Once Chicken told me how his father had knocked his mother downstairs with the baby in her arms, only she'd got her own back, for she had broken a chair over his head, and then drenched him with a bucket of cold water. I didn't know whether the other drunkards quarrelled with their wives or not. Captain Lingdale's wife was a very quiet woman. She went to chapel regularly, and was always clean and nicely dressed, but she looked sad and Mother often said how sorry she was for her, for being married to a man who was not only a drunkard, but didn't believe in God. It stood to reason that a drunkard could not have a happy home. Three of the drunkards I knew had been sea captains, and had lost their positions because of drink and were now very poor. Another, Bob Walsh, had been ship's cook, and while he still went to sea now and again, he couldn't keep a position for long, and he and Mr Burton were drinking companions, only Bob himself wasn't married at all, and lived with his old mother, who, like Mrs Lingdale, was respectable and a good chapel-goer. All these drunkards looked unhappy even when they were drunk. They were lazy, and when they stood on the Slipway, or in front of the lifeboat house, they spat all over the place, and used bad language, no matter who was in hearing distance.

I knew of course that drink could make some men jolly. Nearly all the Bramblewick sailors I knew were gloomy, and scarcely ever spoke when they were sober. Yet if you passed by the pubs, you heard them laughing and singing songs, and when the pubs turned out, particularly on a Saturday night, nearly all the men would go down into the Dock, and go on singing. If I was asleep this always woke me up, and although I knew it was wrong to do so, I couldn't help listening to the words of the songs they sang. They were sailor songs. Some of the words were swears and some of them dirty and disgusting, but I liked the tunes, and always they ended up by singing the hymn, *Lead, Kindly Light*. After this, while the men were shouting "good night" to each other, there would very often be the sound of quarrelling, then of fighting, and I'd hear Mother saying to Dad downstairs, how disgusting it all was, and how she wished she had never come to live in such a place.

Once I heard Dad make an excuse for the sailors who got drunk. He said he had heard one of their wives saying that it was because they had such a lot of anxiety when they were at sea. They were nearly all on small sailing ships, trading along the coast or to the Baltic, and Holland and France, and in winter they encountered dreadful storms. In one of these storms no less than seven Bramblewick sailors lost their lives, and their bodies had never been found. It wasn't surprising, Dad said, that some of them yielded to the temptation of drink, although it was a great pity; but Mother didn't agree with this, and said it was all the more reason why they should lead good Christian lives; and that she was glad that they were not all like that, and that several Bramblewick captains were staunch teetotallers, and these were the ones who had done well for themselves. Then Dad had mentioned Captain Haines, who was very rich, and that he wasn't a teetotaller, and that he swore, too, and had that thing on his mantelpiece. But Mother could always beat him at an argument, and she made him admit that there was no excuse for anyone to touch strong drink, and that it would be a very good thing if all public-houses were closed by the law. I often thought this, too. If there weren't any public-houses, Mike would never be tempted to go on the spree any more, and there would be no danger of him being destroyed. Mr Burton might get regular work, and be able to support his family and move into another house; and Chicken and his little brothers and sisters would always have plenty to eat. I didn't understand why God didn't stop all drink being made, or make it taste nasty, or why He didn't strike all the pubs with thunderbolts, until Mother told me that He didn't do His work by miracles like these, but through the hearts of men, making them see their folly and the sinfulness of their ways. It was no use just feeling angry with them; we must show by our own example the one true way to happiness and eternal life. That was why all staunch teetotallers should wear the blue ribbon, no matter how they were scoffed at by those who drank.

Well, I was a teetotaller, for that time I had stayed with Uncle Fred he had made me sign the pledge, and said a special prayer for me when I had done so, that I should never even be *tempted* to break it. He had given me a piece of ribbon to wear in my coat, but I had lost it before I got home, and I was glad Mother had never made me wear another, or it would have got me into a lot of trouble with the boys. But I never saw the brewer's dray coming down the Bank without thinking of all the misery it caused, and wishing something would happen to it: and when Mike got over his spree, I wished stronger than ever that God would work a miracle with Mike at least, for he was in bed a week, and he had spent all the money he had saved from the summer's fishing; and he was so shaky for at least another week that he couldn't stand for his picture, and Dad said it would perhaps mean he wouldn't be able to finish it in time to send it to the Academy, particularly if he went on the spree again.

One morning a very unusual thing happened at school. Slogger was late, and when he did appear, he had with him a funny little man in dark clothes and a black hat, just like Uncle Fred wore. He had white whiskers, too, and he wore spectacles; and but for his collar he looked exactly like a clergyman. We all stood still and stared at him, and to our great surprise he said, in a funny voice:

"Good morning, boys."

Slogger would never have dreamt of speaking to us outside the school in this friendly way, and no one answered: we just stared, and the man stared too, and seemed a bit surprised; but Slogger soon had the door unlocked, and let him go in first. During the rush to get in I heard one boy say "It's the school inspector," and another, "It's a chap come to take our photographs," and I felt jealous at this, for though I wasn't very proud of Dad being a photographer, I didn't like the idea of a stranger coming and taking away his trade. Both boys were wrong. An even greater surprise was waiting for us inside. Slogger's desk had been moved almost up to the window, and in its place was a table, which I knew belonged to the chapel vestry; and on this was a flask of water, several bottles, and a box. Slogger had taken the gentleman to the fire, and they were standing warming their backs at it, and talking. They went on doing this after the last boy was in, and we all stared at them, and there was quite a lot of whispering until suddenly Slogger said sternly, "Silence. Arms folded," and left the gentleman and went to his desk.

His desk looked very funny being by the window, and Slogger himself looked different. His cheeks were redder than I had ever seen them, and the first time he tried to strike the tuning-fork he hit the register instead of the desk, and it didn't make a sound at all. It worked the second time, but he actually gave us the hymn we had sung yesterday, instead of the right one, and he could scarcely get us to sing it at all, for we couldn't take our eyes off the table or get used to there being someone else in the school and things out of place. As soon as we had finished the Lord's Prayer, and opened our eyes, Slogger marked the register very quickly; then, instead of giving the order for the sum books, he said:

"Arms folded. Silence."

When there was silence, Slogger coughed, and wiped his mouth with his handkerchief, and then, fidgeting with his moustache, he said, in a voice quite different from his ordinary voice:

"Now, boys, instead of doing your ordinary lessons this morning, I want you all to sit very still, and pay attention to what this gentleman has got to say to you. He has come to talk to you on a subject of very great interest and importance. We all know what an evil thing strong drink is, and the harm it does. We all know what a disgusting sight a drunkard is."

I couldn't help turning round to look at Chicken when he said this, and I was sorry, for nearly every other boy did the same thing, and Chicken blushed. But Slogger didn't box anybody's ears. He just coughed very sternly, and this made us all look to him again, and he went on to say that the gentleman had come to tell us about strong drink, and what a bad thing it was and how much better it was never to start taking it, and to remain teetotallers all our lives. We were to pay very close attention, all the time, and if anyone whispered or didn't pay attention, he would be punished later.

Slogger stopped and we all looked at the man, who smiled at us, and then walked from the fire to the table. Slogger quickly moved back to the fire, took the *Yorkshire Post* from his stool and put it on the mantelpiece, and sat down. For a minute there was dead silence. Then the man coughed and smiled again, and began to talk. He was altogether different from Slogger. He began straight away by making a joke about Bramblewick, and saying its streets made him think of a rabbit warren, and that he quite expected to see a big rabbit popping out of one of the dark alleys. I thought this was funny, but I didn't laugh, because Slogger always punished laughing. None of the other boys laughed either, but we all paid close attention, and he went on to make another joke, saying that he hoped we weren't feeling disappointed that we weren't starting our lessons, but that we were to listen to a temperance lecture instead. This did make me laugh, but quietly, and I was careful Slogger didn't see me. But no one else laughed, and the man didn't make any more jokes, but got on with his subject. He didn't just talk. It was more like an object lesson. He asked questions, and those who knew the answers put their hands up. He asked if anyone knew how many kinds of strong drink there were, and different boys answered beer, whisky, brandy, rum, and other kinds. He asked if anyone knew what any of these drinks were made of, and what they called the people who made them. Grab answered that they called a man who made beer a brewer, but no one knew what it was made from, so the man told us it was made from hops and barley; and that whisky was made from corn, and brandy from grapes, and rum from sugar; and he said that we must remember that they were made from things that were good to eat to begin with, and didn't make people drunk. He then went on, sometimes asking questions, sometimes just talking, to say how, when these foods were treated in a certain way, they weren't foods any longer, but were changed into liquid which had in it a terrible poison, and this poison was called alcohol. And the strange thing was that men took drink and paid a lot of money for it, just because of this poison, which was the thing that made them drunk.

I was already horrified. I had heard Mother say that drink was a poison, but I didn't think she meant a *real* poison, like the stuff murderers used to kill their victims. And I was more horrified when the man opened his box and took out a bottle and a little dish. He held up the bottle, which contained a clear liquid, and he said that this was the very stuff he had been talking about; and he said the word Alcohol very loudly, and made us repeat it all together. Then he poured a little of it on to the dish, and said we were to watch him very closely. He struck a match and put it near the dish, and the liquid began to burn, with a blue flame, and he waited until it had all burnt away. Then he asked us if we thought that any man in his right senses would drink whisky, or rum, or beer, if he knew that with every glass he was putting stuff like that inside his stomach. We all answered, "No, sir," and he went on to tell us more things about alcohol. He said that the first thing it did when a man swallowed it was to work through his stomach to his brain. It might make him feel happy, and make him want to sing and shout; but the next thing it did was to make him want some more, and while this might make him feel happier still, it was more likely to make him want to quarrel and fight, and use bad language, even to commit a crime. And again it would make him want to go on drinking. He might be a poor man with very little money, but the alcohol would make him forget that, even though his wife and children were starving. And when he had spent all his money and got sober again, he would feel ill because the poison was still working inside him and it would make him crave for more, so that at the first chance he would start again.

I daren't look at Chicken. I knew he must be thinking about his father, but I was thinking not only about him, but about Mike, and I knew now what Mike had meant when he said that drink would destroy him.

The next thing the man did was to show us another bottle, but it was a big one, and as well as fluid it contained a white object that looked like a piece of tripe. He asked if anyone knew what it was. I put my hand up, but a seventh standard boy whose father was a butcher answered:

"Yes, sir. It's a bit of salt pork."

The man smiled at this, and said it wasn't a bad answer because it did look like salt pork, because of its colour and because it looked tough, but actually it was a bit of liver, and the fluid in the bottle was alcohol again. Then he asked if anyone could tell him what colour liver was and whether it was soft or hard. The butcher's boy, without waiting to put his hand up, said that fresh liver was soft, and brown in colour; and this pleased the man, for he smiled again and held up the bottle for us to see, and shook it, so that we heard the liver rattle as though it was a bit of rock. Then he went on talking. Human beings had livers as well as animals, he said, and the liver was close to our stomachs, and had a lot to do with the digestion of our food. Now we could see what liver looked like when it was soaked in alcohol. It turned white and tough, and that was just what happened to a drunkard's liver, in the end. It went hard, and wouldn't do its work properly, and this was another of the many ways alcohol affected the human body. Now, did anyone want further proof that all these drinks we had talked about were poison? We all answered, "No, sir." He still kept the bottle with the liver in one hand, but he held up the glass water jug in the other, and he asked us if we didn't think that the safest and best and most health-giving of all drinks was that which Almighty God had provided so bounteously on every hand – *pure water?* We all answered, "Yes, sir." There was a silence, but before the man went on, Grab, who had paid attention as well as anybody, put up his hand to ask a question. The man asked him what he wanted, and Grab said:

"Please, sir, is it a human liver in the bottle? Out of a dead man?"

I had been wondering if it was myself, and I was glad when the man said it wasn't. He said it was just cow's liver, but that wouldn't have made any difference to the way alcohol would have made it tough. He didn't tell us any more about alcohol, though. The next thing he said was that he hoped we would not forget anything he had told us, and that we would all make up our minds now never to touch strong drink, and the best way to help us to do this was to sign the temperance pledge. He took a book from his box, and it was the same sort of book Uncle Fred had. You signed your name in two places, and one part of each page could be torn off, and this was the pledge itself. He put the book on the table, and then smiled at Slogger, who got up, and walked towards him, and then stood and looked at us. He was still very red in the face, and fidgety. He said:

"Now, boys. You have heard all the gentleman has told you about the evils of strong drink, and I hope that you won't forget any of it, and that you all realise now what a foolish thing it is ever to touch strong drink, and that it is a deadly poison. As it is now five minutes to playtime, you will go out now, and come in five minutes early. I hope that every boy will want to sign the pledge, and we will begin at Standard VII, and each boy after he has signed will walk quietly out. The rest keep your arms folded and be silent."

I thought I had better not say I had already signed the pledge, in case the other boys should think I was just trying to get out early; and, anyway, I felt that I wanted to sign it again now that I really knew what a terrible thing drink was.

I had never known Slogger do so much punishing as he did that morning. The man stayed talking to him nearly until the end of playtime, so that he had no chance to read the *Yorkshire Post*. And as soon as he had gone Slogger came out to the playground to call us in, and he boxed several boys' ears before we got into school. I thought that we should miss sums altogether, but he ordered the books to be given out at once, so that it was just as though school was starting, and as soon as everyone was at work he went to the fire and started reading. With the other boys the chief trouble was they couldn't help looking at their pledges, and after Slogger had punished two or three of them for this, he said we had to pass them along to the end of each desk, and then one boy collected them and put them in the cupboard where they were to stay until dinner time. But it wasn't easy for anyone to settle down after such an unusual morning. I couldn't give my mind to doing sums. I couldn't help thinking about drink being a poison and making a man's liver go hard, and about Mike and *his* liver, and whether it had already got so hard that the next time he went on the spree it would destroy him. I thought that if Mike died it would be the most awful thing that had ever happened. I felt that I must go and see him the very moment we got out of school, and tell him about his liver, and show him his danger, and persuade him never to drink again. Perhaps he would be so frightened that he would sign the pledge himself.

I did see Mike, but it wasn't until the next day. He was in his warehouse, cutting up pieces of lead to go on a new salmon net he was making. He listened attentively to everything I said, and kept nodding his head as though he agreed with everything, and he looked very sad.

"Och – it's all true," he said, when I'd finished. "It's all true. It's the devil's own poison is the drink. I've wished a thousand times I'd never learnt the taste of the stuff. And there's dear Tom lying in the grave, and he might be with me now, helping to make this net, if it hadn't been for drink. It's a good thing the man came to tell you about it all, and show you the evil of it. My own stomach is not recovered yet from all the drink I took a while back; for if I eat a good meal, I feel sick for long after, and maybe it's the liver that's going hard, for I've heard the liver is the most important organ of the body, as important as your heart. Och – I'll think twice before I'll touch a drop of the stuff again. I'm a better man without it ... But what's the use of my signing the pledge? If I broke it it would only add one more sin to the heavy burden I shall carry to the grave. It's no good at all my signing the pledge. Most likely it would be through that the devil would get me again by tempting me to break it, when I might hang out against the desire for the drink itself."

I felt more worried than ever. Boozer, having spent all his money, had gone back to sea; but another drunkard called Will Sedman was home, and the next Saturday night there was a terrible fight in the Dock between him and a farmer: and a young sailor who joined in got his head split open by falling on a kerb; and (although I didn't learn all about it till Chicken told me next day at Sunday School) he had to be carried home on a hand-barrow, and his wife fainted when she saw him, for she thought that he was dead. I could scarcely sleep at all that night. In spite of what Mother told me, I prayed to God that he would stop drink being made, or take the alcohol out of it, so that it wouldn't make men drunk, and want to fight, and make their livers go hard; or that if He didn't do this, He would at least stop Mike drinking again, and make him sign the pledge.

The temperance man must have thought that Bramblewick was a bad place for drinking, for Mr Thompson had just finished his first prayer at Sunday School, when he came in, and Mr Thompson shook hands with him, in a friendly way, and then told us that we were going to have a temperance lecture instead of the ordinary lessons and hymns. He told us the same things as before, only he didn't show us the liver, and he was more religious, and said a long prayer when he had done. And just before the last hymn, Mr Thompson said that the gentleman was going to preach a temperance sermon in the chapel that night and that a lady was coming from Burnharbour to sing some special solos, and that he hoped we should all tell our parents, and be sure to come ourselves, or we should miss a great treat.

Dad was always in a bad temper on Sundays. He didn't go to chapel, but to church, and he had to go three times, because he was a sidesman. The first service was at eight o'clock in the morning, so that he had to get up at seven and go without his breakfast. This made him hungry, and when he had his breakfast he felt sleepy, and he'd try and settle down in his chair for a nap; but there was always something to interrupt him, and he'd have to go off to church again at ten o'clock. He couldn't sleep when he got back because of mother getting the dinner ready. Unless it was fine and dry he didn't like to go for a walk for fear of dirtying his best clothes. Besides, his best boots were tight, and hurt his corns. And he wouldn't go to the studio on a Sunday, in case someone would see him, and say he was going to work. So usually he just sat and kept awake, and read the Bible, and snapped at me if I made a noise or tried to play, and he wasn't much better after dinner, although sometimes he said his head was aching and went to bed. I was really quite glad to go to Sunday School in the afternoon, and even chapel wasn't as bad as being at home.

Although I hated the clothes I had to wear, which were the same as my weekday ones, only new, I liked to see Mother dressed up, and I thought she looked lovely. She wore a flowing skirt, and a little black bodice with dozens of buttons on it, and a gold brooch instead of her silver one. She had a dark coat to go over this, and she wore a dark velvet hat and a veil. She smelt of lavender, as there was a bag of lavender in the chest where she kept her clothes. But she got very solemn as soon as she started getting ready for chapel, and she would never speak to me once on our way there, and clutched me tightly by the hand, as though she thought I might run back home.

I was glad that we were not late that night. The chapel was a big place, shaped like a horse-shoe inside. There were pews downstairs, but all the congregation sat in the gallery, and the pulpit and organ and choir seats were on a high platform facing this. Our pew was in the first row, so that to reach it you had to walk down a long staircase, from the back, and everyone could see you if you were late, and stare at you. But there was scarcely anyone there when we arrived, except Mr Thompson, who stood at the door. I didn't look at him, because the jelly business wasn't quite off my mind, and I thought Mother must be thinking of it, too: but he shook her hand just as though he hadn't seen her for months; and he patted my shoulder as we passed, just like someone would pat a little dog.

As soon as we got into our pew, Mother leaned forward and closed her eyes for silent prayer: and then she sat bolt upright, and stared straight in front of her. But I watched the people coming in. Mr Thompson shook every grown-up person's hand, even if they were his own relations, and patted the shoulders of boys and girls. Captain and Mrs Haines came in, and sat in a pew on the opposite side of the gallery to ours. I thought of the thing on their mantleshelf, and I looked at Mother to see if she was looking at them, but she wasn't. Old Mrs Walsh, Bob's Mother, was already in her pew, although of course he wasn't with her. The fishermen Fosdycks went to church, and the Grahams went to the Congregational chapel, but the three Stainforth brothers came in with their wives, and sat together in the same pew, and behind them came old Mrs Wain, who started fidgeting with her handkerchief the very moment she sat down. Mrs Wain was a widow, and she had lost two of her sons in a collision in the English Channel, and the only other son she had was in Australia and she hadn't seen him for twenty years. She lived in a cottage all by herself, and I heard one of the boys say that she drank rum just like a man, only it never made her drunk; and that she had a lot of dolls and talked to them just as if they were babies; and whether this was true or not, there could be no doubt that she was queer in her head, for sometimes you could see her going from room to room in her house, pulling down the blinds, and then pulling them up again and peering out and laughing, and she was always very fidgety. I saw Mrs Lingdale, Boozer's wife. She sat in a pew by herself, and she was dressed all in black, and as soon as she had said her silent prayer, she sat bolt upright just like Mother, staring straight in front of her. Several retired Up Bank captains and their wives came in, and two more widows whose husbands had been drowned in that terrible storm;

and Mrs Fosdyck with Grab and Len and Kid, and their two sisters. But there weren't many other children. Chicken never came to chapel; and most of the women were alone, for their husbands were away at sea, and in spite of what Mr Thompson had said about our being in for a treat, the congregation wasn't bigger than usual, and to my great surprise, Slogger wasn't there at all.

But I soon lost interest in the congregation; for the lady organist came up and took her seat, and she was followed by several other ladies who were in the choir, and then by a lady I had never seen before; and everyone in the chapel, even Mother, stared at her, as she took her seat close to the organ. I thought straight away that I had never seen such a lovely lady. She had a face rather like Mother's, only it was very pale, and she had very large dark eyes; and while I couldn't have told what sort of clothes she was wearing, I knew I had never seen any that looked so nice. She was tall, but she wasn't a bit fat. She was young, but she wasn't a girl, for I hated girls and thought they were all silly. She was just lovely; and when the organist leaned towards her and showed her a hymn-book, she smiled, and that made her look lovelier still.

I couldn't take my eyes off her, even when the temperance man came up and walked between the choir seats to the pulpit; and all through the singing of the first hymn I watched her and could think of nothing but how lovely she was. I knew, of course, that she was the lady Mr Thompson had told us about who had come from Burnharbour to sing. I would have known this by her voice, if nothing else. It was deep, yet you could hear it clear above the voices of the congregation and the choir, and it was soft and smooth, so that even the organ notes seemed rough compared with it.

I closed my eyes when the hymn was finished and the man began to pray, but I could still see her. I could still hear her voice, and I didn't hear a word the man said except "Amen," and as soon as he had said that I opened my eyes and looked at her just as she raised her head and opened her eyes, and I knew at once that she was going to sing her first solo, for she was holding a sheet of music in her hand. The man sat down. The organist began to play. The lady stood up, and she began to sing, and it was lovelier than ever, because there were no other voices, and the organ played so softly you could scarcely hear it at all. I don't know what it was she sang. I couldn't make out the words. I only knew that I had never listened to anything so lovely; I had never seen anyone I liked so much. I felt suddenly that I could have done anything that lady asked me to. I could have run errands for her, got great bunches of primroses and daffodils, caught fish for her, given her all the treasures I found on the shore. I noticed Grab, staring at her with his mouth half-open, and I felt that if he had dared to call out after her in the street, I could have gone up to him and slapped him in the face and fought him until he was unconscious. I felt I could have done anything brave, like saving someone from drowning, or being caught in a burning house, or being charged by a mad bull. But more than anything I felt I wanted to do something good, noble, religious. Although I couldn't make out the words, I knew it must be a sacred song, and I felt it must have something to do with temperance, and that by singing she was trying to do what the man did by talking; showing people what an evil thing drink was, and how much better it was to be teetotal. She stopped, and I wished it had been a concert, and that I could have clapped and shouted. Everyone was very silent and just stared at her till the man prayed again, and when he'd finished and another ordinary hymn had been sung, he began his sermon.

What he said wasn't very different from what he'd said at school and Sunday school, but he didn't show the liver, and there was even more religion in it. I listened very attentively, because I felt the lady wanted me to; but I went on looking at her, and whenever he said something he had said before, I started thinking how I could do something very good and noble connected with temperance. I wished I was bigger and that I could do what the man was doing; that I was a temperance lecturer, but with a more powerful voice, so that I could make everyone listen to me; that I could go and stand in the Dock, even on a Saturday night, and make all the drunken men stop singing and quarrelling and fighting: and have them go down on their knees and ask God to forgive them, and then promise to give up drink forever and sign the pledge – even Boozer, and Mike, and Mr Burton and Bob Walsh, and Ned Sedman. I thought this would be a wonderful thing to do. The lady might even be with me to sing. But I saw that I would never be able to do anything like this until I was grown up, and by that time the lady would be quite old, and her hair might be white and her voice cracked, and I tried to think of something I could do now, while I was a boy. I thought of setting fire to one of the Bramblewick pubs, but I knew that I daren't do a thing like that. I thought of doing something to the brewer's dray, so that when it started down the Bank it would run away and upset so that all the drink would be spilt. But that might kill the horses, and perhaps the driver, and it would be murder; and I went on thinking, and suddenly I remembered how I had often seen barrels of beer and cases of other drink standing outside the Dolphin, in the little alley between the pub and Thompson's shop, and I became terribly excited with a secret idea.

I went on thinking about it all the time the man was talking, so that I only knew he had finished when he sat down and the lady got up again to sing another solo. This time I did know what it was, for although the tune was different to the usual one, the words were *Rock of Ages*. It was lovelier than ever: and although the congregation just stared at her, and Grab was actually sucking a sweet and looking towards the chapel door, and Mrs Wain went on fidgeting with her handkerchief, and neither Mrs Lingdale nor Mrs Walsh, nor any of the women who had drunkards in their families, seemed to be a bit upset, I knew Mother was almost crying, because I could feel her shaking, and I was nearly crying myself, but only because it was the last solo, and that soon we'd be going home. And I went on thinking about my secret idea all through the next prayer, in which the man prayed that a great temperance revival would sweep over the country and over the district of Bramblewick, and through the singing of the last hymn, when the collection was taken; and when this was over, and the man pronounced the benediction, I didn't close my eyes, but peeped through my fingers at the lady, whose face wasn't hidden, although her head was bent and her eyes were closed; and I wished like anything that she knew what I was thinking about and how I liked her.

Then everyone got up, and the congregation started to go out, and the choir began to sing the going-out hymn. Usually I liked this hymn better than any other, for I didn't like chapel really. But I wouldn't have moved if Mother hadn't nudged me, and all the way up the staircase I kept turning round to look at the lady, and didn't notice Mr Thompson until he patted my shoulder again, and smiled at Mother, and said, "Good night. God bless you." I took a last look at her as we turned down the chapel stairs, and I could hear her voice sounding clear above the others, until we got into the street, and I felt very sad, and I think I would have cried if it hadn't been for thinking of the deed I was going to do for her sake, when the first chance came.

I expected that after the visit of the temperance lecturer, and the special chapel service, everybody in Bramblewick would be talking about drink being a deadly poison, and that the temperance revival would have started. But it didn't seem to make the slightest difference. Ned Sedman, Mr Burton, Bob Walsh, were all drunk on Monday, and Chicken told me that his father had got hold of his pledge and put it in the fire, and at school on Monday I heard Grab say that it was all lies about beer and other drinks being a poison. *His* father wasn't a teetotaller, and he wasn't going to be one, either. He'd already had a taste of rum when he was on board ship, and it was champion stuff. He only wished he had a glass of it to drink every day! I knew this was only boasting, but I was careful not to say anything to start another row with him, and I thought that this was all the more reason why I should carry out my plan. I went on thinking about it all the time, and about the lovely lady, and every time I passed the alley between the Dolphin and Thompson's shop I looked to see if there were any beer barrels there. I didn't say anything about it to Mother, nor to Chicken. It was all a dead secret.

A bad storm came on on Monday night. It woke me up, for although there was no skylight in the cliff side of the attic roof, the roof itself was higher than the edge of the cliff, and when the wind blew from the sea it rattled the tiles and made howling noises in the chimney; and when the tide got up, and big waves broke against the cliff it was like thunder, and the whole house shook. It didn't frighten me very much because I was used to it, and I knew that our house was built on the shale itself, and not on the clay which covered the shale in places, like the houses at the top of Chapel Street which had fallen over. Besides, whenever there was a storm, I thought of what might be washed up on the shore, and how the clay along the south cliff would be falling, bringing down more treasures.

But a storm always caused a lot of excitement in Bramblewick. If the cobles had gone off before the storm broke, everyone who had nothing else to do would stand on the slipway or behind the breakwater, watching the cobles trying to reach the Landing. It was very hard and dangerous work for them if they were fishing at the south end of the bay, when the wind turned north-east, and sometimes you'd be certain they were lost when they disappeared from sight between the great waves rolling on to the scaurs on each side of the Landing.

No cobles were off in this storm, however, and the excitement was about some ships with Bramblewick sailors on board, which were known to be somewhere along the coast, including the ship Grab's father was in. Grab and Len and Kid didn't seem very worried about their father being in danger; in fact, they boasted about it, and Grab even said he wished he was on board and that he wouldn't mind being shipwrecked and rescued by the lifeboat or the rocket brigade. But his mother was anxious, for I heard her in Thompson's shop asking an old captain how many days it took for a passage from Leith to London, and if he thought her husband was overdue, and she said she wished she'd get a wire from the owners to say it was all right.

Boozer's ship, too, was somewhere out along the coast. I had heard that he never got drunk when he was at sea, and that he was a very good sailor, but that he was rough with his men, and used worse language when he was sober than when he was drunk; and that even during a storm he would boast that he was not afraid of God driving his ship ashore, and that there wasn't a God at all. The strange thing was that in his whole life he had never once been shipwrecked, while some Bramblewick captains, who never drank at all and were religious, had been shipwrecked dozens of times. I didn't *wish* that anything would happen to him, of course, but when I heard the other boys talking about him, I felt it wouldn't be surprising if he was wrecked in this storm, and drowned, and I thought if he was it would be a lesson to the others who drank and led wicked lives.

The wind blew very strong all day Tuesday, and the sea was so rough that when the tide was up, big waves broke right over the breakwater, and rushed up into the Dock, so that the cobles had to be moved up the Road, behind the lifeboat-house. Everyone expected that there would be a wreck, and news came that there had been several wrecks on various parts of the coast, and a lot of pit props washed up on the shore, and one of the fishermen found a lifebelt. But there were no wrecks at

Bramblewick. Mrs Fosdyck got a wire that her husband was safe in port; and it was heard that the other ships were all safe. And, instead of Boozer being wrecked, news came that he had actually saved another ship from being driven on to rocks; and that he would get a big sum of money for having done this. By Wednesday the storm was over, although the sea remained quite rough. The wind changed to the south and it rained all day.

All this time I had scarcely ever stopped thinking about my plan, and several times Mother asked me if I had anything on my mind worrying me. I should have liked to have told her, but I thought that, after all, I might not be able to do it, and if I did it would be all the better if it came as a surprise. It was raining so hard after tea on Wednesday that Mother wouldn't let me go out. Dad was in a good humour, however, for Mike had sat for him all afternoon, and he was very pleased with the progress he had made, and he had lent me his saw. I had a candle in the coal-place, and I was sawing wood there, until it was nearly suppertime, and I was very happy, for I liked sawing wood, and it pleased Mother because of the coal it saved, and also because she hadn't to worry about my being in bad company, or getting into trouble. I was still thinking about the lady and my plan, but I hadn't heard the brewer's cart, and I didn't even wonder whether there might be any barrels standing in the alley: I didn't even imagine that I might have to go out. I was quite surprised when Mother shouted to me to open the street door and see if it was raining very hard. It wasn't raining very hard, but it was dark and gloomy in the street, and the wind was strong and the sea made quite a lot of noise on the breakwater. I shouted up the stairs that it wasn't bad, and Mother shouted back, asking me to put my things on and go and get some milk as she hadn't enough for supper. I didn't want to go, for I was halfway through a log, but it was better than having to get water, and I hurried upstairs for my things and the jug and the money.

We got our milk from a man who had a small farm at the back of the village, but he lived in a cottage halfway up the Road. I ran down towards the Dock. Thompson's shop was closed, for it was early closing day, and Mr Thompson, I thought, would be at the mid-week chapel service, to which Mother never went unless there was something special. I passed the shop and the alley was just on my left, and there, standing just where I had seen the beer barrels before, was a barrel and a wooden case. I stopped and suddenly I felt terribly excited. There was no one about. The only sound I could hear, except for the noise of the wind and sea, was the sound of men's voices in the bar room of the Dolphin, the street door of which was closed. It wasn't a very big barrel. I thought for a moment it might be empty, but I tried it with my hands, and I knew by its weight it was full. I thought that perhaps instead of having come by the brewer's dray, it and the case had come from Burnharbour by the carrier (for this very often happened) and the landlord of the Dolphin didn't know about it, or was leaving it till later to put into his cellar. I looked down the Dock. The cobles were still hauled up behind the lifeboat house. Between me and the slipway top, up which the broken seas were rushing, was all sloping ground. I saw that if I could once tip the barrel over, it would start rolling, and there would be nothing to stop it going into the sea. But I thought I'd better get the milk first, so that I could rush straight home. I was so excited that when the milkman's wife opened the door and asked me what I wanted, I actually said, "A pint of beer, please," and I felt my cheeks go burning hot when she laughed at me and said, "Eh – you come to the wrong spot for beer, haven't you? Do you mean milk?" I said "Yes – I mean milk, please," but I stuttered, and I thought she was looking at me in a very curious way, and I began to feel quite frightened about what I was going to do. As soon as I started back, I got more frightened, and I thought I'd better not do it if I met anyone, for when it was found out, everyone would hear about it, and if anyone had seen me near the place, they would tell and I would be blamed. I thought I had better go straight home, and not look up the alley.

But I didn't see anyone; and when I reached the place I couldn't help looking, and the barrel was there, and still there was no one about. And suddenly, although I was more frightened than ever, I made myself think about the lady, and the temperance man, and about beer being a poison, and all the suffering it caused, and how it made

Chicken's life so unhappy, and was destroying Mike, and I moved towards it. I put the milk jug down, close up to the wall of the shop; and then I took another quick glance up Cliff Street, then down the Dock to the slipway; and with all my strength I heaved against the barrel, and turned it over on to its side, and let it go.

The sound of the wind and sea was strong: yet it seemed to me that as soon as the barrel started rolling, there came a dead calm, for the noise it made rolling over the cobble pavings was like the noise of a cart. I seized the milk jug and spilt quite a lot of milk over my hand, I looked round in time to see the barrel rolling down the Dock, crash into the wall on the opposite side of the slipway, and then rebound and roll down the slipway, into the rush of an incoming sea. Then, with the milk still spilling on to my hand, and down my coat, I ran up the street, opened the door and shut it again, and stood inside, shaking with fright. But in a moment, before even Mother shouted at me, I was excited again, and bursting with pride at what I had done. Mother had opened the door at the top of the stairs.

"Are you wet, Sonny?" she shouted. "Come on, hurry upstairs and get your things off."

I went upstairs. Dad was in his chair by the fire reading. Mother was at the fireplace. Dad didn't look up, but Mother looked at me, and she must have known that something had happened, for she made a sound of surprise, and said, quite frightened:

"Whatever's the matter? Have you fallen and

hurt yourself?"

I didn't say anything for a moment. I just stood looking at Mother, and feeling prouder and prouder, and Dad, too, turned round and looked at me, although he didn't get up from his chair. Then I said, trying to keep my voice calm, "Mother, I've destroyed a barrel of beer, all by myself."

I had thought that the first thing that Mother would do would be to put her arms round me and kiss me, and say how brave I was, and how proud she was of me. But she just looked surprised, and so did Dad; and Dad got up and said:

"You've what? You've *what?*"

And then Mother said in a very funny voice: "What do you mean, Sonny?"

I began to feel a bit frightened again, but I said:

"Well, you know that sometimes, when the brewer's dray or the carrier's cart comes to the Dolphin, they don't take the barrels right in, but leave them in the alley between the Dolphin and Thompson's shop?"

"Yes?" Mother said quietly.

"They *don't* leave them there," Dad interrupted, before I had time to go on. "They only put the empties there for the dray to call for them."

He began to look quite angry, but Mother told him to hush and not interfere, and let me go on. But Dad had made *me* feel angry, for he was very fond of contradicting, and proving other people were wrong when they said things, and I answered almost cheekily:

"Well, this one wasn't empty, anyway. It was

full. I know it was, because it took me all my time to move it."

Neither of them said anything to this for a moment. They just stared at me; and then Dad said, sharply:

"What do you mean – *move* it?"

I wasn't afraid of him being angry. I was frightened because Mother looked so queer and upset. But I knew it was no good my pretending I hadn't done anything now, and I felt that as soon as I told the whole story, they'd both see I had done right.

"I turned it over," I said. "It was a barrel of beer, standing just between the Dolphin and the shop. Beer contains poison. The temperance man proved that. You ought to have seen the piece of liver he showed us. It contains alcohol, and as well as making people drunk, and commit crimes, it kills them in the end. So I thought it would be a good thing if I rolled the barrel over, and let it roll into the sea. And I did. It went right down and hit the wall, and then a wave washed it away. And it's gone forever."

I stopped, and looked at Dad and Mother, expecting that at last they would say what a good thing I had done. But Mother only looked more upset than ever, and Dad angrier. He started to pace up and down the room, and suddenly he turned on Mother, and said, angrily:.

"Well, he's got us into trouble now and no mistake. What are we going to do about it? The man who keeps the Dolphin is related to all the wealthiest people in the place. We'll never hear the last of it. It's going to cost us pounds' worth of orders. We'll have to pay for it, too. It will mean the police, if I'm not mistaken. What are we going to do about it? *You're* bringing the boy up."

Mother didn't say anything. She looked as though she was going to cry. Then Dad suddenly turned on me:

"Are you telling the truth?"

"Yes, I am. It's all true."

"Where exactly *was* the barrel?"

"It was where I said, in the alley between the Dolphin and the shop."

"Was it nearer to the public-house, or the shop?"

"To the shop. But they always leave them there."

Dad just looked at me for a moment, saying nothing; but I was already beginning to think I might have made a dreadful mistake. The next thing he said was:

"Are you sure it was a barrel of beer, and not something else? Had it any label?" and before I had time to think whether it had or not, he turned on Mother again, and shouted:

"Do you know what the boy's done? Do you know what he's done? That barrel must have belonged to Mr Thompson, not to the Dolphin at all. I saw the carrier's cart in the Dock. The carrier must have put it there because the shop was closed, and Mr Thompson being out. It makes it even worse. It must have been a barrel of vinegar!"

*   *   *

It wasn't a barrel of vinegar I had rolled into the sea. It was treacle; but Dad was right about it belonging to Mr Thompson, and I might have known that myself if I hadn't been so excited, and anxious to do something against drink, and please God and the lovely lady. Mother put on her things, and went down, and she caught Mr Thompson just as he was getting back from chapel. I never knew exactly what she said to him, or what he said to her, but he must have been a bit angry at first, because of treacle being such expensive stuff. Her face was very red when she came back, but when Dad asked her what had happened, she just said that she had seen Mr Thompson, and explained everything, and that he had been very kind, and that there was no need to say any more about it at present, although she would have to talk it over with me later when I went to bed.

She did have a long talk with me when I went to bed. She said that she understood why I had done it, and that the *idea* was really a very noble one, and that she wished that someone would destroy all the strong drink there was in the world, and never let another drop of it be made. But that could only be done by the law, and the law was made by men, and until men could be brought to see what a wicked thing drink was, it would go on, and it was just as much against the law to destroy a barrel of beer that belonged to someone else as it was to destroy a sack of flour. So really, although I had *meant* to do good, I had done something wrong, and it had been a worse wrong because I had injured Mr Thompson, who himself was a good Christian and a staunch teetotaller: and it was a fortunate thing that he was such a kind man, and that he wasn't going to tell the policeman, as he would have had a perfect right to do; and he wasn't going to make Dad pay for the treacle, but was going to let him do some photographs instead.

She kissed me goodnight very lovingly. But as soon as she had gone, I started to cry, and I went on for a long time. Yet it wasn't because I was sorry for Mr Thompson, or because I felt I had done anything wrong. I didn't feel that I had done anything wrong. I had tried to do something for temperance and it wasn't my fault I had made a mistake. I felt angry with Mother. I felt I hated Dad. They were both always going for me for telling lies, but when I had told the truth, it only got me into trouble. If drinking was against the word of God, as Mother often said it was, why should it be wrong to stop men drinking by destroying their drink, even by setting fire to the pubs? Perhaps Grab was right when he said it was all a lie about drink being a poison. How was it that some of the Bramblewick drunkards were quite old when they had been drinking all their lives? And if it *was* wicked, how was it that Boozer had not only escaped from the storm, but rescued another ship, and made a lot more money which he'd be able to spend on more drink?

I stopped crying, but I went on feeling angry,

and I didn't feel a bit sorry for what I had done. Instead, I felt wicked, and I thought of a lot of swears, and said them aloud, and didn't feel frightened of God, when I had done this, and I began to think of other wicked things I might do, and would do, just to pay Dad and Mother back. I thought that the next time I found a penny scratting, I would buy another packet of fags and smoke them; that I would go round Garry Nab just as often as I liked; and that if Mother asked me, I'd just tell her a lie. I thought I'd swear and say even the dirty words that Grab and the other boys said. I thought I would never run any more errands for Mother unless she made me. I'd just show her how wicked I could be, and that would teach her not to blame me when I'd tried to do something good. The only thing that frightened me about this was that it might make her want more than ever to send me away from Bramblewick to stay with Uncle Fred and go to a nice school. But I felt too wicked to be very frightened about this, and I went on feeling wickeder and wickeder. And the strange thing was that while I thought of the lady who had sung at chapel quite a lot, I didn't feel any more that she was lovely. I thought that she'd be just like Mother when you got to know her, very religious, and strict, and always wanting you to be nice and not enjoy yourself. I felt that I wanted to be wicked for the rest of my life.

BOOK TWO

I

DAD DIDN'T JUST go on painting a bit more of a picture every day until it was finished; not if it was an important picture like the one he was doing of Mike. One day he'd say he'd got it just right, and that he wouldn't touch it again, and he'd be in a very happy mood, whistling and humming as he went about the house, making jokes with Mother, and talking to her about all that was going to happen if the picture was accepted by the Academy and then sold for a large sum of money. But the next day when he came to look at it, he'd see something he didn't quite like, and start altering it whether Mike was there to stand for him or not, and instead of getting it better, he made it worse, and this would make something else look wrong, and he'd get into a temper, and perhaps scrape all that he had painted during a week. Three times at least he completely scraped off Mike's face, and when he came to put the coble in he got it wrong so many times that at last he gave it up and had Mike standing by a stone instead, with a bit of scaur and the sea behind him, and only a small coble sail showing on the sea itself.

It wasn't until the beginning of next March that it was finished, and I don't think Dad would have stopped work then if Mike hadn't got cross and said he wouldn't stand anymore, because he was sick of him saying it was finished, and then scraping it out again. He said it gave him rheumatics keeping still for so long, and that it was twice as hard as digging a grave. I didn't like it quite as much as I did the first time Dad had said it was finished, but I did think it was a lovely picture, and very like Mike, and Dad, although he said he wasn't quite sure that he had got the expression right, seemed very proud of it, and said it was easily his best work and was sure it would be accepted.

But he was very worried. No one had given any orders for photos or pictures since Christmas. The picture had to be sent in by the end of March. He hadn't got a frame for it yet. When it was framed, he would have to get a packing-case, and then pay carriage. And there was another expense; for it couldn't be sent straight to the Acadamy, but had to go to an agent, who would unpack it, and take it to the Academy himself, and charge quite a lot of money whether the Academy accepted it or not. Dad got angry whenever he talked about this to Mother. He said that the Government didn't give any encouragement to artists. Instead, it did all it could to make it difficult for a man to get his work known to the public; and that there must be hundreds and hundreds of very great artists who, because they were poor, could never get into the Academy, and would probably die unknown. He said it would be an awful thing if, after all the work he had put into the picture of Mike, it couldn't be sent off. He said that unless he *did* get an order for something before long, he'd have to explain the position to Mr Fenwick, and ask him to make a frame and a packing-case, and put it down on his account. But Mother said he mustn't dare to do such a thing, for he already owed him for some more paints, and we were in debt to Mr Thompson again, too. She was sure God would send the money some way.

I felt miserable when I heard Mother talking about how poor we were. We weren't as poor as the Burtons were, of course, for there was always something to eat in the house, but I knew how worried she was when we were in debt, and, in spite of all the wicked things I now did quite regularly, like swearing and going to forbidden places and telling lies, I tried very hard to help her by getting wood from the shore, and bits of coal and cinders that washed up; and I took her all the English coins I found scratting, including a shilling, and one day I got ninepence from the rag-and-bone man for some brass, and only kept a ha'penny of this to buy a hook to catch some fish for her. It was a small hook with a length of fine gut to it, and I thought it would do for trout, as well as for the fish you caught down the scaurs; although if I did get some trout, I didn't know how I would explain to Mother how I had got them.

I knew that you had to have a licence to fish for trout, and this cost one-and-sixpence, and if you got one you still had to get permission to fish in the becks; and as the becks belonged to the squire, and he wouldn't let anyone else fish in them but the miller, it would only have been a waste of money. Besides, the licences were sold by Mr Thompson, and even if I had saved up and bought one, he would have told Mother, and as she forbade me to go near the dam (which was the best place for trout), it would have just got me into trouble, and of course, would have stopped me getting her the fish, when she needed them so badly.

I had fished in the dam, but only with a bent pin, and I had never caught anything. But Mike had told me what sort of worms trout liked best, and how to find them, and one evening I arranged with Chicken that we should have a try. I'd got some worms before school and kept them in a tin in my pocket all afternoon. It was now nearly spring and primrose time, so that if I had wanted an excuse for hurrying off after tea, I had only to say I was going to get some primroses. But Mother didn't make so much fuss about where I was going to, now that the evenings were longer, for she hadn't found out any of the wicked things I had done, and believed that I never went anywhere except on the south cliff and shore. She just said jokingly that she wondered what treasures I would bring back with me, and whether I had seen a rainbow, and was going to hunt for the box of gold that was supposed to be buried where one end of it touched the ground. This made me a bit angry, because I had once seen a rainbow with one end touching the shore just by Garry Nab, and I had spent hours scratting there without finding as much as a brass button. But I knew that she was more worried now than ever, because of having no money, and because Dad was getting so unhappy about the picture, so I just laughed, and said it might be gold and it might be something else.

As usual, Chicken had a lot to talk about as we hurried along the cliff top, and I did listen closely to one thing he said. He had heard that Boozer was expected to arrive back on the five o'clock train. He hadn't been home since the storm, and the business about the ship he had saved had been taken to the law courts, and Boozer had been given more than a hundred pounds for what he had done, and as well as that he had been given a spy-glass as a present for saving the lives of the men who had been on the ship.

"I reckon he'll be tight every day for months," Chicken said, "with all that money. Father's looking forward to seeing him. He's scarcely had anything to drink for nearly a week, and Boozer always treats him and Bob Walsh. It'll be a queer thing if Father is able to get upstairs by himself tonight."

The dam was higher up Garry Beck than the mill, at the beginning of the oak wood, which reached for about half a mile inland, covering both sides of a narrow dale. To reach it we had to leave the cliff path a little beyond the place where we had made the bonfire and the wigwam, and take another path leading down a rough bank into the wood itself. We stopped at the top of this path, for it gave a clear view of the mill (which was also a farm). The miller was a tall, scraggy old man, with fierce eyes, like Slogger's. I was afraid of him, because he hated people even going into the wood for flowers, and in summer he often scared visitors almost out of their wits by shouting at them, although they did not know they were trespassing. He had a very loud voice, and it wasn't very long before we heard it, for although we could not see him, he was in one of the farm buildings, and he seemed to be doing something with his pigs. I thought this was good, and I told Chicken that he must not speak or make any other sort of noise and we started down the bank, climbed over a gate, and got into the wood safely. I could see the deep muddy water of the dam, fringed with reeds and willows below us, and I was very excited.

Although the trees were just starting to bud, they grew so close together that we could see scarcely any sky, and it was just like dusk under them. The air was very still, so that even a twig breaking sounded like a cracker, and, when suddenly a trout jumped in the dam, I gave a jump myself and started trembling all over. But I wasn't really frightened. I was just excited. We crept nearer to the dam, and got to a place from which we could see the dam, and also the path which led to the dam wall from the mill. We stopped here and I whispered to Chicken that he mustn't come any farther, but just watch the path, and that if he heard anyone coming along it he was to whistle softly, then wait for me to join him, and we could run up the wood another way. He looked a bit frightened and he didn't answer, but kept his lips pressed together, and nodded his head. I made my way to a clump of hazels where I had noticed a nice whippy stick. I cut it and cleaned it, and sat down and took out my line which was made up of pieces of grocery string saved from parcels. My fingers were trembling and it got raffled, and I had to waste a lot of time undoing the knots, and when I got it clear I had a dreadful fright because I couldn't find the hook and thought I must have left it at home. All the time I was looking through my pockets the trout kept jumping, and I had almost started to cry, when I did find it, and it caught in my pocket lining, and I had to waste more time cutting it out with my knife. I don't think I had ever felt quite so excited as I did when at last I had got everything ready, and with the hook baited, I moved to the edge of the dam.

In some places the bank was quite clear. In others the reeds and willows were so thick you couldn't see the water through them. The place I chose was just a narrow strip between two of these clumps, and I had just room to move my rod, and let the worm fall clear of an old willow trunk that had fallen into the water itself. And the worm had scarcely sunk from sight when I saw the line straighten and move sharply away. I felt a tug, and knew I had hooked a fish. Mike had told me that trout were like salmon, very strong and cunning, and that if you hooked one, you mustn't try to pull it straight in, but let it kick about until it was tired. I didn't think of this, now. I just jerked at the rod with all my strength, and with a loud splash the fish came out of the water on to the bank, and I left go of the rod and pounced on it with my hands.

I thought when I looked at it I had never seen anything so lovely. It was all silvery and speckled red, and while it wasn't as big as some of the fish I had caught on the scaurs, like billet and codling, it was much plumper. I hoped I could catch another. I unhooked it and just held it up for a moment for Chicken to see; then I put it in my pocket, and re-baited the hook, and threw it out again. And again it was almost instantly seized by another fish. This time I didn't stop to admire it or to hold it up for Chicken. I could think of nothing but of getting it off, and into my pocket, and re-baiting the hook for still another. Again it was seized, and this time by a bigger fish that resisted my first efforts to jerk it out, by rushing under the half-sunken log. But I watched it until it cleared, then I moved backwards so as to drag it up the bank. It broke away from the hook and tried to flap back to the water, but I pounced on it and got it just in time, and put it, still flapping, into my pocket.

I had almost forgotten Chicken. I was just mad with excitement. I couldn't have believed that trout were such easy things to catch. I wanted to go on and on, catching more, filling all my pockets with them. The only difficulty was baiting the hook when my hands were covered with slime and scales and keeping the line from raffling, in my excitement. I caught at least six more, and the last of them I had to put in my breeches pocket, because the others were full. And then, just as I was getting a worm out of the tin, I heard Chicken coming towards me. I turned angrily, but one look at his face told me that he hadn't just left his post because he was sick of waiting. He was pointing his hand up the wood and then towards the mill. I moved towards him. As soon as we were near enough, he whispered fearfully:

"There's *two* chaps coming. One from the mill. One down the wood. I daren't whistle. Which way can we go?"

He clutched my arm, and we stood, listening. Quite loudly now I could hear footsteps and breaking twigs, from the mill path and from the wood, where, had the miller come, I thought we might escape. The trout were still flapping in my pocket. I thought for a moment of taking them out, and throwing them back in the dam, but at once I saw there would be no time. We would have to hide; and quickly, too. I saw that unless the men actually walked along the edge of the dam the nearest clump of willows would hide us. I got down on my hands and knees, and signed to Chicken to follow. The ground was muddy and wet, but that was good, for it made no sound. Taking care not to make the upright branches shake, I squirmed along, Chicken following close, until we were in the heart of a clump. Here there was actually a shallow pool, that had been left when the dam had been full. We had to kneel in this, but we were quite hidden. The footsteps drew nearer. I knew that those from the mill must be the miller's, and I wasn't surprised when I heard the squire's voice hailing him, although it frightened me more than ever. I had never had anything to do with the squire. He was like the miller, very big and stern-looking; but he was supposed to be more fierce, and to hate trespassers even more. I had heard that he had once caught a young farmer poaching on his land, and had thrashed him with a stick until he could hardly walk. I felt that if we were caught now it would be the most dreadful thing that had ever happened in my whole life. But I was too frightened to cry. Chicken got hold of my hand again, and we just waited, and all the time I could feel the trout flapping in my pockets, but I daren't start throwing them away.

They got close together and stopped; and then started talking, but they were near the dam wall, and I couldn't hear everything they said; but first of all they were talking about the sluices, which were worked from a place just the other side of the wall. Then I heard the word "trout", and I felt that they both must be looking at the dam, where the fish were jumping loudly. I thought if they had really come to fish, we were bound to be discovered; but that if they did go below the wall we might squirm out quietly, and then run up the wood; and I looked round to see if we could easily get out of the clump the way we had come. And as I turned I was horrified to see, quite close to us, a large black dog, standing among the reeds, panting, with its tongue lolling out, staring straight at me, and looking as though it was about to spring. I don't know whether I shouted or not, or whether Chicken did when he saw it. I think we were too frightened even to get our breath. I thought it was just going to leap on us and kill us. And it did leap, and it landed almost on top of my body; but instead of biting me, it began licking my face, and pawing at me, and making funny little whining noises, and then it started on Chicken and rolled him right over into the muddy pool. I thought it was funny after; but I didn't then. When Chicken got up it licked him all over his face with its big sticky tongue, and then it started on me again, and I daren't do anything to stop it. The miller and the squire were still talking. Suddenly they began to move towards us, and I distinctly heard the squire say:

"Yes. Get all the willows cut close. There isn't room to throw a fly. I'll be coming along one evening this week. There seem to be more fish than there have been for years."

And then he said:

"Where's that bitch of mine got to?" and he shouted, " Nell, Nell – Nell!"

It was just then that the dog seemed to find out the fish in my pockets; for it left off licking my face and started pawing at my coat and sniffing. I daren't try to stop it. There was no flap on my coat pocket, and it suddenly pushed its nose in and pulled a trout clean out. Then, as the squire shouted again it bounded away, into the reeds and out of sight. Almost at once I heard the squire swearing at it, and going for it with his stick. But it must have swallowed the trout, for neither the squire nor the miller said anything about it.

They couldn't have been more than a dozen strides away from us now, and I knew that our chance of escaping up the wood had gone. I thought that the next time they moved they'd be right on top of us, and even if we were hidden the dog would show them where we were, particularly if it was hungry and it wanted another trout. But although they went on talking about the weeds and willows being cut down, they didn't come any nearer, and the dog stayed with them, and at last they started walking slowly back towards the wall. They stopped again; but soon they were moving down the path to the mill, and their voices became faint.

Chicken was crying, and I was nearly crying myself with relief. I gave him a sharp nudge, however, and started to crawl out of the clump. We waited at the edge of it, listening. Then, not caring about the noise we made, we dashed up the wood, over the gate, and ran as fast as we could for the cliff top.

I'd never been so glad to be anywhere, as out of that gloomy wood. I couldn't think of anything else until we were completely out of sight of it, and neither of us spoke until we reached the place near to the wigwam. Then we sat down just below the cliff edge. We were out of breath. We were wet through and plastered over with mud. My face was sticky, and I could still smell where the dog had licked me. But I could also feel the trout, no longer flapping, but wet and cold in my pockets, and I pulled them out and laid them on the grass. The sight of them made me feel better, and Chicken stopped crying at last, and wiped his face with his coat sleeve. He didn't say anything about the trout, though.

"God. I *was* frightened," was the first thing he said. "I've never been so frightened in my life. I thought that dog was going to kill us, first time it jumped. It's a wonder they didn't find us. *By* – we'd have got a hiding if they had. I couldn't whistle, you know. They came so sudden. What are you going to tell your mother, when she sees you all covered with mud?"

I was already thinking about Mother, and the sight of the trout, while exciting, gave me a new fear. I mustn't even let her guess where we had been. Yet if I took her the trout she would know that I couldn't have been anywhere else than Garry Beck, and she'd guess I'd been at the dam. But would she know they were trout if I didn't tell her? She didn't know very much about fish. She didn't know the difference between a flounder and a dab, or a billet and a codling. There wasn't so much difference between a trout and a billet except for the red spots. I might even scrape the spots off. I tried to do so with my knife, and although it was now dusk, and that might have helped to hide them, it did seem that they didn't show so plainly. I shared them out with Chicken, and I scraped all mine, and put them back in my pocket; and then, as there didn't seem to be anyone on the shore, I thought we'd best go down and wash the mud from our boots and clothes in a pool before going home. As we were already wet, getting a bit wetter wouldn't matter, and it would make it look as if we had been fishing on the scaurs.

We ran down the cliff. We washed each other's breeches, and I washed my face to get rid of the smell of the dog. We hurried along the shore. There was no one on the slipway, and I left Chicken in the Dock. Thompson's shop was already lit up, and as I passed it I saw Grab just filling a basket with groceries which Stan Thompson was handing to him from the counter. I felt very proud and superior to Grab. I thought that he daren't have gone fishing in the dam, and been nearly caught by the squire and the miller. There was a light in our own shop, too. Although I was so cold and wet, I'd never felt happier and prouder. The only thing Mother could be vexed about was my wet boots and breeches, and I was sure she wouldn't be vexed when she saw the fish and knew what a good supper we should have. She'd want to cook them straight away, and if she dipped them in batter, as she usually did, she'd probably not look close enough to see any spots, and anyway, she couldn't prove I hadn't caught them down the scaurs.

But as I stepped through the street doorway, which was open, I got such a surprise that I forgot all about the trout; for there, in the shop, talking to Dad in a very loud voice, was Captain Lingdale. His back was towards me. I couldn't tell if he was drunk or not, but I thought he must be, by the way he was shouting, and by the way Dad was standing as far back in the shop as he could, and looking very anxious, as though he was praying that Boozer would go away. Although Boozer was shouting so loud, the only sense I could make out of what he was saying was that he wanted *three* of something. And all Dad did was to keep on saying:

"Yes, Captain. Yes, Captain."

I went slowly upstairs, still trying to make out what it was Boozer wanted; and there was Mother, standing in the living-room doorway, looking more anxious than Dad. She didn't ask me where I had been, or notice that my clothes were wet. She clutched hold of my arm, and whispered anxiously:

"Is it Captain Lingdale?"

I whispered back "Yes." I felt frightened myself. I thought Boozer might want to fight Dad. I wondered if I ought to run and fetch the policeman, or Mike. Mother kept clutching me and we both stood listening, but I couldn't make out anything except that Boozer wanted *three* of something, until he shouted:

"Come on and have a pint on it. Come on."

Then Dad said:

"No, thank you, Captain, I'm a teetotaller, you know. If you'll leave the photo, I'll see what I can do tomorrow."

And then there was a bang, and I thought Boozer must have struck Dad a blow, for there was silence for a moment. Then Boozer shouted:

"All right – take that then. Take that on account... I want a drink. I'm going."

Then I heard him tramping heavily out of the shop, and he gave the street door a bang that made both of us jump. We heard Dad moving about, and Mother shouted to him, asking him if he was all right. He didn't answer, but he started to come upstairs, and we moved back into the room, and Mother stood waiting for him. When he appeared his face was very red, and he looked as though he had had an awful fright. But he looked excited, too. Neither he nor Mother spoke for a moment, and Dad just stood at the stair-top, holding a photo and a piece of paper in his hand and staring at them as though he was bewildered.

"What did that dreadful man want?" Mother said at last. "What did he want?"

Dad held up the photo, and I saw that it was a photo of Boozer himself, wearing a captain's cap, and holding a spyglass under one arm, and looking quite sober and respectable; and Dad said:

"Didn't you hear what he wanted? Didn't you hear what he said? He wants three portraits painted from this photo. Three-guinea size. All exactly the same. He wants them to give to his friends as presents, because of that ship he saved. That's the telescope that was presented to him. And he insisted on my having this on account. He banged it down on the counter, and then stamped out. Look – it's a five-pound note!"

He held the piece of paper up. I had never seen a five-pound note before, but I knew that it was the same as five sovereigns, and I thought that it was wonderful. I thought that Mother would just shout with joy, that such a wonderful thing had happened, when she and Dad needed the money so badly. It was more wonderful than the purse. But Mother didn't look a bit happy. She looked exactly as she did when she found out that I had done something wrong, and then she said, very solemnly:

"We're not going to take it, of course. How could we take money from that dreadful man? Just think of his wife and what she must suffer from his drunken habits, and seeing him waste his money. He's drunk now, or he wouldn't have wanted you to paint pictures for him. He's not responsible for his actions. But I'm glad he gave you the money. It will mean so much saved for his poor wife. I'm going to take it to her at once."

I think Dad must have felt a bit angry and disappointed, because he must have thought that all his anxiety about Mike's picture was over; but he must have seen that Mother was right, for all he said was, "very well," and he put the note down on the table, and went over to the fire and sat down in his chair.

Mother at once started to put on her hat and coat. Then she looked at me and said, but not crossly:

"Sonny, your boots are wet through. Get them changed at once."

I thought I'd better not say anything about the fish yet. She picked up the note, and without saying another word, went out. Dad didn't say anything either. His face was still very red, and he just sat staring into the fire. I lit a candle and went up into the attic and changed my boots and stockings and breeches; then came down, and Dad was still in the same place, and he didn't seem to notice that I had been out of the room. Mother kept the dishes in a dark corner, and I took out the trout, and put them on a shelf with a piece of paper over them, for I thought Dad might know they were trout if Mother didn't. I kept very quiet so that he wouldn't start asking me questions. It wasn't until I heard Mother opening the street door again that Dad moved, and then he only got hold of the poker and stirred the fire, and he didn't say anything when she came in. She looked very angry and upset, and her breath was going very quickly. She didn't say anything, either, for a long time. She took off her things. Then she put her apron on, as though she was going to start getting supper ready, and I thought I had better tell her about the fish. She looked quite pleased for a moment and said how clever I was, and asked me if I had changed my things. But I knew she was thinking about something else all the time, and she scarcely looked at the fish, and started mixing some batter. And it wasn't until she got this ready that she spoke to Dad. Then all she said was:

"Never in all my life have I felt so humiliated."

Dad didn't say anything. He never did when Mother was upset like this; but just waited for her to go on. She put the pan on the fire, and some fat in it; and when her back was turned I quickly dipped all the trout in the batter, to hide the spots. Then she did go on:

"I thought that Mrs Lingdale would at least

have been grateful for our having saved that money from being wasted in drink. I thought that she of all persons would have understood why we couldn't take the money or even the order from a man who was under the influence of drink. I explained the position as nicely as I could. I tried not to hurt her feelings. And all she said was that her husband knew how to look after himself and his money as well as anyone else in Bramblewick, drunk or sober, and that if he wanted to order three pictures of himself, and pay five pounds on account, it was his business, not hers. And when I offered her the note, she actually slammed the door in my face, and left me there, standing!"

Mother turned to get the fish, and she started cooking them. Dad watched her in a funny way, as though he couldn't make up his mind what to do; but at last he said:

"Well – and what did you do? Have you still got the money?"

"Yes, of course I have," Mother said quietly. "It's still in my purse."

Dad waited a bit, looking this time at the fire; then he said:

"Well – and what are we going to do?"

Mother didn't speak until she had got all the fish in the pan, then:

"I think what we ought to do is to write a letter to Captain Lingdale himself, telling him that you can't do the pictures, and send the money back."

"Just so that he can spend it on drink?" Dad said, looking up quickly. "I don't see how that's going to do any good. I think it would be stupid. I do, really. I think it would be stupid."

"Then you really want to paint three pictures of that dreadful man?" Mother answered. "You're quite willing to be employed by him?"

Dad looked a bit bothered, and didn't answer for a moment, then he said:

"I'd certainly not like to have him sitting for me in the studio. But I don't see very much harm in doing a picture from a photo; although I do hate that sort of work, particularly having to do it three times over. I'd rather do fifty coffin plates. But seeing what the money would mean to us just now, I think it would be most wrong to refuse. It would mean that I would be able to send off Regan's picture, and think what that may lead to. If it was sold we might be able to get out of Bramblewick before the winter, and actually go to the continent. It would be a foot on the ladder, if nothing else. It would be a very much better thing for us to have the money than for it to be wasted in drink."

Mother went on cooking the fish. Dad just sat staring into the fire. At last she said supper was ready; and it wasn't until then that she told Dad that perhaps, after all, seeing it would only be spent in drink, he'd better keep the money, only she hoped that he wouldn't put one of the pictures in the shop window, for the whole village to see, and that Captain Lingdale himself wouldn't set foot in the shop again. If Dad was out, *she* wouldn't go down and speak to him. She didn't want to have anything to do with the business at all. She didn't want to see the pictures.

We sat down to supper. Dad's face was still red, but he soon became very cheerful. He said that he had never in his life tasted such delicious fish. He asked me what they were and where I had caught them, and when I told them they were billet and that I had caught them down the scaurs, he said just like he had said about the purse, that he'd have to come with me one day. I was glad that both he and Mother believed me, and I didn't worry a bit about my telling such a lie. I was glad, too, that Mother had agreed to Dad keeping the money, and doing the pictures. I did want Mike's picture to go to the Academy, and be accepted and sold; but I couldn't help feeling frightened when Dad talked about our leaving Bramblewick and going abroad, for if I didn't go it would mean my having to stay with Uncle Fred in Liverpool, and go to another school. In spite of everything I did like Bramblewick. I thought it would be awful to live in a place where you couldn't be near the sea, and know whether the tide was up or down, or whether it was rough or smooth, or search for treasures or be "first on". It would be awful to leave Bramblewick, and never see Mike again, or go off with him in his coble in summer. And while I didn't like Chicken so very much, I had got used to him; and if I knew that I was never going to meet him again at the bottom of the cliff path, I'd feel terribly sad. I thought that I'd rather go to school with Grab and the other boys than with boys such as I had seen in Bramblewick during the summer, who were always dressed up in their best clothes, and never used bad language, and were always well behaved.

And Dad seemed so certain now that the picture would be accepted and sold. He went on talking about it all through supper, and after supper he helped Mother to wash up, a thing he only did when he was in a very good temper. And then he got hold of a book about Italy that someone had lent to him, and started to read it aloud, while Mother sewed, and I had to keep still and quiet. It wasn't very interesting and I was glad when it was time to go to bed.

II

I NEVER SAW the three pictures of Boozer. Neither Dad nor Mother mentioned the subject again while I was listening; but I know that he did them, and that he must have got the whole money for them, for he had a real English gold frame made for Mike's picture, and I got a new pair of boots, not seaboots, of course, and for a long time I never heard Mother worrying about being in debt.

Dad thought that before the picture was sent away, it would be a good thing to have it in the shop window. He said it would be a splendid advertisement for him. He put it in one morning and it was there when I got home from school. He had cleared out all the photographs, and put it in the middle all by itself. I felt proud of it. It looked twice as good now it was framed; and I was proud to see several people looking at it, and hear them say what a good likeness it was. But, as usual, I went down on the shore before dinner, and when I got back there was Grab and most of the other boys outside the shop shouting and laughing as though they were making fun of the picture; and when I got near they started to laugh and say mocking things at me, asking me where I got my new boots from, and why my father didn't paint a picture of me and put it in the window, and Grab actually tried to kick my backside as I stepped inside the door. I thought that if Dad was going to let the picture stay in the window, I'd have nothing but trouble.

But as we were having tea that afternoon, Mike came into the shop and called Dad. He was very angry. He said that Dad must take the picture out of the window at once; that all the people in Bramblewick were talking about it, and making fun of him. It wouldn't have been so bad if the picture didn't show him in his old clothes, looking no better than a tramp, or a man selling bootlaces from door to door. He didn't mind at all the people in London seeing it, for none of them knew him. But he wasn't going to be disgraced in the village, where he was as good as any other man, and could fight the best of them. Dad was a bit angry too. He told Mike again that he didn't understand and that it was the old clothes he was wearing that gave character to the picture; but Mike said he didn't want to understand that, and if he'd thought that he was going to make a show of it like this, he wouldn't have stood for the thing so many times, when he'd rather have been out working. So Dad at last said he'd take it out; and he did, but he was in a bad temper when he came upstairs, and he went out as soon as he had had his tea, and it wasn't until after supper, when he started reading the book on Italy, that he became cheerful again.

He just kept it in the shop after that, until the day came for it to be sent off to the agent in London. He had got a new packing-case made by Mr Fenwick, but before the picture was put in it he had to fix the label on the back of the frame, with his name and address on it, and what the picture was called. He didn't know quite what would be the best name for it. He thought YORKSHIRE FISHERMAN sounded all right, but that didn't agree with Mike being an Irishman. He thought if he called it IRISH FISHERMAN, then this wouldn't agree with the background being a scaur, and the sea with a coble sail on it, and Mike having a Yorkshire guernsey round his shoulders. Mother said he should just call it Mike Regan; but he said that would be just the same as calling it IRISH FISHERMAN because of it being an Irish name, and that what he really wanted was something poetic, so that it really wouldn't matter whether Mike was Irish or Yorkshire, and in the end he called it AN IDLE HOUR.

But even this did not trouble him so much as having to fill up the form which had to be sent to the Academy itself, for he had to say how much money he wanted for the picture if it was sold. The biggest sum of money he had ever got for a picture was six pounds, including the frame. Mother said that he ought to charge ten, and that she'd be very pleased if it sold for so much. Dad said he had never heard of anything so ridiculous; that if a picture was accepted by the Academy it proved that it was worth a large sum of money. Of course, he didn't expect that he would get so much as an R.A. or even an A.R.A., or an artist who had exhibited many times and whose work was well known. Artists like these would charge anything from seventy-five guineas for a picture as big as AN

IDLE HOUR. An R.A. would probably charge two hundred guineas for it, and it might prove to be worth five times that amount when the artist was dead. It would be a mistake to ask too much, but it would be an even bigger mistake to ask too little, for this would show that he hadn't much opinion of its value himself. He said he thought it oughtn't to be a penny less than fifty guineas, and he wrote fifty guineas in the space on the form, but only in lead pencil, and he rubbed this out and put in forty-five, and then twenty-five, and he inked this in. Then he scraped twenty-five out and put in thirty, which he said was neither too much nor too little, although if it was sold, he'd be certain to wish he'd put forty-five at least.

It wasn't easy for me to know what to say in my prayers the night after the picture had been sent off. I did want it to be accepted and sold. I did want Dad to be famous and rich so that Mother could have a really nice house to live in, and not have to scrub floors and wash up dishes anymore and do photos; and that I could buy anything I liked. But I didn't want us to leave Bramblewick, and above everything, I didn't want to live with Uncle Fred. But it wasn't easy to say in my prayers that the reason why I didn't want to live with Uncle Fred was because of him being so religious. That would be like an insult to God. I got out of it by just praying that the picture would be accepted and sold, and that the money would make Dad and Mother and me happier, in the way that we wished most. I felt that God would understand exactly what I meant by that. Yet I felt that I was now leading such a wicked life that there wasn't much chance of my prayer being answered at all. If it did turn out all right, it would be in answer to Dad's and Mother's prayers and not to mine.

It worried me, what was going to happen, whenever I thought of it, but it would be three weeks before Dad got word from the Academy, and the bird-nesting season had now begun, so there were plenty of other things to think about. I loved springtime. Although Mother still said I hadn't to go farther along the shore than Garry Nab, or into the Garry Wood, there was a valley higher up the beck called Brocketts, which you could get to by a lane; and although this was really farther from home, she said I could go there, and this gave me an excuse for going almost anywhere I liked, for all I had to do was to bring some primroses back with me and say I had got them there. There were so many in Brocketts that I could pick a big bunch in a few minutes, and I could spend all the rest of the time bird-nesting.

Mother didn't actually forbid me to go bird-nesting. She didn't say it was a sin against God to take birds' eggs; but the first time I had shown her one she looked very sad, and asked me to imagine myself a little bird spending days and days gathering bits of grass and wool, and making the nest so warm and cosy for its eggs, and then flying to it one day and finding the eggs gone and the nest torn to pieces. Wouldn't it be just like some robbers coming to a home and setting fire to it and murdering the children? I didn't think it would be quite so bad as this, because eggs weren't the same as children, and anyway, people took hens' eggs away from them regularly, and the hens didn't seem to mind or they wouldn't go on laying more eggs in the same place. But I did see it was cruel to take all the eggs from a nest, and I wouldn't have thought of touching the nest itself, or the little birds when they were hatched. It didn't seem to make any difference, if you took just one egg, for the mother went on sitting just the same, proving that she couldn't count; and as I didn't want more than one egg of each kind for my collection, I was sure I wasn't doing anything wrong. But I kept them in a box under a chest of drawers in the attic, where, since I'd shown Mother the loose plank, I kept my other treasures, and whenever I did bring some eggs home, I always hurried straight upstairs, and never said a word about them.

I made Chicken keep to the same rules, and made him promise that whenever we found a nest he should keep it a dead secret, and never go to it by himself. The other boys didn't worry about not taking more than one egg, of course. They robbed every nest they found; even robins' (which was supposed to be very unlucky) and thrushes' and wrens'. One of the loveliest nests I ever found was a chaffinch's, and it was quite close to the village, in a patch of bushes behind the gas house. It was in a holly bush, built in the fork between two branches, made of moss and lichens, and lined with wool and feathers. It had three eggs when we found it, a lovely pale green colour with queer brown marks, as though they had been painted with a brush. We waited until it had another egg and then we took one, but the Mother didn't mind, for next day she laid another. The bush was so close to where the other boys played, I hadn't much hope it wouldn't be found; and when we went to it one day there were three boys near it, blowing the eggs, and the nest had been torn to bits. One of the boys was a cousin of Grab's, but not so big as Len and Kid, and I kicked his backside for him. Grab hided me for this later, but I didn't mind. I'd have gone for Grab himself if I'd *seen* him robbing such a nest and tearing it up for no reason at all.

Yet the other boys, while they robbed plenty of blackbirds and thrushes, and robins, close to the village, were not so interested in bird-nesting as we were; and most of the nests we found at Brocketts weren't touched by anyone except us and they weren't the nests of such common birds. We found a water-hen's nest on a branch close down by the beck, with twelve eggs, and a barn owl's nest in a hollow tree with two. Garry Wood was quite near to Brocketts, and while we had to keep a sharp lookout for the squire and the miller, we spent a lot of time in it and found, among other things, a pheasant's nest with fifteen, a carrion crow's, a magpie's, and a sparrow-hawk's. The crow's was in a very tall beech tree and it took me a long time to climb to it. The magpie's wasn't so high, but when I got to it I found it was nearly all made of thorn twigs and that it had a thick pile of these over the top, so that I could hardly get my hand into the nest itself. The hawk's was actually on a tree branch that overhung the dam itself, and I was really very frightened climbing to it, for in one place I had to go under the branch and go along hand over hand like a monkey. But the eggs were the loveliest I had ever seen. They weren't pointed, but almost as round as a ball, and they were marked with lovely red and brown patches. I took the loveliest one and I had to hold it in my mouth while I climbed down, and for a long time it was the most precious egg in my collection.

We found a dipper's nest (made like a wren's, of moss, and in the shape of a ball, with only a tiny entrance to it) under a little waterfall in the beck, so that the birds had to fly through the water to reach it. We found the nests of wood pigeons, wagtails, tree pipits and creepers, warblers, goldfinches, yellow-hammers, blue-tits, and redstarts. We heard a green woodpecker one day, and actually saw it chipping a hole in a dead trunk, while it hung on to the bark with its claws; but later, when the hole was finished, and the bird laid its eggs, it was so deep we couldn't get at them.

Whenever we went to Brocketts the air was full of the songs of blackbirds and thrushes, and finches and linnets; and there was nearly always a skylark singing in the air, and a cuckoo calling, and crows cawing in Garry Wood, and lapwings making their queer cries over the fields. It was all so exciting that the very minute we got out of sight of the village, I could forget all the things that troubled me, like

Grab, and going to school, and Mother hating Bramblewick, and what might happen if Dad became rich.

But Dad himself was already beginning to get very anxious about the Academy. There were two deliveries of letters every day; and he'd always be in the house now when the postman came. If the postman knocked at the door he'd give an awful jump, and rush downstairs to see what had come. Usually it was just a bill, or a circular, but he'd go very red when he opened it, and give a sigh when he saw what it was, and he'd say, "Well, no news is good news," and Mother would go for him for expecting to hear news about the picture before the proper time, although I knew she was anxious too.

It was on the second Sunday after the picture had been sent off that a terrible thing happened at Bramblewick. Since the fine weather had come I had got into the habit of playing truant from Sunday School on the Sundays that Mr Thompson didn't take it. The other superintendent was a very old man with weak eyesight, and he was so stupid that he wouldn't have noticed if his own grandchildren were present or not. What I did was to pretend to go early, then run straight past the school, round to the bridge, and back along the alleys above the road to the gas house and meet Chicken in the usual place. It meant, of course, that we couldn't go very far from home; and if Mother asked me what we had learnt at school I had to invent something; but this was easy, and I could always show her one of the little text cards they gave away at Sunday School, that I'd saved from one of Mr Thompson's days, and not shown her before.

On this day we had gone along the cliffs to look at a skylark's nest to see if its eggs were hatched. We came back along the cliff path, and I was afraid I was a bit late. I decided to go straight down past the top of the rubbish shoot and through the Dock. As soon as we got round the coastguards' cottages, we could see that something very unusual was happening. There were a lot of people in the Dock, all talking very low but excitedly, and the fishermen, although they were in their best clothes, were taking the chocks from the wheels of one of the small boats, and preparing to launch her. With them was the police sergeant, and Mike, and two coastguards; and suddenly I saw the doctor coming down the Road, very quickly, carrying a small case in his hand.

We ran down and stood among the people who were watching and it wasn't long before we heard someone asking what was the matter, and another person answer:

"It's Tommy Brewster. He's tumbled over Low Batts cliff. He was on there bird-nesting with some other lads. They came running back and said he'd tumbled over. The tide's up so they can only get to where he is by boat. I doubt it'll only be his dead body they'll fetch back with them, though. He must have dropped from top to bottom."

I was very frightened. I knew Tommy Brewster, although I had never had much to do with him, for he had left school and was serving his time with another Bramblewick grocer. His father was a sea captain and was now away at sea. He lived quite close to the chapel. Everybody, even the sergeant and the other men, looked frightened too. They didn't talk much. The way they looked at each other, as they started to launch the boat, was like the way the bearers at a funeral looked when they were carrying a coffin out of a house. And suddenly I noticed Mrs Brewster herself standing with another woman who was holding her arm. She wasn't crying. She was just staring at the boat, and breathing hard, and her face was white. I thought of Mother, and what she'd feel like if she'd just been told that I'd fallen over the cliff. I thought I'd better rush home and let her know that I was all right, in case someone told her, and didn't say who it was; and I did this, but I didn't want to be kept in, so I just shouted up the stairs what had happened and hurried down again to the Dock before she had a chance to call me back.

The sea was smooth. The tide was up. The boat was already launched. The doctor and the sergeant and the coastguards had got in, and now the fishermen pushed her off, and they started rowing as fast as they could towards Low Batts Point, which was the north point of the Bay. I found Chicken standing with a group of other boys and I went up to them. Grab was there, too; and also a bigger boy, who had left school. I soon learnt that this boy had been with Tommy when the thing had happened. He seemed very proud of himself at being able to tell the story. Even Grab was listening in silence.

There had been several other boys, but all of them big. They'd gone to Low Batts to see if they could find any gulls' eggs. They'd seen a gull fly off from under a ledge, just below the cliff top beyond the point, at a spot called Castle Wall, and Tommy had said he was going to try for an egg. It wasn't very steep there, but just below the ledge the cliff went almost straight down to the bottom, where it was all hard scaur and fallen rocks. Tommy had gone down, and at last he'd shouted that he could see a nest but couldn't tell whether there were any eggs in it, until he got nearer; and it was just then his feet seemed to slip. He tried to save himself and hung on to a sod with his hands. But the sod broke loose, and he started sliding down, feet first, and the next moment he was out of sight. He never shouted, the boy said. They didn't hear any other sound. The last they saw of him was his straw hat, still on his head, and then they saw a lot of dust come up, and then all the gulls in the cliff went flying out to sea, screaming just like they did when the lifeboat gun went off. A few minutes later they saw a coastguard coming along the cliff top, so they ran and told him what had happened, and after he'd tried to look down and see where Tommy was, he'd started running back for Bramblewick, and they'd all followed him. But the coastguard had said that Tommy would be dead for certain.

By this time the Dock was almost full of people, crowding on the slipway top, and looking over the breakwater at the boat which was moving quickly towards the point. I saw Dad and Mother, looking very anxious, but I kept out of their way. At last the boat got out of sight round the point. It was a long time before she appeared again, moving south. I didn't hear anyone speak when she did. It was just as though everyone was in chapel, and the only sound you could hear in the Dock was the cawing of some jackdaws among the chimney-pots, and this made me feel more frightened than ever about what had happened, for it made me think about my eggs, and particularly about the crow's, and the sparrowhawk's and the risk I had run in climbing to them. Suppose the branch had given way, and I had fallen into the dam, and I had been drowned. I thought that no matter how much I wanted a gull's egg I would never risk climbing for one.

The boat drew near. As the tide was high and the sea so smooth it didn't come in between the posts that marked the landing scaurs, but straight in under the village cliff. Soon we could make out the doctor and the sergeant sitting in the stern, and something very white near them. This was Tommy's straw hat, but Tommy himself was lying stretched out on the thwart, quite still, and now and again the doctor was looking down at him, but the sergeant was staring straight ahead, and I had never seen him so stern and solemn. Chicken gripped my arm.

"He's dead," he whispered.

I didn't say anything.

The boat grounded at the bottom of the

slipway. We could now see Tommy quite distinctly. He was lying face upwards. There were bandages over his head; and these and his face were covered with blood. At once one of the Fosdycks, although he hadn't got his seaboots on, jumped out of the boat and waded ashore, and began to walk quickly up the slipway. He was red in the face and looked very anxious. Some of the people on the slipway moved towards him and started asking questions. He waved them out of the way. But I heard him say in his gruff voice:

"We don't know yet. He's breathing, that's all we know. I'm going for the stretcher from the lifeboat-house. Some of you had better let his mother know, and tell her to get a bed ready for him."

I hadn't seen Mrs Brewster since I had come down the slipway, and I daren't look round for fear of seeing Mother. The other fishermen had now got out, and they heaved the boat in. The stretcher was brought down and very carefully Tommy was lifted on to it. The sergeant came up the slipway and made everyone stand back, and I couldn't see any more because of the grown-up people in front of us. But after Tommy had been carried up, those who had been in the boat stood on the slipway, and one of the fishermen was telling the people how they had found him. He was lying on the scaur at the cliff foot. The doctor and the sergeant got to him first. It seemed he was dead. But it must have been his hat that saved him from being killed outright. It was banged so hard down on his head, the doctor had to cut it away, and the rim of it had cut him all round his forehead, and that was where the blood had come from. He must have turned over when he was falling, and landed straight on his head. The doctor said none of his bones was broken, so far as he could tell. But although he was breathing, he didn't think there'd be much chance of saving his life, and the fisherman said he didn't think there was, either. The last bit of cliff where he had fallen was undercut, and he must have dropped clear for at least as high as a house. If he did live it would be a miracle.

Gradually the people went away, and suddenly I saw Mother looking for me, and I went to her. She gripped my hand and held it tightly all the way home. As soon as we got inside she started to cry, and then she asked me if I had ever gone along Low Batts cliff by myself. I had been once or twice, but never gull-nesting, so I told her I hadn't. She said that she hoped this would be a terrible lesson to me, never to disobey her about going to places that were dangerous. She wanted me to promise that I would never go along the cliff, either by myself or with other boys, and that for her sake I would never run into danger. I promised I wouldn't, and I really did mean it. I thought that not for all the eggs in the world would I venture near Low Batts cliff again; and she kissed me and then she went on talking about poor Mrs Brewster and what she must be feeling like, seeing her dear boy lying there, perhaps already dead, and that I must pray in my heart to God that he *wasn't* dead, but that He would save him and make him well again. I had been praying this all the time, of course, for even if it had been Grab who had fallen over the cliff, I wouldn't have wished him to die. I thought death was horrible for anybody, even for your worst enemies.

Mother didn't have any tea, and I didn't feel hungry. At chapel that night, the preacher said a special prayer for Tommy, actually mentioning his name, and when Dad got back from church he said the Vicar had done the same thing. Before I went to bed he went out to make inquiries, and he learnt that Tommy was still breathing, but unconscious. Mother let me have a candle to take to bed, in case I felt frightened. I did feel frightened. Every time I closed my eyes I could see Tommy Brewster slipping down the cliff, feet first, until I could see nothing but his straw hat; or him falling head over heels, and landing on his head on the scaur; or him being carried up the slipway; or lying in his bed, unconscious, with his mother watching him. And when I didn't see him I saw myself climbing to the hawk's nest and the branch giving way; and I could almost feel myself being drowned. I kept on praying for Tommy, and several times I repeated to myself the promise I had made to Mother, never to run into danger again. Yet I couldn't help wondering what a seagull's egg looked like, and thinking what a wonderful thing it would be to have one in my collection, and I actually imagined finding a nest on the cliff near Garry Nab, where I could get at it safely; although I knew, of course, that gulls never did breed in places like this, but only in cliffs that were steep and dangerous.

III

TOMMY BREWSTER'S STRAW hat had saved his life, although everyone said it was a miracle, and Mother said it was God Himself who had protected him and saved him from being dashed to pieces on the rocks. He regained consciousness next week, and although he was still very ill, and hadn't to be moved, the doctor said that he would get quite well again in time.

It was a great relief to everybody, but Mother scarcely ever stopped talking about it, and she started getting more worried than ever about me when I went out after tea, and she made me promise again and again not to go near the cliffs. Dad didn't seem so anxious, but then he was worrying about the picture, for he said that he might hear about it any time now. The first post came before I went to school. The postman was an old man who was very absent-minded. Sometimes he'd go right past a house he had a letter for, so that the people would think there was nothing for them, then he'd find the letter and come back and take them by surprise. Sometimes he took a letter to the wrong house. If I was awake, I could hear him coming down Cliff Street, banging hard at the doors, and crossing from side to side of the street, and I could tell by his footsteps whether he was coming to our house or not.

Nothing had come by next Friday, and when I

got back from school, Dad was in a very bad temper. He said that the letter must have been sent off by now, and that he thought it was quite likely that the postman had lost it or put it in the letter box of some empty house, so that perhaps he wouldn't get it for days and days. He thought it was a disgrace that we should have a postman who could do that sort of thing, and that it was time someone complained about it. Mother agreed, and I could tell how anxious and worried she was, because she made the tea without putting any tea in the pot, and I was very glad when the meal was over and I could get out. The weather was still fine and warm. I had arranged with Chicken that we should go to Brocketts again, walk down Garry Wood, and then, if the coast was clear, try for some more trout as well as look for nests.

But when I met Chicken, he told me that Len and Kid Fosdyck and some other boys had already gone along the cliff top, and he had heard them say they were going to Brocketts. I knew we would get into trouble if we followed them, particularly if we found them going near any nests we knew of, so I thought that for once we'd go somewhere else, and I thought of a quarry near a farm about half a mile inland from Low Batts Point, where we might find some sand martins, for there was a bed of sand above the stone itself, and I'd once seen some holes which looked as though they might be nests, although this had been in winter time.

We had to go up the Bank, past the new houses, and under the railway line; and then up a little road called Dark Lane, which was a famous place for birds' nests. We hadn't been to it this season because of the other boys, and we soon found signs of where they had been, for there were dozens of thrushes' and blackies' nests pulled out and lying on the ground, and eggshells everywhere. The lane led up to a farm which stood on a high hill, and this hill sloped down again towards the sea at Low Batts Point. The farm we were making for was nearer the sea than this one and was called Low Batts Farm. To reach it we had to leave the lane soon, and cross over some pasture fields; but I thought we had better dodge the farm itself. The quarry was on the seaward side of it, and beyond the quarry was a thick patch of whins. We made for the whins and worked our way back, and we had just got in sight of the quarry when we were startled by a shout, and saw the farmer, carrying a gun, coming towards us. We ran back into the whins, and hid, but we soon heard him coming again. The fields we had crossed from the lane were his, so I was afraid of going back that way. Below us the whins reached down to the railway line, and beyond the line were more fields reaching to the cliff edge, and as that seemed to be our only safe way home, we set off, and soon reached the railway. I did think then that we might have walked back along the line and got off before we reached the Bramblewick signal box, but this was one of the very things Mother had always forbidden me to do, and it would have got us back very early, and I thought it would be all right if we went down to the cliff path so long as we didn't go near the cliff edge.

It wasn't until we had reached the path that I thought of Tommy Brewster, and that it would be very interesting to see the actual place where he had fallen. I had heard about it so many times I was certain I should know it when I saw it. It was farther from the village than the place where we had struck the path, but that didn't matter. I asked Chicken if he'd like to see it and he said yes, so we set off.

We weren't quite at Low Batts Point yet. Looking back, we could see the whole of Bramblewick Bay as far as High Batts, and Browe and Garry Beck woods, and quite a lot of the village itself, and the new coastguard station on the hill above it. But we couldn't see any people either behind us or ahead. At first the cliff edge was guarded by a stone wall standing well back from it, so that even when we looked over we couldn't see the actual cliff, so that it was quite safe. Yet we heard the gulls, making that queer chuckling cry they make in nesting time, and now and again one of them would soar close over our heads, as though it wanted to see what we were up to. It was a wild place and I liked it better than Brocketts. When we got round the point, the whins grew thicker, and we saw rabbits scurrying across the path to their holes in the cliff edge, which was now guarded only by a fence of posts and old wire cable that must have come from a shipwreck. In places we could see the cliff without looking over the fence. It was high and very steep, and soon we came in sight of a very steep bit which I knew must be Castle Wall. We stopped where the path took a sudden twist, and looking between the wires, saw a little slope with a ledge sticking out from the bottom of it; and just as we looked a gull flew out from under the ledge, and swooped down screaming towards the sea, and it was joined by others, all screaming. I knew it must be the very place where Tommy had fallen.

"Don't go near the edge," Chicken said.

I knew better, of course. But there was plenty of firm ground even on the other side of the fence, and we could see clearly without even leaning against the wires. We could even see the marks of Tommy's feet, and the place where they must have started slipping, and where the sod had given way; and the first thing I thought was how stupid he had been to try and get to the ledge, for no one could have possibly reached under it unless they had been fastened with a rope.

"He must have been a fool," I said.

"Aye, I think so, too," said Chicken. "*I* wouldn't get over that fence for a million pounds. It's a wonder he wasn't killed. I reckon we ought to be getting home now; now we've seen it. It makes me feel frightened. What if all this ground suddenly gave way!"

I thought this was a silly idea, and I told Chicken not to talk daft. It couldn't fall unless there was an earthquake and earthquakes only happened in foreign countries. Still, I did move back from the fence a bit, and I think I'd have agreed to start back home then if I hadn't noticed, beyond Castle Wall, a place where the cliff wasn't so steep, with patches of grass growing on it halfway down to the rocks. It wasn't far. I thought that if there were any nests there we might easily be able just to *see* into them and I was longing to see what a gull's egg really looked like.

Chicken didn't look very pleased when I told him what I wanted to do, but he knew better than argue, for I'd have just told him I wouldn't let him come with me anymore. We set off, and it took us a few minutes to reach the place I had seen. It was altogether different from the rest of the cliff, for there wasn't an actual steep edge. The fence itself ran straight on; but at the seaward side of it was quite a broad piece of uneven ground, with grass and whins growing between patches of bare shale. I remembered Mike telling me there were some old jet mines somewhere beyond Low Batts point, and it looked as though this was the very place, for soon we found what must have been a cave, only the crumbly shale had fallen in, almost closing its mouth. It was exciting. I almost forgot the gulls for the time being, although they were screaming fiercely enough close above our heads. I wondered if we could find a real cave that we could get into and explore, and we went on looking until at last we were quite near to the cliffs again. And then I saw a gull's nest – with two eggs in it.

It was in the cliff, of course. There wasn't a sign of nests anywhere on the ground where we had walked. It was below us, about as far down as the dam had been from the hawk's nest, but it wasn't much steeper than the rubbish shoot that I went down almost every time I wanted to be "first on", and there were tufts of grass growing almost the whole way down to it. The only real difference was that it looked a bit more slippery, and that below the nest, instead of there being just the shore to jump to, the cliff was steep, and there was a long drop below, at least as high as Bramblewick church steeple.

We stood very still – the ground where we were was almost level – and I pointed to the nest. I was too excited to speak. Chicken, however, had seen it, and he suddenly clutched my arm.

"Eh," he said, "you're not going to have a try for it, are you? Let's get home."

I didn't take any notice of this. I was frightened. I wished we hadn't seen the nest at all, then we could have gone back and perhaps never troubled any more as to what a gull's egg looked like, or whether they ever were found in a place where you could get at them. I knew now that if I didn't have a try, I'd always be thinking of it, and wishing I had, and that I'd very likely come along the cliffs again and perhaps try to get to a nest in a really dangerous place. And this wasn't dangerous. So long as I kept moving, and didn't let my feet stay too long in one place, it would be perfectly safe. I'd have thought nothing of it if it had just been the shore below, and not that long drop. But if I didn't look down I shouldn't see the drop, and if I didn't think about it, there was nothing to frighten me. I thought I would do it.

"You stay where you are," I said to Chicken. "Look out for anyone coming along the cliff. It won't take me a minute."

I'd never seen him look so frightened. He clutched at my arm, and tried to hold me back. I felt vexed and nearly hit him, and I made him leave go. Then, taking a quick look at the nest, I started down, keeping to the grassy spots and avoiding those where the shale was bare, for I knew they were slippery. It was easy, and I knew it was always easier to get up a cliff or a tree than get down, for getting up you could see where you were going, while getting down you had to guess, or trust to your feet to feel for the holds. The grass was dry and it wasn't strongly rooted; but I knew how much weight I could put on a sod before it started to give way, and I took care to keep moving. It wasn't until I was just above the ledge where the nest was that I found anything difficult. The sods ended here, and the shale, although not very steep, was crumbly. But I turned over, and clawed at it with my feet and hands, and using my belly as a brake, I slid down it on to the very ledge where the nest was, and the next moment I was on my knees beside it, looking at the eggs, touching them.

They were lovelier even than the sparrow hawk's. They were twice as big, and sharply pointed. They were pale green, and spotted with red and brown and black. They were warm, too.

Quite close to where I was two gulls were wheeling in the air, screaming fiercely, and I thought these must be the parent birds watching me. I wondered whether I should take just one egg or both and take one for Chicken. I lifted both of them out, then I thought it would be luckier if I left one, so I put it back and put the other in my coat pocket; but as I had two pockets, I thought better of it and got the other egg, too, for I might easily break one getting back, and it would be nice for Chicken to have one, and the gulls would very likely desert the nest now they had seen that someone could get to it easily, so that the egg would be wasted.

I looked up then. Chicken was standing where I had left him and he was still looking very frightened. He shouted at me in a squeaky voice:

"Are you safe? Come on back. Come on back."

I shouted that I was all right, and then, making certain that the eggs were safe, I turned round, and looked up the bit of shale I had slithered down, and reached my hands to what looked like a good hold. It was a bit of hard rock stuck in the shale itself, but it gave way before I had put scarcely any weight on it, leaving a hole, which was too rounded to give support to my fingers. I tried another place, but it was no better. The nearest sod was at least six inches higher than I could reach, and this didn't look very strong, for I had loosened it a bit coming down. I was frightened. The ledge itself was about a yard wide and was safe for my feet; but although I tried again and again, I couldn't get a hold with my hands in the shale. I got my knife out and tried to cut a handhole. The shale was so soft that I couldn't cut a square enough hole in it to give a grip. I tried to cut a foot-hold, thinking that if I could only reach up to the sod it would be all right; but again I only made a hole with sloping edge from which my foot slithered.

Suddenly I heard Chicken shout:

"Are you all right? Are you all right?"

I looked up and saw that he was crying, and he must have seen how frightened I was, for he shouted:

"Are you stuck? Shall I run and tell the coastguards? You'll fall back over the cliff if you're not careful. Shall I go?"

I think that if I had known there was someone near, who could have come and hauled me up with a rope, I'd have shouted back, "Yes," and that I'd have stuck tight on the ledge and waited for them, even if it had meant everyone knowing about it, including Mother. But the thought that Chicken might have to run all the way back to Bramblewick, and that it might be dark before anyone came, and that I'd have to be alone on the ledge all that time frightened me more than anything. I looked at the sod again, only six inches out of reach. I looked along the ledge to see if there was anything loose I could get so as to build up a place to stand on. There was nothing but loose shale and earth; and then suddenly I thought of my boots and my coat, and the fishing line I had put in my pocket when I had thought of our going to the dam. My body was shaking, and my breath was going very quickly, but I tried not to think of the cliff below. I changed the eggs into my breeches pockets. I took off my boots and coat, and with the boots inside, made a tight parcel. I scraped up the loose shale and earth into a heap and put the bundle on top and stamped on it to make it firm. I stood on it and reached up and found I could touch the sod. I set to work on one of the foot-holds again, and deepened it and thought it would hold if I didn't put all my weight on it or stay too long. I fastened one end of the fishing line to the bundle, tied my knife to the other end, and after several tries, managed to throw the knife up so that it held on something above the shaley bit. Then, taking care not to touch the line, I got my fingers buried deep in the roots of the sod, stuck my foot in the hold as hard as I could, and pulled myself up, and found myself on safe ground once more.

But I daren't look down again, not even when I hauled up my coat; not even when the bundle fouled something, and I thought the line was going to break. I kept my eyes upwards, and I just tugged at it as though it had been a fish caught in some weed, and when it did clear, I didn't stop to unfasten it, but hauled it after me the rest of the way to where Chicken stood waiting. I didn't even stop then except to pick up the bundle. We moved as quickly as we could to a clump of whins on the other side of the fence, and then I sat down and I started to cry, and I went on crying for a long time, for I couldn't think of anything but what a narrow escape I'd had, and what a relief it was to be on level ground out of sight of the cliff. Chicken was crying, too, but not so much as I was, and he was the first to say anything.

"You oughtn't to have gone," he said. "You oughtn't to have gone. I thought you'd never get back. I thought you'd be killed. I reckon we oughtn't to go after gulls' eggs any more. It's too dangerous. Tommy Brewster would have been killed if he hadn't had a straw hat on his head. And you hadn't got a hat on at all. I reckon that eggs aren't worth losing your life for."

I remembered the eggs and took them from my pockets. I was still crying, but I soon stopped. I didn't let Chicken hold them at first, although I was going to give him one, but I let him touch them, and he had to agree that they were lovely. I laid them down very carefully in the grass, and put my boots and coat on. It was very nearly dusk. I thought we had better hurry home as fast as we could; but I had to blow the eggs first, for they would be safer like that. I had a pin and I did it very carefully. When Chicken saw the first yolk, he said:

"*By!* It looks like a hen's egg, doesn't it? I wonder if it's good to eat!"

He tasted it, but he didn't like it.

I felt all right now. I had got a seagull's egg, and I knew there wasn't another boy in the place had got one. I was quite safe, after all, and no one could have seen me: Mother would never know that I had been along the cliffs, and there would be no need for me ever to come here again. I thought we'd best go straight up to the railway line, and keep to it all the way back, so that even if anyone did see us, they wouldn't think we had been on the cliff.

It didn't take us very long to reach it, and when we did we ran, keeping to the cinder track clear of the sleepers. The line got nearer to the cliff as it drew near the new houses and the signal box. Actually it would have been quicker for us to leave it here, and get on to the cliff path; but I thought it would be safer to keep to it as far as possible; and we had to get some primroses yet. There were plenty on the line side, and some violets, too. We started picking them, and then Chicken startled me by pointing over the railway fence to the cliff-path and whispering:

"Eh – there's your mother coming."

My heart almost stopped beating with fright. It *was* Mother. She had just got over a stile, and was walking along the path towards Low Batts, as fast as she could go. I knew she was looking for me. I knew that somehow or other she had got to know that I had gone along the cliffs. But I didn't trouble to think how. I thought how terrible it would be if she just went on and on, and never found me. She would be certain to think I had fallen over. I knew I would have to show myself. Quickly I gave Chicken my egg, and told him he must look after it until tomorrow and that he was to rush along the line and not bother about me. He gave me all the flowers he had picked, and I put them with mine. Then I waited till Mother was well past me, and I got up to the fence and shouted:

"Mother – Mother!"

She stopped and turned and then came quickly towards me. I held out the flowers so that she should see them clearly: but she didn't take any notice of them. She couldn't speak properly, either, she was so out of breath. She just got hold of me, and gripped my arm so hard I nearly shouted; and it wasn't until we got over the stile, and had reached the first of the new houses that she started asking me where I had been and if I had been looking for gulls' eggs in the cliff. I didn't say anything because I didn't know how much she did know; but when she told me that one of the coastguards had seen me and another boy through his spy-glass going along the cliff near Low Batts point, I knew it was no good pretending I had only been near the railway, so I said I had been on the cliff with Chicken, who had gone home another way, but that I hadn't been looking for gulls' eggs, and that we'd spent all our time looking for other nests and flowers, and that I had actually got quite a lot of violets for her. I said I wouldn't have *dared* to have gone after gulls' eggs seeing what had happened to Tommy Brewster.

She didn't say anything to this, but only gripped me tighter. I felt myself starting to cry again, and I was glad we didn't pass any of the other lads as we walked down the Bank, and along past the chapel home. Dad was out. As soon as we got in, Mother said I was to go straight to bed. She came up with me, and started going for me again. She said she couldn't have believed I could have been so cruel as to frighten her like that. Even if I hadn't actually been bird-nesting, or climbing it was enough that in spite of all my promises, I had gone along the cliff. It meant that she could never trust me again: never – *never*. That whenever I was out she would think of me getting into danger and being killed. The only thing she hoped and prayed for was that Dad would sell the picture, and that she could send me off to Liverpool. If it was sold it would be the first thing she would do.

She left me and didn't even kiss me. I lay in bed crying. I heard Dad come in; and I thought I heard her telling him what I had done, and him saying it was her own fault, because she didn't thrash me; and then several times I heard the words "Liverpool" and "school" and "Uncle Fred". I don't think I had ever felt so miserable. I felt I had done for myself altogether. The only nice thing I could think of was the gull's eggs, but thinking of them only brought me back to thinking how they had got me into trouble and that if I had just gone to Brocketts everything would have been all right. I knew that Mother didn't want me to go to get rid of me, but only because of my being bad. I wondered whether the letter would come tomorrow, saying the picture had been accepted. I wondered how long it would be before it was sold, and Mother packed me off. If she did so at once it would mean that I would miss the very best time of all the year in Bramblewick; and what I had been looking forward to more than anything; for very soon now Mike would start cleaning and painting the

Shannon Rose, and then she'd be launched for the salmon fishing; and I knew he would let me go with him whenever I wasn't at school, and the sea was calm enough.

It was a wonder I got to sleep at all, I was so unhappy. Yet I did, for one moment I was thinking about Uncle Fred and how I hated him, and the next I was looking up at the white-washed ceiling of the attic, and it was broad daylight, and I could hear the postman rapping loudly on our door. At once I was wide awake. I heard the door open and the postman's voice, and then the door being slammed again, and Dad coming up the stairs. I got out of bed and tip-toed down to the top of the living-room stairs, and held my breath, for fear of missing anything he said, for I just knew it must be the letter come at last.

"What is it?" Mother said.

"It's from the Academy," Dad answered in a funny voice. "I think you'd better open it."

"Don't be stupid. Open it yourself."

There was no sound at all for a moment. I thought that the next thing I'd hear would be Dad, giving a great shout of joy like he had done before when he had got some good news. But it was Mother who spoke next, and she said very anxiously:

"Well – what is it? What is it?"

And Dad answered in an awful voice, almost crying:

"It's been rejected. It's been rejected, after all."

BOOK THREE

I

ALTHOUGH DAD WAS very disappointed and upset about the picture, and was bad-tempered for a long time after, he didn't give up hope that one day he was going to be famous: and when the picture came back from the agent, and he took it out of the packing-case, he said that it was even better than he had thought it was, and the only reason why it had been turned out was that its style was unusual. The judges hated anything unusual, unless it was by an R.A. or a well-known artist. In fact, some of the best artists never got into the Academy, which showed what stick-in-the-mud people the judges were. But he would have another try, and perhaps this time not do a portrait, but a landscape, and he thought he'd start making some studies for it at once. Mother said it would be much better if he spent all his time doing sketches that would sell when the summer visitors came, and that it was better to ask one guinea for a picture and *get* it, than ask thirty and not get anything at all; particularly when the frame and the cost of sending it to the Academy had to be counted. She thought that if we had a good summer there was just a chance that she would be able to send me to Liverpool in the autumn.

I hoped, of course, that we would have a good

summer, but I hated the idea of leaving Bramblewick more than ever, and again I tried very hard to be good, or at least to make Mother think I was good. The bird-nesting season was now over, so I wasn't tempted to go near the cliffs again, and anyway, I had got my egg hidden with the others under the chest of drawers. I had plenty of fights, but if someone made my nose bleed I always stayed out until it had stopped. And while Chicken and I had several adventures, and once went right on to High Batts, looking for firewood, and were nearly caught by the tide, I was so careful that I was certain that Mother never found out anything, and I hoped that even if we did have a good summer she wouldn't send me away.

Mike got very excited when the salmon fishing season drew near. He kept the *Shannon Rose* in a little grassy hollow behind the gas house, turned bottom up, and with an old sail tied over her to protect her from the weather. He would have liked to have started fishing before the Bramblewick men, but, although the law allowed them to begin in June, there wasn't so much money to be made with salmon then as with lobsters, so they went lobstering until July; and as they went off at a different time of day for this, there wouldn't have been anyone to help Mike with his coble, so he had to wait for them. They didn't like Mike, and he didn't like them, although they were forced to help each other. They were a jealous lot, he said. The way they went on, the whole Bay might belong to them and no one have a right to fish in it but themselves. They were the same with everyone who came to the place to live. You might have your father and your grandfather born in the place and yet you'd still be a foreigner, unless you did everything exactly the same way they did it. He once told me that I ought to be proud I wasn't born in Bramblewick, and proud of my Mother, too, the way she stuck out against them all.

But it wasn't just because Mike was a foreigner the other fishermen hated him so. There were certain places in the Bay that were much better for fishing than others, and it was a rule among the fishermen that the boat that got to a berth first on Monday morning should keep that berth for the whole week. The *Shannon Rose* was a very heavy boat. The other men used very light cobles for salmoning, so usually Mike had to take the very worst berth. Yet in spite of this, he was a better fisherman than any of them, and often got more fish than all the others put together, yet they couldn't say it was because he was fishing in a better place.

Mike was very fond of the *Shannon Rose*. She was an old boat when he had bought her, and there was something peculiar in the way she was built that gave her a list, so that when she was moving she made you think of a seagull with a broken wing, swimming. But he'd got used to this, and he said it made her easier to pull, and he'd never put ballast in to make her float even. Every year, before he launched her, he gave her a fresh coat of paint. This year he let me help him, and it was almost as exciting as bird-nesting. First she had to be washed all over and scrubbed with sand: and when everything was dry her bottom planks were tarred, then her side planks painted, each one a different colour, white, red, and blue, with a narrow band of yellow along her gunwale. When this was dry he would ask Dad to come and paint her name and the register marks, and Mike would stand watching him, and get vexed if he didn't do it exactly as he wanted it; and this year they had another argument as to whether there ought to be a full stop between *Shannon* and *Rose*. Mike said there ought to be one, and it didn't look finished unless there was. Dad said there oughtn't because it was all one name, but Mike got his way again.

Chicken helped, too, although of course he wasn't allowed to do any painting, and he didn't like it as much as if we were off together somewhere. He was always dropping hints about other things we might be doing, and one day I got vexed with him and told him to go off by himself. This was on a Saturday after Dad had finished painting the name, and the coble was turned up on her keel ready for launching, and I was helping Mike to paint the oars. Chicken nearly cried, and later I wished I hadn't been vexed with him, and that we had gone off somewhere together. I didn't see him at all on Sunday. But on Monday, just before school, I met him in the street, and I could see that he had been crying. I asked him what was the matter.

"Haven't you heard about Father?" he said.

I told him I hadn't heard anything.

"He's been taken bad," he said. "Bob Walsh brought him home on Saturday night. They were both of 'em tight of course, and Mother didn't think much about it when father fell down on the kitchen floor and started moaning. She made Bob help her to get him up to bed, but he kept on moaning and saying he'd got a pain in his back, and he never got to sleep at all, so first thing in the morning she made me go and get the doctor. The doctor said he'd got inflammation of the lungs. Last night he got worse and worse, and I had to fetch the doctor again. Father was spitting blood and making such a row, and he was asking God to have mercy on him for his sins, for he knew he was going to die. The doctor said he didn't think he would live through the night. He's alive this morning, but he's still spitting blood and moaning ... *By!* It's awful hearing him, and Mother's crying, and our kids have had to go off to someone else's house, and I had to go too for my breakfast. I hope father won't die. He's all right when he isn't tight. He'd give you anything."

Although I didn't like Mr Burton, I felt very sad and sorry for Chicken, and as I had a ha'penny in my pocket I was saving to buy a book with, I asked him to take it and buy some sweets, but he wouldn't and started crying again as we went up towards the school, and he kept on saying he hoped his father wouldn't die. But just after playtime, when the copybooks were given out, there was a knock at the school door. Slogger went to see who it was, and although we couldn't see, we could tell by Slogger's face that it was something important. He went very red, and as soon as the person had gone, he looked down the school and said in a very quiet voice:

"Burton, go home at once."

I think Chicken must have known what it was, for he burst out crying. and he let his slate fall as he got up, making a great clatter. Slogger didn't say anything to him for this, of course, but he boxed another boy's ears for turning round, and he said that he would keep the whole school in if we didn't get on with our work at once. I thought that Mr Burton must be dead, but I didn't think then what a difference that was going to make to Chicken and me.

He *was* dead. That night Dad brought the coffin plate from Mr Fenwick, and he started to paint it as soon as we had finished supper. For once he didn't say that I ought to be in bed, but I think that was because I kept very quiet, and he didn't notice me watching him. I still didn't feel sad about Mr Burton even when I saw Dad painting his name on the plate; but I felt sadder and sadder about Chicken. No matter how bad a father was, if he drank and swore, and didn't work to give you food, you couldn't help loving him a bit, and the way Chicken had cried showed that there *had* been something in his favour, although I had never heard Chicken say that about him being all right when he was sober before. I had never heard him say anything good about him.

Mother, too, looked sad, and very solemn, and she must have been thinking about Chicken, and his little brothers and sisters, for she said:

"Well, perhaps, it's a mercy he has been taken. Of the dead say no evil, but that man must have been a sore trial to his wife, and I think she'll really be better off without him, because for all her faults she's a hard-working woman, and I'm sure that if it hadn't been for her, the children would have starved to death long ago. I wonder what will happen to her and her poor little children now?"

"From what Mr Fenwick told me," Dad said, "they'll have to leave that cottage. The rent's owing for nearly two years and the man who owns it will be only too glad of the chance to turn them out ... Fancy, it's that other drunkard, Bob Walsh, who is paying for the funeral. I'm surprised he's got the money, for he hasn't been to sea for a very long time. I should think he's wheedled it out of his old mother."

"Oh – what a terrible curse drink is," said Mother. "Just think of what those poor little children must have suffered. I think we ought to make up a parcel of food for Mrs Burton, and leave it on the doorstep again."

"I think they'll be all right for tonight," Dad said quickly. "They're being looked after by a neighbour, some relation of old Mrs Walsh. There'll be no one in the house except the body."

I didn't see Chicken the next day, and although I did the day after, I didn't get a chance to speak to him because it was the day of the funeral. I scarcely knew him, he looked so clean; and he had got some clothes I had never seen him in before, and new black boots. I think someone must have given him the clothes, for they were a lot too big for him. He looked very sad. I didn't go to the funeral, for it was during afternoon school time. Dad and Mother went, and they got back just before I did, and they were talking about it when we were having tea. Mother said she was surprised at the large number of people who had been there, and the number of flowers. Mrs Burton had cried all the time, and so had Chicken, but the other children hadn't gone. Bob Walsh had been among the mourners, and Mrs Lingdale (Boozer himself was back at sea), and Mike, of course, had been there to fill in the grave. Then she said that she had heard someone saying that they had heard that Mrs Burton had been offered work at Leeds, and that she might be going there with her family at once. It seemed that a clergyman who had visited Bramblewick last summer, and knew all about the Burtons and how Mrs Burton and the children were ill-treated by the father, had written offering this work, and a place for her and the children to live in. It would be a splendid thing, Mother said, if this could happen. What a contrast it would be, after that wretched drunkard's home!

I didn't really believe yet that this meant that Chicken was leaving Bramblewick; but I went out to see if I could find him after tea. He wasn't anywhere about, and as Mike wasn't at the coble, I went for a walk by myself on the shore, and I ran right into Grab, almost in the same place where I had given Len a hiding. He must have been to the mill or one of the farms, for he was carrying an empty basket.

He grinned at me in his sneery way.

"Now, Worms," he said, mockingly. "You look a bit lonely. I hear you've lost your mate. Did you know Chicken's mother has been chucked out of her house?"

I was as polite to Grab as I could be, for I didn't want him to hide me. I was feeling miserable enough as it was.

"They haven't gone away yet, Tom, have they?" I asked.

"No. But I bet they'll be out of it before the week's up, and good riddance to them. They're only foreigners. I notice you call me Tom. Do you call me Tom when you're talking about me to Chicken?"

I didn't answer. I thought that at least Grab was going to kick my backside or twist my arm. But he didn't touch me. He just said boastingly:

"I'm going to sea when the summer holidays start. I'll bloody well kill you if you touch our Len or Kid again when I'm away. I'm going out foreign. I hope we have a lot of bad weather. I shan't be sick. I never am. I reckon I'll be going to sea altogether when I leave school."

I was glad when he walked away. I went home without seeing Chicken. He wasn't at school next day, but after tea I met him in the old place. He was all dressed up, just as he had been for the funeral, and the first thing he told me was that he was going away to Leeds by the first train in the morning; and that he had to go back now, for his mother said he hadn't to get his clothes mucky. They weren't at home. Everything had been packed up and sent to the station.

I had never felt so sad. It was lovely weather, and it would have been just right for going to the mill dam. But Chicken said he daren't go because of his clothes and because he had to hurry back. I scarcely knew what to say then. When I did try to say something I got a lump in my throat, and Chicken, who usually went on talking without stopping, didn't seem to be able to speak either. But he pulled a bag of sweets out of his pocket, and asked me to have one. They were peppermints, very big and hard. He took one, too, and we went on sucking at them, neither of us speaking, and not looking at one another. Then at last Chicken said:

"Well – I'll have to be going now – because of Mother. I've never been farther than Burnharbour in a train before. I've never been in a town like Leeds. They say there's shops everywhere, millions of them."

"Aye. It'll be like Liverpool," I said. "Only there's docks at Liverpool."

"Aye," Chicken answered. "I reckon it will be champion, looking at all the shops ... Well – I'll have to be going. I hope you'll catch some trout if you're going to the dam. I hope the squire doesn't catch you."

Suddenly I felt I was going to cry, but I tried

hard and stopped myself, and I held out my hand, but Chicken didn't get hold of it properly; he just touched it, and said again, stuttering a bit:

"Well – I'll have to be going."

He turned and walked down the steps towards the gas house. I turned the other way and started to whistle, but I couldn't make a proper tune, and suddenly I looked again, and Chicken was out of sight. And then I couldn't stop myself any longer. I just sat down by the side of the path and cried and cried. I couldn't think of anything except that Chicken and I would never go off on another adventure together; that he had gone, and that I'd never see him again.

II

I WENT ON being miserable about Chicken for a long time. Wherever I went, along the shore, or the cliffs, or to Brocketts, there was always something to remind me of him; and I couldn't bear going near the place where we had always met, and where he had left me for the last time. I couldn't think of any of the things I had disliked about him, such as his dirtiness, and the way he was always chewing something, and him talking too much. I could only think of how he had always obeyed me, and how I could always trust him. Whenever I was alone I could imagine I could see his face; sometimes I could hear his voice, particularly if I was walking along the shore when the seas were rushing up over the shingle, or I was listening to the sound of the beck in Garry Wood.

I didn't tell Mother I was miserable about him. I knew she would have tried to comfort me; but I knew she never liked my having Chicken for a friend and that she was really glad he had gone away. Although she didn't say anything about me, I heard her telling Dad one night, how much better it was for Mrs Burton now that she had found regular work, and that she had got a decent home for her children. She had heard that her work was actually looking after a chapel and a Sunday School room. What a contrast that would be to the life she had led in Bramblewick! What a different influence for her children to be brought up in!

The worst of it was that although the other fishermen had stopped lobstering, the weather, after being fine and warm for a long time, now started being very bad, with the wind blowing from the sea almost every day, so that no one had started salmon fishing. The *Shannon Rose* had been launched down to the Dock, but she hadn't been in the sea at all. I thought that the weather was bound to be fine again when the summer holidays started, and this was about the only thing I could look forward to, for school had become worse than ever. The boys teased me about Chicken. I had some sort of a fight almost every day, and Grab, perhaps thinking to pay me in advance for what I might do to his brothers when he went to sea, was always kicking me or twisting my arm, or throwing something at me. I don't think Slogger boxed my ears more than he did anyone else's, but he did it often enough to make me almost wish sometimes that I was at the nice school Mother wanted me to go to.

Mike got very grumpy about having to wait so long to start fishing, and I'd see him walking along the cliff top chewing at a straw, and looking angrily at the waves breaking across the Landing mouth; and if I asked him when he thought the *Shannon Rose* would be launched he'd swear and say:

"Och – don't ask me that now. Ask the other fishermen. They're the lords of the place. She'll be launched when they decide the weather's all right for *them,* so maybe she'll not be launched at all except back to the place where she'll stay the winter, and all the painting we did will be in vain. Now if my brother Tom was alive, we'd be independent of the whole damned lot of them, for I'll swear the two of us could have launched the coble by ourselves, and hauled her up too, with the help of blocks and ropes."

Mike didn't have a regular fishing partner. None of the real Bramblewick fishermen would go with him, of course. Sometimes he had a sailor who was out of a ship. Sometimes he had to put up with a man who knew nothing at all about fishing; and this year I was surprised to hear that his partner was Bob Walsh, who seemed to have been more sober since Mr Burton's death. I didn't like Bob any more than I had liked Mr Burton, although Chicken had said that he was kind-hearted and that he had often given him pennies. He had a thin pale face and watery eyes, and a drooping moustache that was stained brown in the middle through drinking beer. I don't think Mike liked him, either, and he was only having him as a mate because he had to have someone to pull the oars while he was shooting or hauling the nets.

It was only a few days before we broke up for the summer holidays that fishing began. The wind blew strong off the land all one morning, and the boats were launched in the afternoon. They had all got to their berths and shot their nets by the time we left school, and I could see the *Shannon Rose* anchored farthest away of any of them, close to High Batts cliff. It was quite warm again, and there wasn't a cloud in the sky. The wind had almost dropped, and there were patches of sea that were dead calm, so that it looked as though the real fine weather had come at last, and might go on right through the holidays. I knew, of course, that there would be no chance of my going off with Mike until the holidays came; for the boats landed very early in the morning and the men went to bed until dinnertime, and didn't go off again until the afternoon. Still, it was exciting just seeing the *Shannon Rose* afloat, and as soon as I had had tea, and run one or two errands for Mother, who was busy doing some prints, I took off my shoes and stockings, and, with an old pair of shoes on, ran down to the shore.

The tide was out, and the scaurs were bare. Already there were quite a number of visitors staying in the place, and there were strange people sitting on the sand under the cliff and a few out on the scaurs, where I saw Dad sketching, with a lady and gentleman standing behind him and looking at his work. In summer Dad usually painted subjects where the visitors could see him, and he didn't mind them watching him, or even talking to him and admiring his work; for very often that was the way he'd get them to buy a picture, particularly if they liked the subject itself; although if they asked the price of what he was doing he'd never tell them, but ask them to come to the shop. By doing this they might see something else they liked and spend twice as much money, and even give an order for a portrait, which was the work Dad liked doing best.

I didn't like the visitors myself. They sat down by some of the best scratting places, and if you started scratting, they watched you and asked you silly questions. The Bramblewick boys shouted after them, particularly if they wore unusual clothes, and I did this myself sometimes, although I was careful not to shout out after anyone who might be a customer.

I didn't know quite what to do now. I thought that, anyway, I would keep clear of Dad, and as there were no visitors at all on the scaurs beyond Garry Nab, I'd wander on that way, and see if I could find some crabs under the stones at low water. I hadn't got very far when I saw a very curious-looking gentleman with a boy, walking towards me. The gentleman wore a check suit, and a soft straw hat, and as he drew near I saw that he had a funny moustache with its ends brushed upwards, and he was wearing what I had never seen before except in the pictures in *Comic Cuts*, an eyeglass. He walked very stiffly, with his chest sticking out, and he carried a cane with a silver knob under his arm. The boy, who was about my own size, was walking just behind him. He had shoes on his feet, but bare legs (which were very white) and he wore a white guernsey and a straw hat like the gentleman's, only smaller. His face was white, too, but he had flashy black eyes, and I thought he looked very stuck-up and cheeky.

Although I knew it was not a polite thing to do, I stopped and stared, and I couldn't help laughing a bit at the gentleman, because he looked so funny with the glass stuck in one eye. I wondered how he kept it from falling out. He didn't look at me as they passed, and it wasn't until he had passed that I noticed the boy looking at me and pulling a face. I pulled a face myself, and then did just what Grab did in school when he wanted to show that he was going to hide me as soon as we got outside: I shook my clenched fist at him. The boy did the same thing at me, but just then the gentleman made a sort of cough, and the boy looked ahead again. I stood staring at them until I was nearly out of hearing distance, then I shouted "Glass eye!" but not very loudly, and I don't think they heard me, for they didn't turn round.

I went on towards Garry Nab, I didn't feel angry with the boy, but I wondered if he and the gentleman, who I supposed was his father, were staying in Bramblewick, and if I should meet the boy by himself, and if so have a fight with him. He didn't look very strong, and I was certain I could beat him. I walked round the Nab, although Mother still forbade me to do this. There were some visitors sitting in the cove, so I aimed down the scaurs where there was no one at all; and when I got down to low-water mark I started turning stones over. I didn't find any eating crabs, but there were plenty of interesting things to look at, like sea-slugs and brittle-stars and sea-urchins. I felt happier than I had done since Chicken had gone. Whenever I looked up from what I was doing I could see the *Shannon Rose,* and I could even make out Mike, sitting in the stern. One of the Bramblewick boats was anchored quite close to where I was. One was about half a mile farther south, and the other was between that one and Mike. Soon I saw Bob Walsh walking along the shore from the direction of High Batts, and I thought that Mike must have put him ashore so that he might go and get his supper before the night's fishing began.

I went on turning stones over, and wandering from scaur to scaur, thinking about various things, like the holidays, and if the weather would keep fine for them, and how different it would be with Grab away all summer, and if Dad would sell enough pictures for me to go to Liverpool (although Mother hadn't mentioned this for a long time). I thought about Chicken and wondered what he was doing, and whether looking at shops made up for scratting and bird-nesting, and being on the shore. I thought about the funny gentleman with the eyeglass and the boy who had pulled a face at me; and it wasn't until I began to feel very cold that I noticed that the weather was changing. The sun, although it was low, had been shining brightly. Now there were clouds in the sky, moving very quickly from over the sea, and hiding the sun as they passed. I could feel puffs of cold wind, too, and looking towards Low Batts I noticed that where an hour ago had been calm water the sea was quite choppy and rough.

I didn't think just then of the boats being in danger. I only felt disappointed and angry, for I knew at once that the weather was turning bad; that a north-east wind was getting up, and that soon the whole Bay would be white with breakers. I knew that once a north-east wind did get up it never stopped for at least three days, and that all the boats would have to be hauled up into the Dock again. It would just spoil everything!

I hadn't brought my stockings; I had been wading in my shoes. I was soon shaking with cold, and thought I had better go home. Then I looked at the boats and saw that the men in the nearest one, Luke and Tindal Fosdyck, were standing up, looking towards Low Batts, and then at their nets which ran in almost to the scaur ends, where little waves were starting to break. Then I saw Luke Fosdyck start to haul the anchor, while Tindal shipped the oars. They were going to haul their nets and get back to the Landing before the wind got worse.

I changed my mind about going home. Mother would only keep me in if I looked cold. The tide had started to flow. I walked up to the cliff that divided Garry Beck from Browe Beck cove; then climbed up a little way to a grassy ledge where it was warmer, and where I had a good view of the whole Bay. It was near to Browe Beck cove. The wind now was blowing quite strongly and the sea was getting rougher. Real waves were breaking on the big scaurs at Low Batts Point. The Fosdycks had started hauling their nets, and their coble was pitching and rolling. The other boats also had started hauling, and, although he was such a distance away, I could see that Mike was doing the same. Suddenly I thought about Bob Walsh being ashore and that Mike would have to do the hauling all by himself, and then have to pull the whole way home against the wind and rough seas. Would Bob know that the weather had turned bad? Should I run back, and try and find him? I looked along the shore towards the village. The visitors were all moving that way and I could just make out a man coming down the slipway, and soon I saw that it was Bob himself, walking very quick. I noticed for the first time that a block cone had been hoisted on the flagstaff at the new coastguard station with its point up, the sign of a storm from the north. I looked at the *Shannon Rose* and began to feel frightened that something might happen to Mike.

But I knew that I couldn't do anything. I just sat, watching, getting colder and colder and feeling more frightened, for now I could hear the noise of the sea on the scaur ends. Bob Walsh drew near. He was looking anxiously towards the *Shannon Rose*, and walking just as fast as he could. He passed me, but he still had more than a mile to walk before he could reach the place where Mike must have landed him, and I knew it would be difficult for Mike to land again if the sea got any rougher.

Although the tide was flowing it was still a long way down, and the scaurs reached beyond low-water mark in several places, so that before they could get to the Landing mouth all the boats had first to pull out to sea. The Fosdycks had now started to do this, and although their boat was a light one they were having a hard job, for every minute the wind was getting stronger, and the waves bigger. The boat nearest to Mike had also started to pull out, but Mike himself was still hauling his nets. I suddenly thought I would go along the shore towards High Batts, following Bob, for I was anxious to see him get into the *Shannon Rose* to help Mike home. I got down and crossed Browe Beck. Here there was a narrow patch of sand between the scaurs, giving a clear way to the sea, but beyond this the scaurs reached without any break to High Batts, and the shore itself was very rough. All the boats except Mike's were pulling for home before I had got halfway. Bob had left the shore and had got on to the outermost scaur, where the waves were breaking all the time. I saw him waving to Mike. But Mike had at last finished hauling, and now he was at the oars, starting to pull, not in towards Bob, but out to sea, clear of the scaur ends, and it wasn't long before I saw a short wave break right over the bow of the coble.

I stopped again, close up to the cliff. I forgot about the other boats. I could think of nothing else but Mike, for I knew that he was in danger. Even if he had had another strong man to help him it would have been hard work pulling such a heavy coble as the *Shannon Rose* against the wind and waves; and now Bob must have seen that he was too late, for he had started walking slowly back, all the time looking at the coble.

For a long time it didn't seem to make any headway at all. Once it seemed that it was actually being driven back towards the scaur ends; but gradually it did get farther out, and at last it was clear of where the seas were breaking, and instead of going on pulling out to sea, Mike turned a bit so that he was heading for the Landing. But the Landing was more than two miles away. Even the Fosdycks, who had been nearest to it, hadn't reached the mouth of it yet; and now the wind was so strong it would have blown me over if I hadn't leaned against it. It was a real storm.

I stood watching, feeling more and more frightened There was no one else on the whole shore except Bob, and he was now moving towards me, slowly, looking at the *Shannon Rose* the whole time, and keeping pace with it. Mike was making some headway. At each stroke I could see him almost standing off the coble thwart straining at the oars like a horse straining at a heavy cart. He was gradually getting to the gap between the scaurs opposite Browe Beck, and at last he and Bob were opposite me, and I started to walk back too, close to Bob, but he didn't take any notice of me. He looked more frightened than ever. I thought he must be a bit drunk, too, for he was mumbling all the time, and now and again he waved to Mike and shouted. Even I couldn't hear what he said because of the storm, so I knew Mike couldn't; yet I thought he was trying to warn Mike to keep farther out to sea, because beyond the gap the seas were breaking a long way out. The nearest of the other boats was a long way beyond this, yet still a long way from the Landing.

I had often seen the boats rushing for home in bad weather in wintertime, but I had never seen them out in such a storm as this, for it had come on so quickly. Although I watched the *Shannon Rose* all the time I never lost sight of the others. I thought several times that one of them would capsize. I knew, when a great gust of wind came and whipped Bob's hat from his head and nearly knocked me down, that Mike could never pull as far as the Landing. Even if he could, by the time he reached the mouth the seas would be breaking there, and he would not be able to get through. But Mike must have known this all the time. When he cleared the last of the scaurs where the gap came, and where there was sand all the way into the shore, he didn't try any more to keep out to sea. He kept the bow of the coble facing the waves, and the wind, but he stopped pulling. He began to "back", and I knew he was going to try and land on the sand itself, which was now only a few yards ahead from where we were.

The gap, with the tide still only half-flowed, formed a kind of cove. The waves were rolling into it, yet they were not breaking until they reached the sandy shore; and the coble was moving very quickly now. Mike was scarcely using the oars at all, letting the wind and the waves carry him. Suddenly, when a very big wave came, he stopped "backing" and pulled ahead to meet the wave, which lifted the coble almost on end; but as soon as it had passed he started to "back" quickly again, and now he wasn't more than fifty yards from the shore. I heard him shout to Bob.

"Get hold of her now – get hold of her the minute she grounds, don't let her swing or she'll fill."

And the next moment another great wave rose up behind. It seized the coble, and she began to rush in with it stern first, Mike all the time "backing" the oars, and shouting:

"Get hold of her – get hold of her."

Bob had no seaboots on; and he looked as though he didn't much like the idea of wading in, but he did. The wave passed the coble. It curled over, and Bob, who was then only up to his knees, saw it coming and tried to move back out of its way. He was too late. It broke right on top of him, and before he had time to see what was happening the coble rushed in, still stern first, and knocked him right over into the backwash of the same wave. I saw that Mike was safe, for the coble had touched the bottom, but I thought that Bob was drowned. He went right out of sight except for one hand, which clawed at the coble side as he was sucked out past it.

I couldn't see clearly what happened then. I only saw Mike leave go of the oars and lean over the side. The next moment another wave struck the coble, covering it with spray, and turning it almost broadside on, and when I saw Mike again he was standing in the water on the shore side, holding Bob upright with one hand, and trying to push the coble "bow-on" again with the other. But this second wave had rushed back, and for a while the coble itself was almost dry. It was only then that I noticed that Mike had cut his cheek, and that blood was streaming down his face.

He took no notice of this. He had let go of Bob and got both hands on the coble, ready for the next wave. He shouted roughly at Bob to do the same. It came rushing in, and as it broke both of them hung on and kept the coble from being turned.

It was awful for me, being only a boy, and not being able to help my friend. I knew that Mike loved the *Shannon Rose*. I knew that if it did get broadside on it would fill and that all the men in Bramblewick couldn't move her then, or stop her from being dashed to pieces when the tide got higher. I did wade in a bit, but although the coble was almost dry when the waves washed back, it would have been at least up to my waist when even the smallest wave came in; and very soon Bob shouted to Mike that it was no good, and that they'd better give it up, as they couldn't haul the coble in over the soft sand. The other fishermen hadn't got to shore yet, and it might be an hour before any of them came to help. If they weren't careful they'd both be drowned ... Mike swore at Bob when he said this, but I saw him take an anxious look towards the village. The Fosdycks' coble did seem to have got to the Landing, but the other two were still outside. They hung on while another sea washed in, and they hauled the coble a short way, but not far enough to be out of reach of the next one, which broke right over Bob and nearly knocked him down again. I think he would have run in to the shore then if Mike hadn't shouted at him to hold on. He did hold on, but he shouted again at Mike that they'd best give up, and suddenly Mike turned on him and I thought he was going to hit him, he looked so angry.

"I'll not leave her," he shouted. "I'll not leave her. It's mighty pleased the others would be if she was smashed to pieces, but I'll hang on to her until the tide flows and ebbs again if the others don't come and give us a hand. Go to the shore if you're frightened, and leave me to hold her myself. Hang on now – here's another!"

Bob had let go, but he had to hang on again to save himself from being washed away by the next sea that broke. When it rushed back, Mike took another anxious look towards the village, then he turned and it was as though he had seen me for the first time. I could never forget how he looked just then. He had lost his hat. His shirt was torn right down to his waist. He was panting, with his mouth open. His face was white, except where the blood ran down it, and his eyes were wilder than I had ever seen them when he was drunk or fighting. He looked as though he had gone mad. He was hanging on to the boat with one hand. He waved to me with the other, and pointed to the cliff and roared at me.

"Go up to Browe Beck farm, and tell them to bring some horses down. Tell them it's to haul in a boat and save it from destruction. Tell the man I'll pay him a pound if he brings his horses quick. Quick – quick as you can run."

The farm was straight opposite to where we were, standing back from the cliff top with only the red roof of it showing. A road led up to it from the beck itself, but the cliff just below it was clay, and no steeper than the cliff between Garry Beck and the village, and I ran straight to it. It was boggy in parts. There were patches of whin and brambles. But I jumped the bogs, and I forced my way up through the thorns, not heeding the scratches on my bare legs, thinking of nothing but whether I should get to the farm in time to save the *Shannon Rose*. The wind blew furiously. When I reached the cliff top and the first bit of level field, it was like someone running behind me, pushing me along. The farm was now clear in sight, but there was a narrow garden between me and the road which led past it, and two stone walls; and when I climbed over the first I dropped into a thick patch of stinging nettles, and had to walk through them to the garden itself, which was all laid out with vegetables, leaving no path. I didn't trouble about this. On the road itself, harnessed to a mowing machine, were two horses and a man just unharnessing them. I ran to the wall of the road, climbed on top of it, and shouted to the man, who I saw now was the farmer himself. But when he looked at me, I was so out of breath I couldn't speak to him. I just stayed on the wall and pointed to the shore. He stared hard at me, looking a bit angry, then he came up, and climbed until he was kneeling on the top wall, and it was just high enough for him to look over the edge of the cliff to the shore and see the *Shannon Rose,* with Mike and Bob still holding on. And then I managed to say:

"Horses – to pull the coble up. Mr Regan will give you a pound – if you'll haul his coble up."

It was a good job he understood and didn't ask a lot of questions. He just said:

"All right. You can tell him I'll be down as quick as I can ... and don't tramp on those peas when you go back. You've no business coming through that garden. anyway."

He turned to the horses and I didn't wait, but rushed back to the cliff edge and started climbing down again. Mike and Bob were still hanging on, but they hadn't managed to haul the boat out of the way of the waves. I looked towards the village as I climbed down. The first two boats were already ashore in the Landing, and the last one was just coming through the mouth in between the breakers. There was a small crowd of people standing on the slipway. But everyone seemed to be looking at the Landing, and there was no one coming along the beach itself to help the *Shannon Rose*. Perhaps, I thought, they had seen that she had come ashore and that Mike was safe, and that they didn't care so very much whether the coble was smashed up.

The wind seemed worse than ever. Huge waves were breaking along the foot of Low Batts and on the outermost scaurs of the Bay. Before I reached the shore, a wave broke over the coble again, and I saw Mike heaving with all his strength to prevent her being turned, when the spray dashed over him.

I ran to the water's edge, and shouted to him that the horses were coming. He didn't say anything, but he looked towards the place where the road from the farm came down; and every chance he got he looked again; and at last the two horses appeared, with the farmer astride one of them, hitting it with the butt end of his whip.

He didn't waste any time, and they must have been good horses, trained to walking in the sea, for they did just what he wanted them to do. He brought them close down to the coble, and made them back and back until the trace was near enough. And then, when a wave had washed back, and the coble was almost aground, Mike quickly hooked the chains of the trace into the two hauling rings under the coble stern; and when the next wave came in, he shouted, and the farmer, who had got hold of the leading horse, cracked his whip and shouted:

"Gee up, there – gee up!"

Mike and Bob, too, got hold of the coble, and pulled. The horses strained hard, and suddenly the coble began to move, and went on, until she was out of reach of the waves, safe on the dry shore. I couldn't help shouting then:

"Hooray! Hooray!"

And Mike didn't seem to be anxious any more. He shouted to the farmer to stop, and although he seemed to be leaning against the coble because he suddenly felt very tired, and although he was panting, he said in quite a different voice to what he'd used when he was shouting at Bob:

"Wait now. Wait now. Let's have a blow ... Then I'll have you haul her right up to the foot of the road. It will be a high tide with the wind so strong from the sea. We'll get the nets and the other gear out of her first, and let the water out of her through the plug. She's a great weight and it will scrape all the new paint from her bottom going over the rough gravel ... Come on now," he shouted to Bob, who was standing with the water streaming from his trousers, and his teeth chattering, and his body shaking from head to foot. "Give me a hand with the gear, and you'll not suffer so from the cold. The coble's safe, after all, and without the help of the others; although I see they're safe in the Landing, so now they'll all be coming along the shore to help us when we'll not be needing their help."

Mike got into the coble to take out the plug; and as soon as he'd done this, he looked up at me; and although the blood was still trickling down his cheek, and his face was very pale, he looked very happy, and he laughed and suddenly he reached his hand under an oilskin and took out a lovely salmon trout.

"Here," he said. "Here – take the fish. Take it home to your mother. It's the only fish I've got out of all the nets, and it's the first fish of the year. Away home with you now, for you're wet and you'll get your death of cold, with no stockings on your legs and no coat."

I didn't want to take it, seeing it was the only one, and Mike had worked so hard for it, and risked his life and hurt himself; but he got hold of my hand, and pushed my fingers into its gills, and told me again to get away home. I started for home. I *was* cold. My legs felt they had been skinned with the scratches and nettle stings, which the salt water made worse. But I didn't care. I was proud of having helped to save the *Shannon Rose*. I thought this had been the biggest adventure I'd ever had. The only thing that spoilt it was that Chicken hadn't been with me. I could just imagine how he would have talked, and told the other boys. I should have liked Grab to have known about it, even if he had hided me, just for spite. I would have liked that visitor boy to have known about it, too. As it was, I'd have to keep quiet about it, in case Mother found out, for it would never do for her to know that I had spent nearly the whole evening beyond Garry Nab. I would have to tell her that I met Mike coming along the shore and that he'd given me the salmon because I'd helped him to paint the *Shannon Rose*.

But I didn't worry very much about Mother, and I tried not to think about Chicken. I thought of Mike, and that now we would be greater friends than ever. Although the storm seemed to be getting worse, and the whole bay was now white with breakers, it couldn't last so very long. School broke up at the end of the week, and if the weather got fine, I'd be spending nearly all my time in the *Shannon Rose*. Even thinking about Chicken didn't stop me from feeling happy.

III

THE WIND WENT on blowing from the north-east. The sea was very rough. It rained, too, and it was almost as cold as wintertime. Dad was never in a good temper. The weather stopped him painting, of course, and it was bad for business, for the visitors who came into the shop only did so out of curiosity or to shelter from the rain, and Dad didn't sell a single picture or take any more orders for photos. It looked as though we were going to have a bad summer in every way. I didn't see the funny-looking man or the boy again. I only saw Mike once, and I couldn't speak to him because he was with someone; but I went on to Browe Beck several times to look at the *Shannon Rose,* which had been hauled up the farm road clear of the breakers.

Yet I thought it would be better to have the weather bad now than in the holidays, and I felt certain the wind would drop and the sea would be calm again by Monday, although on Friday it was just as bad as ever. We didn't break up until the afternoon, and Slogger made everyone work just as though it was an ordinary day, and actually he was more stern than usual. There was scarcely a boy from Standard IV to Standard VII who didn't get his ears boxed at least once. I don't know how many times Grab got punished for talking and not paying attention. He was more proud of himself than ever. He was going to Hull on the five o'clock train to join his father's ship, and although he wasn't wearing his seaboots he had got a brand new blue serge suit on, and long trousers. Outside school I had heard him boasting to the other boys that he was going for a voyage up the Baltic, perhaps as far as St Petersburg, the capital of Russia, where there were plenty of bears and wolves. *He* wasn't afraid of them. He expected they'd have a very rough voyage across the North Sea. If it was bad weather like this at Bramblewick it would be twice as bad far out from land. *He* didn't care. He liked it rough. He only wished it was wintertime.

I hoped, because of him being so excited about going away and having a new suit on, that he wouldn't bother to touch me, but I was wrong; for at afternoon playtime, just as I was running out, he tripped me up so that I fell full length on the gravel, and scrubbed my knees: and then he twisted both my ears, and kicked my backside, because he said I had tried to trip him. I didn't cry. He asked me if I was going to touch Len and Kid again when he went away. I said I wouldn't unless they touched me, so, as Len was being kept in, he shouted to Kid to give me a smack on the face now to test me. Kid didn't look as though he wanted to, but Grab made him. It was a light blow and didn't hurt much, and I didn't lose my temper, but I said under my breath that I'd give Kid the biggest hiding he'd ever had in his life when the first chance came, no matter what Grab did when he got back from sea. I hated them all worse than ever.

But if Grab had kicked me until I was black and blue, I couldn't have felt really miserable that afternoon. The thought that for five whole weeks there would be no more school almost made me feel sick with excitement. Even if the weather was bad on Monday, it was bound to get fine by the end of the week. Although going off with Mike was the most exciting thing to look forward to, there were plenty of other things to do, like fishing from the scaurs, and hunting for crabs and lobsters when the tide was very low. Mother would be so busy in the shop that she wouldn't be able to find out where I went so long as I was careful. There were miles and miles of shore, south and north of the Bay, that I had never yet explored. The only thing that made me feel sad was thinking about Chicken, and of how excited he would have been on breaking-up day.

There were two lessons after playtime. It was hard to work at them just as though nothing special was happening at four o'clock; and I couldn't understand why Slogger himself shouldn't have felt just a bit different from usual, for, after all, he was going to have a holiday too. Except for him being sterner (and that was perhaps only because all the boys were so excited) he looked as though it was just any other day in the week, and when at last the clock pointed to two minutes to four, he ordered everyone to fold arms, and he walked to his desk and stood there, waiting for silence quite calmly, until suddenly he noticed a boy smiling, and darted at him and gave him a stinging box over the ear. He made us put our hands behind and then fold them again several times. Then, when we had been sitting with our arms folded in deadly silence for at least a minute, and the clock was pointing to a minute past four, he said:

"Stand," and then, "Eyes closed."

Then he said, in just an ordinary voice:

"Our Father..."

And we began to say the Lord's Prayer, not after him, but by ourselves. He stopped us before we got to "Thy Name", and made us start again because we were going too fast. We hadn't got halfway through before he stopped us again, and this time he made us wait for nearly a minute. Then we had another try, and although some of us went much faster than the others, and had got to "Amen" before they had reached "trespasses", he didn't bother any more: and after a moment's silence he said:

"Eyes open."

Usually the next thing he said when everyone was silent was, "Dismiss." But instead of this, he cleared his throat and said:

"Now, boys, as you all know, we break up today for the summer holidays. School will open again on the first Monday in September. Go out quietly, and if any boy shouts in the passage, he'll come back and stay for a quarter of an hour." He waited for at least another half-minute, and then, still in a steady voice, he said the word "Dismiss."

As usual, Standard VII went out first, and while there was no shouting in the passage, there was soon a great noise of cheering outside the school door. I wondered if Grab would wait for me there to give me a last hiding, and if I hadn't better pretend to have lost my pencil, and wait a bit, to give him time to get away. Looking out of the window, I saw that it had suddenly started to rain very heavily, and remembering that he had no overcoat over his new suit, and that he wouldn't have much time for the train, I thought I'd risk it, and when my turn came I went out as fast as anybody, and, reaching the door, I was just in time to see him running along Chapel Street out of sight. There were no other big boys waiting, either. Len Fosdyck, somehow or other, had managed to get ahead of me and was running after Grab. But as I stepped out into the rain, I heard Kid just behind me, so I stopped, and as he passed me, I gave him a good smack across his jaw. But I didn't wait to see if I had made him cry or not, although I heard him shout that he would tell Tom. I had no coat, either. I ran as fast as I could go for home.

The street door was always open in summer. As I stepped in, out of the rain, I saw that the shop door, too, was open, and I had a great surprise, for in the shop, standing with his back towards me, was the funny-looking gentleman I had passed on the shore. The boy was with him, and they were both looking at the picture of Mike, which Dad had propped up on an easel. Dad himself looked very excited and his face was red. But as I looked at him he caught sight of me, and he frowned and made a sign for me to go upstairs and not bother him. I was vexed, for I wanted to have a good look at the boy again. I went upstairs and I found Mother just getting tea ready, but also looking very excited. She asked me, in a whisper, who it was Dad was talking to, and if it looked like a real customer, and when I whispered back that it was a funny man with an eyeglass, she said "Sssh," and held her finger to her lips and tiptoed to the top of the stairs. We couldn't hear very clearly, except when the gentleman seemed to be speaking to his boy, telling him to take his hands off something and keep still. Mother went on getting tea ready. I looked round, saw that the water bucket was empty, and thought it would be a good thing if I went and filled it, for it would please Mother and also give me a chance to look at the boy. But Mother stopped me, for just then there was the sound of them going, and Dad talking to the gentleman very politely, and the gentleman saying that he would be coming in again. Then Dad said, "Good afternoon, sir," and something joking to the boy, and next he came upstairs, so fast that he seemed to be jumping. He looked far more excited than he had done the time Boozer had ordered the three portraits. He was holding a little white card in his hand, and he stopped just for a moment to look at it, then he said to Mother in a shaky voice:

"What do you think? What do you think?"

I knew something unusual had happened, of course, and so did Mother. She said, very excitedly:

"He hasn't bought a picture, has he?"

"*A* picture?" Dad answered. "*A* picture? ... He's taken two sketches – and..." he stopped, as though he hadn't enough breath to go on; then he said, jerkily, "He's taken the portrait of – Mike Regan."

Dad stood quite still when he said this, and then I saw that he was trembling with excitement, and I thought he was going to cry. There *were* tears in Mother's eyes, and I thought I was going to cry myself, although I was only thinking about it being such good news for Dad and Mother, and not about Liverpool and Uncle Fred. Suddenly Mother said:

"How much?"

"They were two-guinea sketches," Dad answered. "I said he could have them for two pounds each when he said he would take both. But if I'd known he was going to take the portrait I'd have let him have them for nothing; I'd have just thrown them in. I noticed him looking at it all the time out of the tail of his eye. He asked me suddenly to put it up on the easel so that he could see it properly. Of course, I could tell at a glance that he knew something about painting, and that he was a very good judge, too. The first thing he said was he didn't like the background. He said I'd got it too high in tone. Curiously enough, I've thought the same thing myself ever since I made that alteration. Well, next he asked me if it had been exhibited. I told him about the Academy. He laughed and said that was just what he would have expected to happen, unless I'd got influence. Then he asked me right out how much I wanted for it. I was so surprised I couldn't answer, and then he asked me what price I'd put on it for the Academy. I told him thirty guineas. He said he couldn't afford as much as that because he'd been buying a lot of pictures lately, so I said, 'What would you be prepared to offer for it?' He looked at it a long time before answering, and then he said, 'Well, I like it very much, except for the background, and if you'll tone that down a bit, I'll give you twenty pounds.'

For a moment Mother didn't speak. She just stood, staring at Dad, with the tears running down her cheeks, and fidgeting with her apron, like she always did when she was excited or upset. Then she gave me a sudden look, and turned again to Dad, and said:

"Twenty pounds. Twenty pounds. Oh – it's wonderful."

"Twenty-four pounds altogether," Dad said. "Don't forget the sketches!" and then he went on proudly, "Well, that portrait's worth more than that. I let it go, but it wouldn't surprise me that, if he ever re-sells it, it will bring him twice as much. He's not a dealer, of course. He's just a private collector, but then most people like that have their heads screwed on the right way. They pick up the stuff that's likely to go up in value when the artist becomes better known. The most important thing is that it's a start. It's not so good as selling out of an exhibition, but from what he told me, he's just the sort of man who *would* have influence. I just feel I'd like to have another go at Mike Regan, a bigger canvas this time. He'd be only too glad to sit for me, now: the weather's bad and he can't get off fishing."

Mother didn't say anything to this, but after another silence she said:

"Did he give you the money?"

Dad laughed.

"No. Of course he didn't. Didn't I tell you I had to alter the background. And besides, you don't expect even a gentleman like that to carry all that money in his pocket, do you? ... Oh, I'm not worried about that. Look at his visiting card. Just see who he is, and *what* he is."

Dad held out the card for Mother to see.

"Look," he went on. "He's a major. Look at his address. The Carlton Club, London. He told me that he'd served in India and South Africa, but I gathered that he's retired from the Army now, and that he's just bought an estate in the south of England, and I expect he's making a collection of pictures for his new home. He's staying at the Station Hotel all August. That in itself shows that he must be a very wealthy man. He's got his young son with him: a very striking looking boy. It was on the tip of my tongue to suggest that I should do a head and shoulders of him in oils, but I thought it better not to seem *too* anxious to push business. That can be broached later.

Dad stopped. He was almost out of breath. He sat down at the table, and I'd never seen him look so happy. Mother looked happy, too, but in a different way. She went on getting tea ready, and didn't say anything more until we were all sat down. Then she said:

"Well, I shan't feel altogether satisfied about it until we get the money; but when we do get it, I shall know that my prayers have been answered. It will mean that my biggest worry will be over."

I didn't look at her then; so I didn't know whether she was looking at me or not; but I knew what she meant by her biggest worry, and that she was thinking about me and sending me away; and I felt a big lump come into my throat, and I don't know how I managed to drink my tea, and eat, and not burst out crying. I couldn't think any more about it being a good thing for her and Dad. I just wished that Dad had never painted the picture of Mike; that the man who had bought it had never come to Bramblewick. I actually wished he would change his mind about taking it, and go away; and I would have prayed to God that this would happen if I hadn't been certain that this would have been going against Mother's prayers, and that God didn't take much notice of my prayers, anyway. Mother didn't say much more. She kept very quiet as though she was thinking; but Dad never once stopped talking all through tea. He talked just the same way as he had done before the picture was sent off to the Academy. He said he was certain that the Major must be a very wealthy man, and very famous, and that he must know hundreds of influential people. It would be almost as good an advertisement as having the picture in the Academy. You never knew where a piece of good fortune like this was going to end. It might easily prove the first step on the way to Brittany or Naples. If only it meant an end to this wretched photography business, and doing pot-boilers for visitors, it would be something. He did so hope he would get a chance of doing a portrait of that striking-looking boy. That in itself would be at least another three guineas, and it would be worth six times that as an advertisement.

The happier Dad sounded, the worse I felt; and it didn't make me feel any better when he suddenly turned to me and asked me if we had broken up at school, and how long the holidays were going to be. When I told him, he said it was a pity the weather was so cold and wet or I might have gone down on the shore after tea, and caught some shrimps; for the Major had told him that his boy had caught quite a lot one day, big ones, too. Perhaps the Major would allow his son to be friends with me. Perhaps we could go shrimping together if the weather got fine again.

I didn't mean to be cheeky, but this made me more vexed than ever; and I said, quickly, that I didn't want to go shrimping, that only girls and little boys did that, and that I didn't want anyone to come with me when I went for real fish, as they'd only be in the way. I nearly said that what I wanted to do to that boy was to have a fight with him and give him a black eye, but it was a good job I didn't, for Dad got angry, and told Mother that I was getting quite out of hand, and that it was high time I *did* go to a school where I'd learn proper manners.

He wasn't angry for long. He was soon talking about the Major again, and as soon as he'd had tea he got up and said he'd dash over to the studio and, as the light wasn't good enough for him to start altering the portrait, he'd try and make a charcoal sketch of the boy's face from memory, while his mind was fresh. He looked at the empty water bucket as he went for his coat, and then looked at me. But he got hold of the bucket, and said to Mother that he'd fill it and leave it at the foot of the stairs for me to bring up. He went downstairs humming a tune, and as soon as he had gone out, Mother, who had scarcely touched her tea, said very quietly, as though she was really saying it to herself:

"Oh – I *do* hope it's true. I *do* hope it's true."

Then she got up and put her arms round me, and hugged me and kissed me. She didn't say anything. I knew that she didn't really want to send me away, and that she knew it would make me unhappy if she started talking about it. But that didn't make any difference to me, for I knew she was thinking about it, and that while she was sad she was also happy, because there would now be enough money for me to go. I felt more miserable even than when I'd parted with Chicken. It was just awful to think that at last school had broken up, and that my troubles with Grab were over for at least a month; that I might be going off with Mike next week, that there were so many exciting things to look forward to; and that now this thing would be hanging over me the whole holidays, that most likely I would be packed off to Uncle Fred before the holidays were done.

I knew it was no good saying anything to Mother, and that it would make things even worse if I started to cry. The only thing that would stop her sending me away, was to go on showing her that Bramblewick didn't have a bad influence on me, that I was really good ...

Dad had come back with the bucket, and he shouted up the stairs. I got up very quickly and ran down. But I didn't get hold of the bucket straight away, for a marvellous thing had suddenly happened to the weather. It had stopped raining. The sun was shining. Stepping out, I saw that the heavy clouds, which had covered up the sky ever since the storm, were being swept away by a strong westerly wind. The air was warm. It felt like summer again. And as I looked down the street I saw Mike just coming out of Thompson's shop, emptying some tobacco into his pouch, and he saw me, and smiled at me, as though he wanted to talk to me. I got hold of the bucket and went up stairs with it as fast as I dare go.

Mother had started clearing the tea-things away, and although I didn't want to waste any time, and hoped she wouldn't let me, I asked her if I could help her to wash up. She laughed quite happily, and kissed me again, and said it was a very nice kind thing for me to want to do, but as it would very likely start raining again soon, I'd best hurry and get out. I very nearly asked her then if there were any errands I could do, but I thought if I did this so soon after asking her if I could wash up she might think I had done something very bad, and start asking me questions. So I told her I was just going to have a look along the shore to see if I could get her any firewood, and I'd got downstairs before she had time to say anything else.

As soon as I stepped out I felt better, for there could be no doubt that the weather had changed. The sun was really hot, yet the west wind was strong, and would soon make the sea smooth again if it kept on. I stopped thinking of the Major and Liverpool, and thought only of Mike and the *Shannon Rose*. I thought, as I hurried down towards the Dock, that as the tide was down, Mike most likely would be walking along the shore to Browe Beck to get the coble ready for launching as soon as the sea was smooth enough, and that might be tomorrow. I thought I'd go down the slipway first to make sure, and I ran, and I must have been looking towards the sea all the way, or I would have noticed what was going on up the Road. I saw at once that Mike wasn't on the shore. I knew he couldn't have got as far as Garry Nab, for it wasn't more than ten minutes since I'd seen him coming out of the shop. I thought that perhaps he'd gone up to see Bob, and fetch him to go along and help with the coble, so I turned up the slipway again. And it wasn't until I had reached the Dock that I saw a small group of people standing very close together up the Road, opposite to the Mariner's Tavern. They seemed to be looking at something on the ground. There was a woman, too, looking out of one of the bedroom windows of the Mariner's; and suddenly a fisherman came out of the pub with a glass, and some of the people moved to one side, and let him pass between them.

I knew that something bad had happened. At first I felt frightened, and I stopped, just staring. Then I felt curious to find out what it was, and I started up the Road. More people were coming out of the cottages. By the time I got to the place, there were so many people I couldn't see anything, although I knew there must be someone lying on the ground, for everyone was looking the same way, and suddenly I heard a man say:

"We'd best get the lifeboat stretcher and have it ready."

And then the people started to move a bit, and a woman who had just come, and was trying to push her way in front of me, said to another woman who had been there all the time:

"Who *is* it? What's happened?"

The second woman turned round and said in a very hushed voice:

"It's Mike Regan. He's had a fit or a stroke. He was just walking up the Road, and he fell down unconscious, as though he'd been shot with a gun. They're waiting for the doctor to come. But I doubt it's over with him."

The doctor came. He made everyone stand back, and although I still couldn't see Mike, I could hear him breathing, very loudly, as though he was snoring. The doctor was angry. He asked if someone had been giving him brandy, and when the fisherman said, "Aye," he swore at him, and told him he ought to have had more sense than do that before a doctor came, and that it would very likely finish him if he wasn't finished already, for he'd had a stroke. Then he said:

"We've got to get him to bed at once. We'll want hot-water bottles, so someone had better go to his home and get things ready. Bring the stretcher alongside him. Try not to wake him up. The rest of you stand back and let him have some air."

I stood where I was. Everyone kept very

quiet, as though it was a funeral, and I could hear nothing except Mike's breathing until the doctor started to give orders again, telling the men who had got hold of Mike when to lift, and how to lower him on to the stretcher. Then he said:

"Right. Lift now, and walk very slowly."

The people stood right back, and the men began to carry the stretcher down the Road towards Cliff Street. I still couldn't see Mike, because of the doctor who was walking close to his side, but I didn't try to move so that I could. I didn't move at all. I felt awful. I felt too awful even to cry, and wasn't thinking then that it was all up with my going off with Mike in the *Shannon Rose,* although I knew it was so. I could only think of how I loved Mike, and of what a big strong man he was, and of how happy he had looked only a few minutes ago when I had seen him coming out of Thompson's shop. I loved Mike best of anyone I knew except Mother. In a way I loved him more than I loved Mother, for he had never once been vexed with me, or tried to make me do anything I didn't want to do. Was he so ill that he never would get better? Was he going to die?

I watched them carry him round the comer of the Road into Cliff Street. But I stayed where I was, with the people standing all about me; and now they started talking. There were a few visitors, but most of them were Bramblewick women. There was the woman who had answered the other woman, and she must have actually seen it happen, for she kept saying that Mike was just walking up the Road, when he fell forward just as though he'd been shot dead. Another woman said that showed it was a stroke. They always went like that, very sudden. Her husband had gone the same way, only he was just sitting by the fire reading the paper. He slipped down on the floor unconscious, and when they got him round he was paralysed all down one side of his body, and of course he never walked by himself again. I went on listening about other people who had had strokes. Some of them had actually dropped dead. Some of them had got quite well after, but then they'd had a second stroke and died. Then one woman said it all depended on what sort of a life they had led, whether they got well again or not. If they were hard workers, and had been straining themselves a lot, it usually left them paralysed for the rest of their lives. But the worst thing of all was if they drank a lot. Mike Regan didn't drink as hard as a lot of men in Bramblewick, but he drank hard enough when he was at it.

I thought when I heard this, how drunk Mike had been on his last spree, and of how ill he had looked at the end of it, and of how he had said that drink would be the end of him; and I thought of how he must have strained himself pulling the coble against the storm, and then holding it on the sand until the horses came. I suddenly felt I was going to burst out crying, and that once I started I'd never stop. I turned away from the women. I thought first I'd go home and tell Mother what had happened, and how unhappy I was. Then I remembered that she had never liked Mike because he drank and swore and fought, and I thought that if I heard her say a word against him I'd hate her. I thought that I'd best go along the shore, as far away from everyone as I could get, so that I could cry without anyone seeing me or asking me what was the matter; and I ran through the Dock, and down the slipway, and started on towards Garry Nab. But there were some little boys playing cricket under the coastguard's wall, and some visitors a little farther on, and I stopped myself crying until I had got a long way beyond them, nearly halfway to the Nab. I cried then, but I also tried to pray. I said over and over again, "O God, don't let Mr Regan die. Don't let him die." Then remembering about his sins, I asked God to forgive them, and said it was only because he had lost his only brother that he had taken to drink, and that he had tried hard not to drink at all, and that he was always sorry for it after. But I knew it wasn't much use praying unless I kept my eyes closed and I couldn't do this properly while I was walking along the rough shore. I thought it might be better if I went up the cliff to the old place where I could pray on my bended knees, as well as with closed eyes. But I feared if I did this I would start thinking about Chicken all over again as well as about Mike, and that I couldn't bear to be alone in that place; so I went on towards the Nab. And when I was crossing the stepping-stones where I had met Len Fosdyck that day, I noticed a boy all by himself down the scaurs, pushing a shrimp net about in a pool. Although he had his back towards me, I saw at once it was the Major's son.

I didn't stop thinking about Mike, and I didn't feel any less sad, but I did stop crying. I looked up the cove, and along the beach. There was no sign of the Major himself. There was no one on the beach nearer than the visitors I had passed, and they weren't moving my way. I looked at the boy again, then I wiped the tears from my cheeks, and with my fist clenched inside my pocket, I moved towards him.

I didn't know why I wanted to hurt him, or why, while I was still thinking about Mike, my sorrow had changed into anger. It wasn't just because he had pulled a face at me. It hadn't anything to do with his father buying the pictures, because I wanted to fight him the first time I had seen him, and I couldn't have hated him as I hated Grab, for he had never hurt me. I just knew I wanted to fight him, and beat him, more than I had ever wanted to fight or beat Grab. I felt I could have killed him.

I was wearing my sand shoes, and he was still pushing the net along the bottom of the pool, stopping every now and again with his back towards me to see if he had caught anything. I had got quite near to him before he suddenly turned round and saw me. He looked startled, and I thought he looked frightened for a moment, although I had kept my hands in my pockets and he couldn't see that my fists were clenched and ready. Yet he didn't seem to be really afraid of me, for while he didn't actually pull a face, he smiled almost in the same way Grab smiled sometimes, and then he said:

"Hello, what do *you* want?"

His voice was soft as a girl's and he spoke like several other visitor boys I had met; the way Mother called "nice", but I thought stuck-up and proud. He looked stuck-up, and proud too, and while he seemed to be a bit bigger than I had first thought him, I noticed he had thin arms, and that his hands weren't knuckly and hard like Grab's. I thought he wouldn't be anything like as strong as I was. I wanted to start on him straight away; I was trembling inside me, but I answered quite coolly.

"Oh, I'm just looking round."

He looked at me for a moment as though he couldn't make up his mind whether I wanted to quarrel with him or not; but I saw him grip the stick of his shrimping net very tightly, and I thought that the first thing I'd have to do would be to wrench that from him, in case he used it as a weapon. Suddenly he said:

"I think I have seen you before, haven't I? Aren't you the kid that laughed at my pater on the beach a few days ago?"

I had heard the other visitor boys call their fathers "pater", and I knew this was another sign of being stuck-up. I didn't answer. I grinned, to show him that I didn't deny I had laughed at his father, and that I didn't care. He didn't look angry, but he didn't seem to be afraid, either, and he went on:

"You're the artist's kid, aren't you? Your pater's that bally ass with ginger whiskers that paints pictures, and looks as though he's absolutely off his chump. My pater and I went in his shop this afternoon and my pater bought some pictures from him. My pater is a Major and he's got a lot of medals for bravery. I am going to be a soldier soon and I shall probably be a General and win the Victoria Cross. Your pater's absolutely off his chump. He asked me if I like sweets, and actually tried to put a ha'penny in my pocket. My pater allows me five shillings a week to buy what I like with. He's got any amount of money. Your pater looks as poor as a bally church mouse, and six times as silly."

The boy said all this with that stuck-up smile on his face, and without seeming to be a bit afraid of me. I don't know how I managed to listen and keep still. Every word he said made me angrier and angrier. And although it was bad enough to hear him call Dad names, it made me feel even worse that Dad, who always told Mother that sweets were bad for my health and would never give me a ha'penny if I asked for it, had tried to force one on a boy he didn't even know, and who could cheek him like that behind his back. I had stopped thinking about Mike altogether. I could think of nothing but starting a fight and paying for every one of these insults.

I took my fists out of my pockets, and let him see my clenched fists. I stepped near to him and I said:

"Your father's stuck-up and silly, and anyone would laugh at him. *You're* stuck-up and silly, and if you want a fight, come on. Let's start. I'll knock the stuffing out of you."

I watched him carefully, to see if he was going to try to run away, or if he was going to try to defend himself with the shrimping net. He didn't show any sign of moving, and to my surprise, he carefully put the shrimp-net on a stone near the pool, and then smiled at me again and came towards me. I got ready for him. He stopped when he was close and said:

"Do you know much about fighting?"

"I have had a bit of practice," I said, trying hard to keep cool, and watching him in case he tried to trick me. "I know enough to knock the stuffing out of you. Come on. Who'll give the first blow?"

He just laughed.

"Bally ass," he said, "we can't start off like this for a proper fight. We can't fight on this slippery rock. Let's get on to a patch of sand, and do it properly. Really we ought to have a ref. and seconds, but we'll have to do without them. What about rounds? I've got a watch, and if I put it somewhere close we can stop and look at it now and again. Shall we say ten rounds of two minutes each, in case one of us doesn't give the other the K.O. first?"

He said all this quite calmly, without a bit of anger in his voice. I didn't understand half of it, because the way we always fight at Bramblewick after one boy had given the starting blow, was to go on until one of us cried. But I didn't like to tell him this just then. I thought it was a good idea to go up to the sand close by the Nab, and I moved towards it, watching carefully in case he tried to run away. I didn't feel in quite such a temper by the time we had reached it. I had remembered about Mike, and I very nearly started to cry again, but when the boy stopped, and looked at me, still smiling, all my anger suddenly rushed back and I said to him quickly:

"Never mind about the watch. Get your coat off, and start fighting. Come on."

I took my own coat off and threw it on the sands. He took his coat off, but not so quickly, and he folded it carefully before he put it down. Then he turned towards me and reached out his hand.

"Shake," he said.

I had never heard of anyone wanting to shake hands before they fought. If I had, I wouldn't have believed it. I thought it was just a trick and I drew my own hand back. He didn't smile any more. He suddenly crouched, with his left fist clenched and reaching forward, and his face, although it was still pale, looking altogether different, not a bit girlish, but like a man's, and full of real anger. Then he said, in an altogether different voice too:

"Come on."

His face was actually quite close to mine. I struck out at it, with my left and right, almost at once, as I always had done in a fight with any other boy. But I hadn't hit his face. He dodged to one side, and lifted his right arm so that my blows glanced from it, and I didn't know exactly what happened next. I didn't see him strike, I only felt a violent, sickening pain in the middle of my body, and the next thing I really knew was that I was lying on my back on the sand, with the boy kneeling beside me rubbing my stomach with his hands and saying, "You're all right, old sport. You're quite all right." I fought to get my breath, and I had such a sensation in my head and body that I thought I was dying. It was dreadful. Every time I tried to get a breath something in my stomach tried to hold it back. I couldn't see properly. Everything was spinning and it was just as though someone was striking matches all round me and throwing them in my face. Yet soon I began to feel better, and the boy went on rubbing my stomach, and at last my breathing came back, and I was able to move and sit up, and think, and the first thing I thought of was not the boy and the fight, but Mike being carried up the Dock on a stretcher and I burst out crying, and put my face in my hands, and I'd have gone on crying and not caring for anything if the boy hadn't suddenly patted me on the back and said quite kindly:

"I say, old sport. I didn't really mean to hurt you like that. I didn't really. You're all right, you know. You only got a knock-out. I've been knocked out like that dozens of times. It's a beastly feeling, but you'll feel perfectly all right again in a minute."

I knew I had been beaten. But I was crying about Mike, not because of that. Yet I didn't want to tell the boy about Mike. I let him go on thinking I was crying with pain, and he went on talking to me. He was really quite friendly and didn't crow a bit although I knew I would have done if any boy had said he was going to knock the stuffing out of me and I had beaten him instead. He asked me if I really did know anything about fighting. I told him that I'd had hundreds of fights but that at Bramblewick we always fought a different way and that we had no rules and that while I always thought it was cowardly to hit below the belt or kick or bite, or scratch, or have a stone in your hand, the other boys did all these things. He said they must be a lot of bally swine and I said they were, particularly a boy called Grab. I was still crying a bit and my stomach still hurt, but I was feeling better and I told him quite a lot about Grab and Kid and Len and I began almost to like him, although I felt I couldn't say anything about Mike in case he might say something insulting, like he had done about Dad.

Suddenly he said:

"It's a pity you never learnt to fight the proper way. You know, you're quite a strong-looking chap, and I should say you'd be very good at it if you had a bit of practice. My pater had a man give me lessons. My pater thinks it frightfully important that a fellow should know how to defend himself. This man was an ex-army sergeant, and he had been a champion middle-weight, though he had run to fat a bit; and he'd got a kid, much bigger than me, and an awful beast, and we had to box together. The kid just loved licking me, but in less than a bally month I could just do what I liked with him, and once I got him in the bread-basket so hard, I really thought I had killed the beast. The sergeant told the pater that he could make a light-weight champion of me. He said he thought I was just wonderful."

The boy looked very stuck-up again when he said this, but I didn't mind it so much as I had done before, and I thought that he must be a wonderful fighter, the way he had knocked me down and I was thinking of what he had said about the other boy, and about my looking strong, and I was already wishing that I could have lessons, and learn how to knock a boy down so easily. I was thinking less and less about Mike and my unhappiness. Nearly all the pain had gone. I got up on my feet, and while I felt very ashamed of myself, I tried to show the boy that I didn't mind him having beaten me. Suddenly he picked up his coat and took a packet of fags out of his pocket. He took a quick glance along the shore, then he offered me the packet and asked me to have one. I took one, of course, although I was feeling just a bit sick, and he lit it for me and as soon as he had lit his own he blew smoke through his nostrils and said:

"Look here, old sport. I'm bally sorry I talked like that about your pater. I really liked him heaps and he seemed no end of a sport. I only talked like that because you laughed at my pater ... Look here, let's be pals. Let me teach you a thing or two about fighting. My pater's frightfully strict, and I don't get much chance to go anywhere by myself; but we could knock about together a bit, and if any of these bally village boys butted in it would be pretty good sport scrapping with them. I'd just love it. Egg them on, you know, and then just give them the K.O. one after the other. I'm absolutely bally certain I could make you a wonderful boxer in a few lessons. All you've got to learn is to keep your head, and how to guard your body, and the right spots to hit a chap for the K.O. I am absolutely certain I could do it. We could go somewhere straight away and do a bit of sparring. Are you game?"

I still didn't understand all that he said. I still hadn't made up my mind whether I really liked him or not. But I was tingling with excitement. I said to him:

"If a boy knows how to fight properly, and he fights a boy much bigger and stronger than himself who doesn't know how to fight, does it matter very much about the other boy being so big? I mean can he beat him?"

"Absolutely bally certain," he answered. "Look at the way you came for me! If you had hit me on the bread-basket or on the point of the jaw with one of your fists, I'd have gone down just as quick as you did ... Now look here..."

He put his fag down on the stone, and signed to me to do the same. Then he suddenly crouched and put his hands in the same position as he had done before.

"Just you stand like this, and remember that you are going to use your right hand for guarding."

I felt a bit scared, but did as he told me.

"I'll tell you what I'll do," he went on. "I'll move my left hand just like I did when I hit you, only very slowly, so that you'll see it coming. Now watch it, and when you think it's near enough see what you can do with your right hand to stop it."

I watched his left hand. He didn't move it very slowly, but I saw it all the way, and just when it got near enough I whipped up my right and knocked it to one side.

"Bally good," he said. "Now, supposing that it's a fight and you have just done that and you find I am swung off my balance and that I've dropped my guard; what can you do with your left hand?"

He'd got his face quite near to mine again, with nothing in the way, and I saw that I could have given him an awful smack if I had liked. I didn't, of course. I just touched him gently, and he said again it was bally good and that I only wanted a few lessons like this and a bit of practice and I would be wonderful. But just then, he took another glance along the shore, and said:

"I say. I don't want my pater to see us like this. He's frightfully strict. Don't you know of a quiet place we could go to where no one would see us?"

He pointed up the Cove.

"Couldn't we go into the wood behind the mill?"

I looked up the Cove. You could see the Mill Farm from where we were. I thought that at this time the miller himself would be milking his cows, and if we kept to a path which ran above the road, we could get into the wood without being noticed. I said this to the boy, and we got our coats on and picked up our fags. Then I remembered the shrimp-net, but when I reminded him about it, he just laughed and said he didn't want the bally thing, as he didn't think much about shrimping, and it only cost a shilling and that he would like to do some *real* fishing if I could show him where to go. I said I knew quite a lot of places, on the shore, and also inland, where you could catch trout, and he got even more friendly and he asked me what my name was, and when I told him the boys called me Worms, he said it was bally silly and that he'd like to call me Tiger and that his name was Charley.

We walked quickly up the Cove. I did feel pleased about being called Tiger and I felt I liked Charley better every minute and that we might be very good friends, and that it would be wonderful if he taught me to fight so well that when Grab came home I could make up for everything by giving him a good hiding. But then I thought of his father buying the pictures and of my being sent off to Liverpool before Grab got back and, whenever we weren't talking, I thought of Mike lying ill, and that he might actually be dying, so that while I was happy about some things I was very miserable about others and I knew I would start crying again the first minute I was by myself.

I told Charley about the miller and what a fierce man he was, and that we would have to go very quietly along the path. It climbed up the hill a bit, higher than the road, and just before it got to the place where you could get into the wood, there was the miller's garden. I'd often been tempted to go into this garden, for there were some apple and plum trees, as well as gooseberry and currant bushes, but it was so near the mill I'd never dared to go. It hadn't a very tall fence and when we came to a part where it was rather thin, Charley pinched my arm and pointed and whispered:

"I say, Tiger, aren't those gooseberries in there?"

I had already seen them, of course, and that they were covered with very ripe berries; and I had also noticed a plum tree laden with fruit, and some pears.

I didn't say anything, hoping that he would hurry on. But he stopped, and now he whispered:

"I say. We ought to have a few of those gooseberries, you know. Shall we just nip through the fence?"

I was afraid of the miller, but I was more afraid of letting Charley think I daren't do anything he dare do, and I whispered back quickly:

"All right. We can get through here. I've done it dozens of times."

I got through the fence before him. He wasn't long in joining me, and when I stopped for a minute to make sure that no one was coming on the road, he got ahead of me, and went straight for the gooseberries and started eating them. I followed him and gave him a warning nudge, not to waste time doing this but to put some in his pocket, and I did so myself, although I stopped every now and again to listen. We gathered quite a lot, and then, just to show him that I wasn't frightened (although I was) I picked some peas. We got some plums then, and a few apples, although they weren't ripe, and then I thought it couldn't seem cowardly if I warned him that we ought to go. We got back through the fence, and ran along it, and soon we reached the place where Chicken and I had got into the wood, the time the squire and the miller nearly caught us.

As soon as Charley saw the dam, he stopped and got very excited. He asked me if there were any trout in it, and if so had I ever caught any. I told him about our adventure, but I didn't boast too much about the trout, and I told him that if he liked we'd come and have a try one evening, only it was no good now because the beck was in flood with the heavy rains, and the dam itself covered with leaves and branches and stuff that had washed down. I led the way deeper into the wood, and all the time we were munching gooseberries and peas and plums. We came to a place under a tall beech tree, where the ground was almost level and there was no undergrowth, and Charley said it was just the place to start my lessons in, but before we began, we'd better sit down and have another cigarette. He gave me a fag, and although we still had plenty of fruit left, he took a packet of chocolate from his pocket, and offered me half. It was a shilling packet, and after I said how nice it was, he actually made me take what was left of the other half, and put it in my pocket. He said that next time he met me, he'd bring me another whole packet and a shilling packet of cigarettes for myself, but I must never let his pater know that he smoked, because he was terribly strict about things like that; and that reminded him that we must be sure and not stay longer than seven o'clock, because they had dinner at the hotel at half-past, and he'd get into awful trouble if he was late. We'd better begin the lessons at once.

The grass where we stood was still very wet, and the trees, shaking in the wind, dripped water on us. We took off our coats and Charley made me stand as I had done before. He told me I could try and hit him just as hard as I liked, so that I would see how he defended himself. After we'd practised this he made me try defending, and although he gave me one or two punches that hurt quite a lot, I kept quite cool, and I surprised him by giving him one good punch in the place where he had hit me first. It made him gasp, and I thought he was going to get angry and pay me back, but all he said was," Bally good, do it again." I didn't try to, and we rested after this and ate some more fruit and chocolate and had another fag; and then we went on practising. When we stopped we were both quite out of breath. Charley said I was getting on very well indeed, and showed that I was a born fighter, and that as soon as I had had some more practice he'd like to see me have a go at one of the village boys. He'd bet anything I'd give him the K.O. I would have liked to have gone on, but Charley suddenly looked at his watch – which was a real silver one – and said he'd have to fly, as it was nearly half past seven. We hurriedly put on our coats, and started back through the wood. We soon got to the cliff path, and ran all the way along it, and every now and again Charley pulled out his watch to see how the time was getting on, and he seemed very anxious.

We ran down the steps towards the village, to the place where Chicken and I used to meet. I told Charley it would be quicker for him to go straight down past the gas-house. I could see he didn't want to lose a minute, but he stopped and shook hands with me, and said he'd been awfully glad to meet me, and that he'd be on the shore tomorrow morning or afternoon and we'd go and have some more boxing lessons, and that he'd bring plenty of chocolate and cigarettes and also some hooks in case it was all right for fishing. Then he said, "So long, Tiger," and he ran down the steps as fast as he could go.

I watched until he was out of sight. Then I sat down by the side of the path. All the time we'd been in the wood, and running back, I'd never really forgotten about Mike, but I'd been so interested in Charley and in my lessons, I hadn't felt so very unhappy. Now I began to feel more miserable than ever. I thought of all the things that the women had said about strokes and I began to wish that instead of going down the scaurs to Charley and fighting with him, and then robbing the miller's garden and smoking fags, I'd gone up the cliff and prayed. Instead of praying for Mike to get well again I'd actually spent the whole evening doing wicked things, including stealing and smoking. Was Mike dying? Was he dead?

I knew that I'd find out as soon as I got back into the village. Mother would know, of course, for Dad would have found out what had happened, and, as he was friendly with Miss Regan, he would call at the cottage to hear the latest news. I did want to know if he was all right. I thought that nothing could make me happier. But I was terrified of hearing that he was worse, that he was dying, most terrified of hearing that he was dead. I began to cry again. I couldn't make up my mind to go home. One moment I wanted to, because of hearing good news, the next I didn't for fear the news would be bad. But soon I knew I'd have to go, because of it being so late and my having told Mother I was only going to get her some firewood and, as I heard some boys coming up the path from the gas house, I dried my face, and started down the path to the coastguard station. I didn't go very quickly, though I tried to pray as I went. I kept saying to myself, "Oh God, I hope Mr Regan isn't dead, I hope he isn't dead," and as soon as I reached the coastguard's cottage and came in sight of the Dock I began to feel that I would hear that he was all right, for everything in the Dock was going on as usual. The fishermen were standing in front of the lifeboat house, smoking and talking and laughing just as they usually did. Some little boys were playing marbles. There were some visitors walking up the road, and Mr Thompson was standing in the doorway of his shop, looking to see if there were any more customers coming, before he shut up. Nobody looked upset, or anxious. I ran across the Dock, and up Cliff Street, and Mr Thompson actually smiled at me as I passed him. But I stopped running as I got near home; and I walked quite slowly to the door. It was open. I didn't make any noise as I stepped inside and I took off my sand shoes so that I shouldn't have to wipe them on the mat. The shop door was closed, but I peeped through the glass panes in it and I saw the picture of Mike still on the easel where Dad had put it to show to the Major. I thought that it looked more like him now than it had ever done before. It looked alive, exactly as though Mike were standing inside, and that if I opened the door he would speak to me. Suddenly I heard Mother and Dad talking upstairs. I listened and caught the word Regan. I began to creep softly up the stairs, until I was almost at the top and, although the room door was closed, I could hear quite distinctly and I could even hear the sound of Mother stirring something in a pan.

I heard Mother say in a very solemn voice:

"Well, I am glad they did get the priest. It would be a comfort to his poor sister at least, but the whole idea of the last sacrament is against what I regard as the true religion. A man shall be judged according to his works, and nothing a priest can do will make much difference when the time for judgment comes."

I heard Dad cough, as he always did when

Mother said something that he didn't quite agree with, and yet didn't want to contradict. I listened breathlessly for him to go on, for I knew they were talking about Mike, and that I'd hear what had happened to him. And at last Dad said slowly:

"Well, well ... It would be a comfort to her, anyway, seeing that she's a Catholic and it's a Catholic custom. Oh, it's all so sad, and I can still hardly believe it. Why, it was only this morning I was speaking to him and he looked as well as I had ever seen him. And to think it should happen not a quarter of an hour after I had sold his picture. I feel at present I shall never have the heart to do the alterations the Major wants. I'm certain I just couldn't if it wasn't just the background he wants altering. I only hope Mr Fenwick won't want me to do the coffin plate. I wouldn't have the heart to do it – I wouldn't, really. I'll just refuse, even if it means losing business. Poor old Mike."

I knew at last that Mike was dead. I burst out crying and I couldn't help making a noise. I heard Mother give a cry.

"That's Sonny."

I heard Dad move to the door; he opened it, and said, "Hullo, Sonny, what's the matter?"

But Mother pushed him to one side, and moved past him, and she must have understood straight away what was the matter, for she didn't say anything. She didn't try to make me move. She just sat down on the stairs by me and told Dad to go away, and she put her arms round me, and let me cry.

IV

MIKE HAD NEVER regained consciousness. It was a stroke, but the doctor said it had nothing to do with drink, and was due to him having lived a very hard life, and exerting himself too much the day he was caught in the storm. Miss Regan had sent a telegram to the priest at Burnharbour, and he'd arrived just before Mike had died, so that, according to the Roman Catholic religion, his soul was saved, although Mother said again and again that this could make no difference if Mike had really led a bad life, and wasn't sorry for it and hadn't asked for forgiveness himself.

The funeral was on Monday, on the very day when I had expected I would be going off with Mike in the *Shannon Rose*, and the weather was lovely, just as I'd hoped it might be, with only a gentle wind blowing off the land, and the sea smooth and the sun shining clear and hot. But the sea had been smooth enough on Saturday for Bob Walsh and some of the fishermen to launch the coble and bring her round from Browe Beck and haul her right up into the Dock behind the lifeboat house, out of sight of the sea itself.

I didn't go to the funeral, but I saw the people waiting in the Dock for it to begin, and I heard Dad telling Mother about it when he got back. It was held late in the afternoon, so that the fishermen, who had of course started fishing again, would be able to change and go. They were all in their best guernseys and hard black hats, and while they looked solemn none of them looked very sad, and that didn't surprise, for they had hated Mike because he was a foreigner, and because he could catch salmon better than they could, and because, next to his brother Tom, he was the best fighter who had ever lived in Bramblewick. I saw Bob Walsh too, all dressed up, and he did look sad, but I thought that this was because he had been hoping to make quite a lot of money for drink, fishing with Mike, and was disappointed, and anyway, he never did look happy, even when he was drunk.

The most surprising thing about the funeral was that Boozer Lingdale was there. He'd got back from sea by the first train on Monday morning and Dad said he looked quite respectable and quite sober, and that he had joined in the service at the graveside just as though he was a Christian, and that when it came to the coffin being lowered into the grave (which was the same grave Mike's brother was buried in) there were tears in his eyes. Yet that very night he was as drunk as ever, and so was Bob Walsh. Some visitors complained to the policeman about the language Boozer was using in the Dock, and tried to get him locked up. And next morning an even more surprising thing happened, for Boozer came into the shop, and said he wanted to look at Mike's picture. When he saw it, he asked Dad how much he wanted for it, and when Dad told him it was sold he asked him if he would paint another like it for five pounds. This time Dad was really afraid of him and he said he would, just to please him and to get him out of the shop; but he told Mother he wouldn't think of doing such a thing and that he thought it was time Boozer was sent to prison because he was a disgrace to the place.

I felt that I would never get over the death of Mike. I felt far worse than when Chicken had gone, for Chicken, after all, was still alive, and it was possible that I would see him again someday. But although when I closed my eyes I could see Mike's face, and hear his voice, just as though he was alive and speaking to me, and I could imagine being out with him in the *Shannon Rose* on the Bay in lovely summer weather, I'd only to open my eyes and look about me, at the streets, or the Dock, or the shore, or the sea, to know for certain that Mike was lying in his brother's grave and that I never really should see him, or hear his voice again. I had heard that Miss Regan was already trying to sell the *Shannon Rose,* and that one of the fishermen had offered her a pound for Mike's nets the very day of the funeral, but that she'd refused, for they were new and had cost over ten.

The weather went on being fine and hot, and the sea scarcely had a ripple on it. All the other boats were fishing, and some of the village boys were lucky enough to get trips in them during the afternoons, but of course I didn't. It was a good job for me I had found a friend in Charley. His father soon found out about us being together, but when he learned who I was he didn't mind, and wasn't so strict about Charley being away from him so often, so that we could go almost where we liked, so long as he was back punctually for dinner. When Mother found out about it, she asked me if Charley ever smoked or swore or used rude words, or if he was naughty in other ways. I had to tell a lie, for really I thought he was wickeder than any other boy I had met, except for swearing, because I didn't think bally was a real swear, and he scarcely used any other word. But I don't think Mother had ever heard him say this, and while she told me that I must have nothing more to do with him the minute he said or did anything nasty, she said that she did think he was a nice boy and that he spoke nicely, anyway, and had evidently been to a nice school, and that she was glad I had found a friend so that I needn't have anything more to do with the vulgar village boys during the holidays.

She still hadn't said a word to me about my going away. But I knew that she was thinking about this all the time, and that she was only waiting for the Major to pay for the picture before she made her plans, and every time he had been in the shop or in the studio, she asked Dad if he had paid. This made Dad vexed. He said that he knew it would be all right. That it was as clear as anything that the Major was very wealthy. People like that usually put off paying for things until the last moment. If he asked for the money, it would look as though he didn't trust him, and that might easily make him angry and spoil everything: for he had made a charcoal sketch of Charley and shown it to the Major, who had been delighted with it, and said he would like very much to see it carried out in oils, and that if it was a success he would very likely buy it. Dad had asked him if Charley might sit for him and already he had done this several times.

Charley didn't say any more rude things about Dad, but he did hate having to sit still in the studio instead of being with me. The only thing that pleased him about it was that he had noticed the model of the native canoe and that Dad had said it would be a good thing for him to hold it on his knee, while he was sitting and that he would put it in the picture; and when he had finished he would give it to him as a present. I told Charley that it really belonged to me, but that I didn't mind if he got it and kept it while he stayed in Bramblewick, only I hoped that he'd leave it with me when he went away. He promised that he would and also he said if he got a chance he would get one or two of the real arrows Dad had hanging in the studio, perhaps even the bow itself, and sure enough, he did get an arrow, and we made a bow for it, but the arrow was lost the first time Charley had a shot with it.

I liked Charley, yet I never liked him as much as Chicken. For one thing, although I took him everywhere and showed him everything he always acted as though he was boss and knew everything better than I did. He boasted, too. He didn't tell me much about his father, but he boasted about him having been a soldier and of how he had won the

D.S.O. in the South African War for holding a fort against the Boers: and I don't know how many times he told me he was going to be a soldier himself and win the Victoria Cross. He didn't pretend that he had been with his father in the war, but he told me quite boastingly that he had been born in India and that his mother had died of fever, and that he had been sent to live in England with an aunt who seemed to be almost as religious as my Uncle Fred; and he boasted how he played tricks on her, and stole money out of a missionary box, and then tried to set fire to the house because she had tried to keep him in. After this he had been sent to a boarding school, the master of which was an old clergyman who made a hobby of growing roses and won prizes with them all over England. The clergyman thrashed him one day for smoking, so Charley got his own back by chopping down nearly every rose bush in his garden. He'd been expelled for this, and had been expelled from two other schools, and since his father had come home he hadn't been to a school at all, for they had been travelling about most of the time.

Sometimes I really hated Charley, for whenever I tried to tell him about any of my adventures, he'd only listen for a minute or two, then he'd suddenly ask me a question that had nothing at all to do with what I was saying, and when I answered, he would start telling something himself. I knew, too, that he had a bad influence on me, for we never went near a garden but what he'd want to rob it. He liked doing damage to things. He preferred breaking through a hedge into a field than going through the gate, and walking through crops than going round by the ditch. If we came across cattle he would throw stones at them, and one day when he saw a haystack standing by itself in a field he wanted to set fire to it, and he was angry with me because I told him I'd tell the farmer if he did. We were always smoking, and although Charley never swore he encouraged me to swear and use other bad words. I was trying hard to show Mother that I was good, because of Liverpool, which was always hanging over me, but all the time I knew I was getting worse, yet I couldn't help myself, and the thing that pleased me most about Charley was that he went on teaching me to box. Every time we went out together we practised. He never talked or boasted when we were doing this. He hurt me, sometimes I hurt him, yet he never lost his temper. He taught me everything the sergeant had taught him. He said I was getting better even than he had expected, and the only thing against me was that I was a bit slow, but that wasn't so bad as being hasty. I began to feel that if I had wanted to I could have beaten Charley, for I never hit him with my full strength. But I didn't want to beat him. The boy I wanted to fight and beat was Grab, and already a lot of my anxiety about Liverpool was that I might be sent away before Grab got home.

We were now nearly halfway through the holidays. Dad had altered the background of Mike's picture, and the Major was very pleased with it. He had nearly finished Charley's portrait, too, and although Dad hadn't dared to ask him outright, he had dropped a hint about the money, and the Major had said he would settle up for everything when Charley's portrait was finished, and that he would pay another ten guineas for this if it turned out as good as it promised. He had also said that if Dad liked he could send it to the Royal Academy next year. He would either let him have it back or he would send it himself and pay all expenses, and he would speak to a great friend of his who was a great friend of one of the judges, so that it would have a good chance of being accepted. There would be no need to say it was sold. The Major would go to the Academy and pretend that he was buying it for the first time.

Dad was more pleased about this than anything, and he told Mother that he didn't care if he never got another order for photographs. He couldn't stop talking about it. And although Mother said she wouldn't feel satisfied until she had seen the colour of the Major's money, she seemed very happy and said that it looked as though our ship was coming in at last: for she had sold two guinea sketches to a visitor lady, and got the money for them, and one or two other customers were what she called nibbling. One morning, as we were having breakfast, she said outright that as soon as the season had ended and the visitors had gone away she might have a little holiday in Liverpool and take me with her. She didn't say anything about leaving me there when she came back. She talked just as though it would be a holiday and that we should both enjoy ourselves, and Dad said he thought it was a splendid idea, and that I should be able to see the docks and the landing-stage and the big ships and go to the museum, which was just what he had said the last time I had gone, so that it only made me feel worse instead of better. Yet I daren't show Mother what I really felt about it, and what I was most afraid of, and I had to pretend that I was pleased with the idea, although actually I couldn't have felt more miserable if I'd been told that the holidays were over and that I was going back to school tomorrow.

That morning I tried harder than ever to please Mother, by getting water and chopping sticks and running errands, although it was lovely weather and I was dying to get out on to the shore and meet Charley. I didn't meet him until the afternoon as it happened, and by this time the tide was up so that we had to go along the cliff tops. He had got some chocolates and fags as usual, but when he offered me a fag I refused it, and when he suggested that we should first go to the miller's garden and get some plums, I told him straight out that I wouldn't and that I wasn't going to do anything that might get us into trouble. I suggested that we should go down the cliff and make a hut in the place where Chicken and I had ours, which was on the right side of Garry Nab. But Charley just laughed the same way he laughed the first time I met him, and he said scornfully that if I was afraid of going to the garden he would go by himself and then he would go to the dam and fish, and that as soon as he got tired of that he'd go and set fire to the haystack.

I knew that it was no good my trying to tell Charley what I had got on my mind and why I was specially afraid of getting into trouble, for he'd have soon interrupted me and started talking about something else. I just stuck to what I had said, and he went on taunting me until at last we were really quarrelling. I thought it would end in a fight because Charley called me Worms and said I was a funk, and I called him stuck-up, and swore at him. I quite lost my temper and wasn't a bit afraid. I was certain I could beat him now that he'd taught me all about boxing, even if he *did* think I was a bit slow. But we didn't fight. We suddenly noticed a boy coming along the path from Garry Nab carrying a heavy basket over his arm, and we both stopped to look at him. I knew him, of course. His real name was Harry Walters, but the boys called him Ginger because he had ginger hair. His mother, who was a widow and rather bad-tempered, kept a small pastry shop in the Road. Ginger was a year older than Grab. He had left school before Christmas. He was big and strong, but slow and stupid, and he'd never been a bully like Grab; and although he had often mocked me because of my clothes, and kicked my backside for sport, I had never hated him much, and since he had left school he had never troubled me at all, perhaps because he had no time, for his mother kept him hard at work the whole day long. It looked as though he had been on an errand for her now and that he was fetching her some eggs from the Mill or one of the farms beyond. Anyway, the basket looked very heavy.

I had no wish to interfere with Ginger. If I'd been by myself, I wouldn't have stood watching him, I'd have just stepped over the cliff edge until he had passed, for I always tried to avoid any of the village boys if I could. I didn't think Charley was going to interfere with him, until he whispered, not very softly, either:

"I say, Tiger. Look at that bally chap's hair. You could light a cigarette with it."

I forgot my quarrel with Charley, I was so pleased to hear him call me Tiger again. But I didn't wish him to get into trouble and I gave him a warning nudge and whispered:

"Ssh. Don't let him hear you."

Ginger was coming steadily along, knocking off the thistle heads with a hazel switch he carried in his free hand, and he didn't seem to notice us until he got quite near, and when he did he just went on switching at the thistles. We were standing in the path right in his way, and I stepped back a bit. But Charley didn't. He had taken a fag out of his pocket, and he was smiling in his most stuck-up way, and just as Ginger was right in front of him, he said:

"I say, old sport. Would you mind if I lit my cigarette on your hair. I haven't got a match."

Ginger stopped. He just looked surprised at first, and he stared at Charley with his mouth gaping in a very stupid way; then he said roughly:

"What did you say about my hair?"

Charley laughed.

"I didn't say anything about it, you bally ass," he answered. "I just wanted to light my cigarette with it ... It *is* on fire, isn't it, or is that its natural colour?"

Ginger was staring for a moment as though he still didn't understand. Then his eyes seemed to flash, and he swore and he struck at Charley with his switch. But Charley must have been ready for this. He jumped to one side, and Ginger, without trying to hit him again, turned on me, and gave me a stinging crack across my bare legs. Before I could save myself he followed this with another crack across my face. For a minute I was dazed with the pain. I couldn't have done anything to stop him hitting me again if he had wanted to. I couldn't even see him properly. Then suddenly I heard Charley, shouting at the top of his voice:

"Go on, Tiger! Fight him. Fight him! Keep cool, Tiger. Fight him properly."

I don't think I *did* keep my temper. I was so angry I wanted to kill him for hitting me when I had done nothing to him. But Charley's voice *did* make me steady and remember the way to fight and I looked straight at Ginger and shouted at him:

"Come on, Ginger. Put that stick down and fight."

He looked surprised, but of course he didn't look frightened and his eyes were angrier than ever. He shouted at me:

"Fight *you?* I'll half kill you if you call me Ginger again."

"Ginger! Ginger!" I nearly screamed at him. "Put

that stick down and come on."

He put the basket down first, then he laid the stick on top of it; and then without any more warning he came for me, not as though he was going to fight, but just like Grab did with me or any other small boy, to get hold of me so that he could cuff me or kick my backside. In the old days, I'd have just put my hand to my face and thought of nothing but protecting myself from the blow. Instead of this, I crouched just as Charley had taught me and I stepped to one side as he reached out his hand, so that his face was close and with nothing to protect it. I don't remember whether I kept to the proper rules of fighting then. It wasn't like practising with Charley, for Ginger wasn't facing me properly, or trying to fight the proper way. I don't remember exactly how I struck him or even which fist I used. But I did strike him and I must have done it very hard, for although he didn't fall like I did when Charley hit me first, he dropped on to his knees, and he put both his hands to his face, and howled, and when I looked at him properly I saw that his nose was bleeding, and bleeding more than I have ever seen a boy's nose bleed before. I wasn't frightened. I wasn't sorry for what I had done. I just looked at him, feeling terribly excited, and I felt even more excited when Charley got hold of my hand and shook it and shouted:

"Bravo, Tiger! Bravo! Ask him if he wants anymore."

I turned to Ginger again. I shouted at him:

"Have you had enough, Ginger? I can easily give you more if you want it."

He was still howling, but he started to get up. I stood back quickly and crouched, for I thought he was coming for me. As soon as he got to his feet he just looked at me once, and he howled:

"You've broken me nose. I'll tell me mother. You've broken me nose."

And then with one hand still holding his nose, and still howling that it was broken and that he was going to tell his mother, he started running along the path towards home.

For a moment or two I didn't notice that he had left the basket. I was too surprised and too excited to think that I had beaten a boy big and strong as Ginger so easily and so quickly. I watched him run and I shouted after him, "Baby, baby, run away," just like the Bramblewick lads had often shouted after me, and I also shouted, "Tell your mother if you like, Ginger, I don't care."

Then Charley shook my hand again and he went on saying, "Bravo, Tiger, bravo!" until Ginger had almost reached the village steps and then I did notice the basket and Charley did too, and he said:

"The bally ass! He's left his basket. Let's see what's in it."

He moved to it and pulled away some brown paper. Then he shouted:

"I say! It's full of eggs." And he picked one up and showed it to me.

I ought to have known by the way Charley looked at the eggs, and then at me, that he was bent on mischief. I ought to have known that I had already done enough to get me into trouble. But my leg and face, where Ginger had hit me with the stick, were hurting more than ever, and I was still terribly excited, and when Charley picked up the basket and said, "I say – let's throw the bally lot down the cliff," I didn't say a word against it. It was a wicked and stupid thing to do, but I just thought how funny it would be seeing all the eggs rolling down the cliff and getting smashed, and it happened we were opposite a place where the cliff, although it was just clay, was very steep for a long way down and had no ledges, or grass growing on it. But I didn't think of throwing them all down together, and I was sure I wouldn't have thrown more than a few. I'd have been too frightened after I had seen one or two get smashed. But Charley was carrying the basket, and when he reached the edge he just gave a shout, and then, before I could say a word, he tipped the basket and let the whole lot go ...

They *did* look funny. Some of them smashed straight away, but most of them went rolling down right to the bottom just like a lot of ping-pong balls and actually bouncing before they smashed, and some seemed not to smash at all, for when it was all over, we could see them lying at the cliff bottom where the steep bit ended. It was only then that I began to think what a stupid thing we had done and I began to feel frightened. Charley was just about to throw the basket down too, but I stopped him, and said that we had better run away as fast as we could, before anyone saw us, and I looked along the cliff path both ways and was relieved that no one was in sight. Charley put the basket down, but he didn't seem a bit sorry for what he had done. He just laughed and slapped me on the back and said:

"Serve the little beast right ... I say, you did give him a smacker though, Tiger, you were just wonderful ... Come on, what shall we do next? Shall we go into the wood and have a quiet fag?"

I thought it was a good idea to go into the wood, and as soon as we had got well away from the basket, I began to feel quite brave again, particularly as Charley kept saying how wonderful I had been in fighting Ginger, and that it'd served him right because of the cowardly way he had hit me with a stick, and I was very glad that our own quarrel had ended. I felt braver and braver when we reached the top of Garry Beck valley. I began to wish we would meet some more village boys and have another fight; and when we looked down and saw the miller's garden, and Charley asked if we should pop in for a plum or two, I just led the way and Charley didn't try to get ahead of me as he usually did. We got in at the same place, and as the gooseberries were now finished, we made straight for the plum trees, and I didn't bother once to stop and listen if anyone was about. I was actually up a tree filling my pockets with fruit, when I heard a warning hiss from Charley. I looked down and saw him pointing down the road towards the mill, and there was the miller's eldest daughter, a very big, strong woman, running towards the garden as fast as she could and carrying a thick stick. I jumped from the tree, and as I did so a rotten branch cracked off with the noise of a gun. The woman gave a shout and I could tell that she was making for the place in the fence where we had got through. Charley had waited for me. I led the way to the opposite end of the garden. We had to start forcing our way through the actual hedge, which was made of thick thorn, and had some barbed wire in it too. Neither of us had stockings on. I was halfway through when my breeches seat caught on the barbed wire and I had to heave with all my strength to get loose. But I got through all right, and Charley did too, and as the woman hadn't got round the corner of the fence yet, I knew she couldn't catch us, and I hoped that we might get into the shelter of the wood without her seeing who we were. But she must have got a clear view of us as we ran, and she must have known who I was from my back view, for just as we got over the gate into the wood I heard her shout my name, and then she shouted in a way that terrified me:

"I know you, if I don't know who the other lad is. You needn't think you've beaten me. *I'll* teach you to come robbing folks' gardens. The police sergeant will be waiting for you when you get home."

V

I WOKE UP next morning before Mother called me (although I could hear her moving about downstairs) and I wondered at first if everything that had happened yesterday afternoon, and when I had got home, had been a terrible dream. But I soon realised that it wasn't, and that I'd done for myself, for almost the last thing Mother had said was that when we went to Liverpool she was going to see the master of a school that Uncle Fred had told her about in a letter, to see if I could go to it, and that she only hoped that not a word of what had happened would ever reach the ears of the master or he would very likely refuse to have me for fear of my having a bad influence on the scholars. The thing that had upset her most of all was that I hadn't just been wicked myself, but that I had led another boy into temptation and that by doing this something even worse might happen, for if the Major found out about it, it might make him very angry, so that he wouldn't want to have anything more to do with Dad.

I knew, of course, I had been wicked. I had been disobedient, I had fought and used bad language. I had let Charley smash Ginger's eggs without saying a word against it; I had stolen from the garden and smoked a lot of fags and I had told Mother a lot of lies. But neither the miller's daughter nor the police sergeant had come last night to tell Mother about the garden, so that she didn't know anything about the worst thing I had done; and about Ginger, I thought it was awful that I should be blamed for it all, for really I had only done what any other boy would have liked to do if they had dared. Yet because of what Mother had said about the Major finding out about Charley, I hadn't dared to say how Charley had first cheeked Ginger, and that Ginger had struck me, and that it was Charley who had smashed the eggs. Ginger himself had told nothing but lies.

He had gone home and told his mother, and the first thing she had done was to make him take her along the cliffs to get the eggs. She'd seen what had happened to them, and when she got back she had come straight to Mother, and gone for her. She wouldn't go inside the shop. She had just stood on the doorstep and talked in a loud voice for everyone to hear. She said that Harry was just walking back along the cliff tops, when I, and a visitor boy, started throwing stones at him, and when he tried to stop us we'd gone for him and one of the stones had hit him on the nose. Harry said I'd thrown the stone and that I'd sworn at him. I had told Mother that this was nearly all lies and I think she had believed me when I said that I'd fought Ginger fairly, and that he'd hit me first. But I had to let her think, that I had smashed the eggs, and this was really the worst part about it, for there were four dozen, and Mrs Walters had needed them for making some cakes for her shop, and she had said that unless Mother paid for them, she'd go to the police station and have me summoned, so Mother had paid her five shillings.

I could see, when I raised my head from the pillow, that it was going to be another lovely day, and it was already so warm that I could scarcely bear to keep a blanket on me. It would be just right for being out on the scaurs, and catching flatfish in the sandy pools at very low water. You didn't catch these with a hook, but walked in your bare feet very very carefully, and when you saw the head and fins of a fish half-buried in the sand you had to tread on it suddenly. Then with your hand you could get hold of it, and throw it out to the dry rocks. I thought that I would have just loved to have tried for some flatfish today. I shouldn't have had to go to any forbidden places. I could have told Mother exactly where I was going, and she would have been as excited as I was if I'd come home with a big plaice or dab. I had once caught a real sole, so big that it had lasted for three meals and Mother had gone on praising for days; and I knew that I got more real pleasure out of doing things like this than anything I did with Charley; and this made me hate Charley, for I really had tried hard to be good yesterday, and it was all his fault that I had got into trouble. I wouldn't have dared to go into the garden if it hadn't been for him. Right from the first he had made me wickeder and now I had to stick up for him for fear that the Major might be angry and not buy the pictures, although it was this very money Mother wanted to send me to Uncle

Fred's school. If I did tell Mother it was all Charley's fault, would it make her feel different about my going to school? Would she want to tell the Major himself and have a row with him, even if this meant he'd get so angry he wouldn't take the pictures? I thought that I'd do anything to stop her leaving me in Liverpool, and yet when I thought how she'd feel if she didn't get the money, and how disappointed Dad would be, I knew I just couldn't, and that I would have to go on taking the blame, not only for the eggs, but for the garden too, when Mother learnt about it.

I could still hear Mother moving about downstairs; but I couldn't hear Dad, so I thought he must be out. He hadn't said very much to me last night. He had left Mother to say nearly everything. He was vexed, of course, about the eggs and Mother having to pay for them, yet the thing that seemed to upset him most was that Mrs Walters would find out who Charley was and go up to the Station Hotel and start a row with the Major himself. And he said that he thought Charley was the last sort of boy to throw stones or interfere with anybody, because he always seemed so nice and quiet. I wondered what Dad would have thought if he'd known that Charley had called him a bally ass and said that he was absolutely off his chump; and if he'd known about the arrow he had stolen, or if he could have seen me trying to stop him setting fire to the haystack; yet I hadn't dared to say anything.

I cried last night until I had fallen asleep and I

had to keep holding my breath to stop myself from crying now, for I couldn't think of anything that didn't make me miserable. I couldn't think of the fight itself (which I was really proud of) without thinking about the eggs. I couldn't think of how I might now beat Grab without thinking that I would be in Liverpool when he came back. Mother had told me to ask God for forgiveness for all I had done, but I hadn't, because it was no use when I still had such a lot on my conscience and hadn't told her the truth, although really by telling lies I was helping her against myself. Besides, I didn't think that God took the slightest notice of my prayers, or he wouldn't have let Mike die. If Mike hadn't died, I mightn't have met Charley at all, or if I had I wouldn't have had time to be friends with him. Everything I thought of brought me back to Charley. I felt I hated him. I felt that if I did meet him again I'd fight him and give him much worse than I'd given Ginger. Then suddenly I thought of him in a different way. I thought of how he'd always said he was my friend, and of how he'd given me things and taught me how to fight. I wondered whether if I told him all that had happened, and what trouble he'd got me into, he would be sorry, and tell his father that he was to blame. It might get him into trouble because of his father being so strict, but that couldn't make his father angry with Dad, and it would show Mother that I hadn't been so bad as she had thought, and that really I had taken the blame for her sake.

That might please her very much and even

make her change her mind about sending me to school. When she learnt how wicked Charley really was it would show her that going to a nice school didn't always make a boy nice. The Major would, of course, pay her what she had paid for the eggs and he would still be friendly with Dad, so that he would get the money for the pictures all right, which she might use for getting some new furniture or for moving into another house, as she'd so often said she'd wanted to.

Instead of hating Charley, I began to feel again that he was my friend and that he would take the blame if I told him everything. I could still take the blame for the fight, but then Mother had never forbidden me to fight if a boy attacked me first. I thought that the best thing I could do would be to see Charley as soon as I could this morning, and I began to feel almost happy. Then I remembered about the garden, and that even if the egg business was settled my troubles wouldn't be over. It would be no good pretending that I hadn't been in the garden, for the woman must have seen me up the plum tree. It was a wonder that the sergeant hadn't come last night. He was certain to come this morning.

Suddenly through the attic window I heard two different footsteps coming to the street door, and then Dad's voice, and I thought it must be the sergeant coming now. I heard the street door open, and Dad say very politely: "Come in, sir," but the next thing I heard was the Major's voice just as the shop door was opened and closed again. I was glad it wasn't the sergeant, but I soon thought it might mean something just as bad, for the Major had never called so early in the morning before. I strained my ears to listen: I couldn't hear anything with the shop door being closed, and a moment later I got another shock, for Mother suddenly opened the living-room door and called for me to get up. Although she said just what she usually said, I could tell by her voice that she was as upset as she had been last night.

I got out of bed and started to dress. I could scarcely fasten my braces my hands were so shaky. I kept wondering what the Major had come for, and whether it was about me and Charley, and when Dad came upstairs to the living-room, I felt worse than ever. Yet I thought I'd best know what it was, so without putting my shoes on I began to creep quickly downstairs, keeping to the corners where the wood didn't creak. I could hear Dad and Mother talking. Yet I couldn't make out a word they said, even when I got almost as far down as the living-room door. They were almost whispering. Then suddenly I heard Mother walking across the floor towards the door and I had scarcely got up to the bedroom before she opened it, and started coming upstairs. I hurried up to the attic and pretended to be looking for my shoes, expecting, of course, that she was coming to see me, and that the Major must have found out everything. But she stopped at the bedroom, and I heard her moving across the floor, and then opening a drawer. She closed it and then went straight downstairs. I was too frightened to try and listen again to what she and Dad said, and anyway, before I could have got down to the door, Dad was going down the stairs, and in about a minute I heard the sound of the street door being opened and closed, and the Major's footsteps in the street. Dad came up again. He and Mother went on talking for quite a long time, yet I couldn't hear anything until Dad almost shouted: "Oh, rubbish, rubbish." And the next thing was I heard him go downstairs and slam the front door.

I had washed, and got all my clothes on, yet I waited for Mother to call me again before going down, and when she did I went very slowly, for I was terrified of what she was going to say. I thought that if she had found out about the garden and started going for me again, I wouldn't be able to stick up for Charley any longer but that I'd just tell her everything.

She was standing at the fire when I opened the door with her back towards me. When she turned I daren't look at her. I daren't look at her when she said: "Hullo, Sonny," and kissed me and told me breakfast was just ready, for very often she was nice to me like this before she started going for me properly. I sat down at the table, still not daring to look at her or say anything, and when she suddenly came behind me and said: "Mind, Sonny, it's hot," and put my plate down on the table I nearly shouted with fright, and I thought I was going to be sick when I looked at the plate and saw a fried egg.

Yet she didn't start going for me. She poured herself out a cup of tea, and went on doing things in the room, stopping every now and then to have a drink; and she asked me if my breakfast was nice and if I had enough sugar in my tea, just as if nothing at all had happened, although her voice was queer, and I knew that she was really more upset than she had been yesterday, and that it must have been something to do with the Major's visit. I wondered whether she was just waiting for me to start confessing to all I'd done. I felt certain the sergeant hadn't been, yet every footstep I heard in the street made me think it was him coming and I knew that I had only to hear his voice and I'd have to tell, and that I couldn't do this without telling everything about Charley. I wasn't a bit hungry. Usually I liked fried egg better than anything, but every mouthful seemed to stick in my throat and choke me, and I had to leave quite a lot. Mother didn't say anything about this. When I sat back she asked me if I had had enough of everything, and then without any anger in her voice she said that she hoped that I had thought over all that had happened yesterday and asked for God's forgiveness and that I'd made up my mind never to do anything wicked like that again. She didn't wish to punish me, but after what had happened she felt that she couldn't trust me not to disobey her, so that for today at least, although I could go out, I would have to come back every hour and shout up the stairs so that she'd know where I was. She didn't ask me to do anything for her and she kissed me again as I moved to the door, yet it didn't make me feel a bit happier to have her so nice and kind. It made me feel worse, for I was certain about her being specially worried and I had an awful feeling that something specially bad was going to happen soon. I didn't want to go out either. I was terrified at the thought of meeting the sergeant. Yet I never stopped thinking about Charley, and that, whatever else had happened or did happen, it couldn't be so bad if he took the blame for the eggs; and I was certain he would be on the shore and that I could find him before the first hour was up. So I hurried out as fast as I could go, and didn't feel so bad when I looked down the street to the Dock and saw that the way to the shore was clear.

But I didn't find Charley. I went along the shore, and up the cliffs and to every place where I thought there would be a chance of meeting him. I came back home when the hour was up and shouted up the stairs, and as Mother just shouted "All right, Sonny," I went off again and this time, although I was more afraid than ever of meeting the sergeant, I went up the Road and up the Bank to the front of the Station Hotel, but he wasn't in sight. I knew, of course, that the Major didn't allow Charley to come out every morning, and that sometimes they went off together for the day, and I wouldn't have thought anything about it if I hadn't been so anxious to meet him.

The tide was very low, and the sea hadn't a ripple on it. It was just perfect for getting flatfish, and the sun was so hot it would have been nice just to wade. Yet, when I had a walk down the scaurs after I had been home the second time, I didn't try a single pool, for fear I might miss seeing him, and the last hour before dinnertime I spent walking up to the hotel and waiting there behind the wall which hid me from the road. But I didn't see Charley.

I didn't see the sergeant either, although each time I had gone home I had expected to see him coming out of the shop, and when I had got back from the hotel, I stood and waited in the mouth of an alley up the street for several minutes before I had the courage to go in home. But I knew he couldn't have called, for neither Mother nor Dad said a word to me when I went upstairs, and they were silent almost the whole time we were having dinner. But they both looked very worried, and I could see that Mother had been crying, and I felt more certain than ever that something bad was going to happen, something that had nothing to do with me. I wondered if it had anything to do with the Major. I wondered if Charley would know what it was. I got up to go out before Dad did, but instead of going straight out I waited for a moment at the foot of the stairs and listened, and the only thing I heard was Dad saying again: "Nonsense, nonsense," then his walking to the door, so I had to go.

I went out looking for Charley all that afternoon, and getting more and more miserable because I didn't find him. I came back home at the end of every hour, feeling just the same about the sergeant when I went in, and not feeling any better when Mother shouted all right. I began to wish that he would come and get it over. I thought that if he didn't come before bedtime, and I hadn't seen Charley before then, I shouldn't be able to hold out any longer, but that I'd tell Mother everything; and when at last I went in for tea and found Dad and Mother just as silent and worried-looking, I felt I couldn't sit still through the meal and not burst out crying. And we had scarcely started tea when I heard heavy footsteps in the street and I just knew it was someone coming to the door, and sure enough, there was a loud rap almost at once, and a man's voice calling Dad's name. It was the sergeant. I was too terrified even to cry. I just sat still, staring at the tablecloth while Dad got up and went to the door. He shouted down the stairs:

"Yes. I'm here. Do you want me?"

"I'd like to have a word with you, if you'd come down," the sergeant answered.

Dad went down. They both went into the shop and closed the door. I don't know how long they stayed there. I could hear their voices, the sergeant's very deep and talking more than Dad, but I couldn't make out a word either of them said. I just sat still, staring at the tablecloth, wanting to cry, yet not being able to, feeling like I did when Charley hit me, yet everything still instead of spinning round. And Mother was still, too. She didn't make a sound until suddenly the shop door opened and the sergeant, without saying a word, went out, and Dad began to come upstairs. Then she gave a little cry, and stood up, waiting. He came up very slowly, just as though he was carrying a bag of coal on his back. He stopped at the stair top and Mother moved towards him, but he came in, and although I daren't look at him I knew that something terrible had happened, and I thought the sergeant must have brought a summons for me to go to the police court and be tried for robbing the miller's garden. And the first thing he said was:

"It's terrible! Oh, it's terrible!"

I did look at him then. I saw him flop down in a chair near the door, and he was actually crying. I started to cry myself, but I stopped the very moment Dad looked at Mother and spoke again in a shaky, crying voice:

"It's the Major," he said. "It's the Major! He's *gone!* The sergeant came to know if I knew anything about him, if he had tried to get any money out of *us*. I thought he was just fooling. I told him the Major had been in this morning and asked for the loan of five pounds, and that we had let him have one. The sergeant said it would be the last we'd see of that money. He's a fraud. He's a criminal. He's wanted by the police in several places for getting money under false pretences. But he must have smelt a rat. The sergeant got to know about him too late. He went off on the nine o'clock train, taking his boy with him. He hasn't paid his hotel bill since he came here. He actually borrowed five pounds from the manageress too, as well as what he got from us ... oh, it's a shame, it's a shame. And the picture – and all he promised to do for us."

Dad put his hands to his face and started to cry again. I looked at Mother. She was standing, just staring, not at Dad, not at anything. Her face was white, but she wasn't crying. She just looked as though she was going to have a fight with someone the proper way, cool and steady and not afraid of anything, and she just said in a steady voice:

"Well, I have always thought it's wrong to judge anyone until they have given proof of their wickedness. But right from the beginning I never in my heart trusted that man. I felt this morning that we were not acting wisely in letting him have the pound. It was against my judgment. Yet I didn't think that anyone could be so wicked and mean as to rob people in our position. I wouldn't have believed that anyone could have done such a thing."

She stopped, but only for a moment, and then she went on just as steadily as before, not looking at Dad or anything, but staring straight in front of her.

"He will be caught and punished. God will see to that. It's very cruel. It's very hard on us. It will mean there will be no trip to Liverpool. That Sonny will have to go on here for the time being. Yet I blame myself for thinking that a man like that could be God's instrument for the answer of my prayers, and I would rather he had that pound that he has stolen from us than we should touch his money, soiled by dishonesty. I only hope that he hasn't defrauded anyone worse off than we are ... That poor boy: imagine what is going to happen to him, with such a father, with such an example before him ... It's no good crying, anyway. We've just got to try and forget all about it, and go on believing that our prayers will be answered in the end. That lady, who is nibbling about the water-colour of the Dock, said she might look in again this evening, and I think I am going to land her. The season's not over yet. Come on. The tea's all getting cold. Come on, Dad."

She looked at Dad, and Dad suddenly got up and instead of looking sad he looked angrier than I had ever seen him look before.

"Oh, how *can* you talk like that?" he shouted. "How can you be so cool about it? The man's robbed us. He's a rogue. He's a scoundrel. He ought to be put in prison. What's the good of talking about a paltry guinea sketch after what he said he was taking? Mike Regan's picture! Twenty pounds! The two sketches. The portrait I've painted of his son. Oh – I'd like to kill him!"

Dad got hold of his hat and opened the door. Then he turned on Mother and shouted at her.

"I don't want any tea. It would just choke me the way I'm feeling now. I'm going over to the studio and I'm going to tear the portrait of that man's boy to pieces."

He clattered downstairs, and slammed the street door behind him. For a moment Mother just stood where she was, staring again and not saying. Then I started to cry, and the next moment Mother had put her arms round me, and she was crying, too. I felt I had never loved her so much as I did then, for although she didn't say anything I knew that she was terribly sad about the Major, and not getting the money to send me to school, and being robbed of that pound, and about the things I'd done, and yet I knew that she was glad that she wasn't going to take me away and leave me in Liverpool. It made me feel sorrier than I had ever felt for the wrong things I had done, that in future I would never do anything that would make her unhappy. I went on crying and I didn't look her in the eyes, but I started telling her the truth about Charley and the eggs, and then I confessed about the garden. And when I'd done, she scarcely said a word against me. She just kissed me, and said that in spite of it having been wicked, and that it was wrong to tell a lie even to help other people, even your own parents, I had been brave, and now that I'd confessed everything, I could start again with a clean slate, and prove that I was just the sort of boy she could be proud of, and that I'd grow to be a good man. She said that she wouldn't ask me to come back every hour when I went out. That from now on she would trust me, and that I'd better have my tea and go out now as the weather was so lovely, and that if the police sergeant came about the garden we should just tell him everything, and she was sure it would be all right, when he and the miller knew I was sorry and that I'd never do it again. I stopped crying and Mother did too. She made some fresh tea and we went on with the meal just as though everything was all right again. I couldn't feel very happy, of course. I knew that Mother must have been feeling terribly disappointed, for she must have believed a bit that she would get the money. I felt very sorry for Dad, for it must have looked to him as though the Major was going to make him famous, and I felt that if I'd been him I'd have wanted to smash up Charley's picture, for he had spent almost as much time on that as he had done on Mike's, and it wasn't likely that anyone would want to buy it. I felt sad about all this; but I couldn't help feeling relieved that I'd got everything off my conscience, and that I wasn't going to Uncle Fred's school after all.

VI

NOTHING MORE WAS ever heard of the Major, although the police did their best to catch him. He had defrauded other people as well as Dad and the Station Hotel. He owed money to several tradesmen in the place, and the very morning he had borrowed the pound from Dad, he had gone into Mrs Thompson's shop, and asked Mr Thompson himself to oblige him by changing a cheque for ten pounds, which Mr Thompson had done. Of course, the cheque was false and not worth a ha'penny, and for weeks after Mr Thompson would show it to anyone who went into the shop, and would tell them the whole story of how he had been defrauded.

I don't know whether Dad did smash up Charley's picture or not. I didn't see it the next time I went into the studio, but I noticed he had put the model canoe back where it had been before, so that I never got it as I had hoped I would. I didn't see Mike's picture again, and it wasn't until a long time after that I learnt that Dad had sold it to Boozer without the frame, which he thought would do for his next Academy picture, and that Boozer had given it to Miss Regan as a present. I never heard Dad mention the Major's name again.

I did miss Charley. In spite of everything, I had liked him. I don't think he knew that his father was a wicked man. I don't think that he meant to be wicked himself. Mother said it was just the poison coming out of him and that probably he wouldn't have been wicked at all if he'd had a mother to look after him. Yet he *was* wicked, and he'd made me do things I wouldn't have thought of doing if I'd been by myself, so that I was really glad that he'd gone, now that I was trying so hard to be good and not yield to temptation. I didn't hear anything more about the miller's garden. I think the woman must have shouted that about the police sergeant just to frighten me. But I was careful always to keep out of the way whenever I saw her, and while I passed the garden many times on my way to the wood, and the apples were getting ripe, I was never even tempted to go in. I went on being good for the rest of the holidays. I helped Mother all I could by doing things in the house and running errands. I caught quite a lot of flatfish for her, and got plenty of firewood. The lady who had been nibbling bought the sketch, and several other visitors bought pictures, but of course that didn't make up for what the Major had promised to pay, so Mother had to give up the idea of having a holiday in Liverpool, and it looked as though Dad would have to keep on taking photographs all through the winter, although he said he was going to start another Academy picture when the visitors had gone: a landscape this time.

I knew that Mother was very pleased with the way I was behaving, for she actually said that I could now go as far as Browe Beck, and into Garry Wood, so long as I didn't go near the dam. I didn't swear any more, I didn't smoke, and I didn't have any fights, although I was tempted to give Len Fosdyck a good hiding one day when he was with Kid and another boy, and they shouted after me. Yet I hadn't forgotten my lessons and my fight with Ginger, and when I thought of going back to school, I wasn't frightened, like I had been before. I wasn't sorry that Ginger had told everybody that I had beaten him with a stone. Nobody in the place knew that I could fight the proper way. I thought that I wouldn't pick a quarrel with Grab. I'd just wait until he started twisting my arms or pinching me, or something like that, then I'd ask him if he'd have a proper fight, and I'd surprise him and all the other boys too. When I had beaten him, there wasn't anyone else who would be likely to trouble me. There were several other boys in the school who'd be very glad to see Grab beaten, who even might be glad to be friends with me, so that I could start again on my own, but whenever I thought of this, I thought about Chicken, and that no matter how many other boys were willing to come with me, I'd never have anyone like him. I often thought of Mike too, and when the last day of August came, and the end of the salmon fishing, I felt very sad: for this was a great day among the fishermen, particularly if it had been a good season as this one had. All the boats, except those used for winter fishing, were launched up, and when this was done every man gave two shillings to the Fishermen's Arms to pay for a hot pot, which was a mixture of several sorts of drinks, and everybody who liked could have some. Usually this had meant Mike starting on one of his sprees, and fighting with someone, and when I saw the men crowding round the Fishermen's Arms, talking and laughing, I couldn't help but look at the *Shannon Rose* still lying above the Lifeboat House, with a notice board fastened to her to say that she was FOR SALE, and thinking about Mike himself lying in his brother's grave in the old churchyard.

It was a Saturday and the last real day of the holidays when the boats were launched up. The weather was still fine, but not so warm, and you could tell by a feel in the air that summer was nearly over and that autumn was coming. Most of the visitors had already gone away on the morning and midday trains. There was scarcely anyone along the beach in the afternoon when the fishermen started drinking. I decided to have a walk along the beach as far as Browe Beck and see if I could find anything, for although the sea hadn't been rough once the whole month, and it was no good scratting, there was a chance of finding something a visitor had lost, like the purse that had got me into such trouble last November.

I walked very slowly, keeping to the cliff bottoms and carefully searching all the little sandy coves where I had noticed visitors sitting or having picnics. There were plenty of bottles and sardine tins and paper bags and orange peel and old newspapers, but I didn't find anything that was valuable or worth keeping as a curio, and I couldn't feel a bit happy. I was sad about Mike, and the other fishermen rejoicing because they had had such a good season. I was sad that the holidays were over. Although when I thought of it, I was quite excited about the idea of having a fight with Grab, and making up for all he'd done to me, there was nothing very nice in the thought of going back to school and having Slogger boxing your ears all day long and having to wear boots and stockings again. It was better than Uncle Fred's school, of course, but even if I did beat Grab and some of the boys wanted to be friendly with me, I was still, and always would be, a foreigner, just like Mike had been.

I got more and more miserable as I walked along to Garry Nab, and still not finding anything, not even a bit of firewood. I thought of Mother and of how good I'd been lately, and that I could now walk on to Browe Beck without having to tell any lies about it when I got home, and that she trusted me, and never seemed to be a bit worried as to what I had been doing. I started to think of the times I'd been bad, and I thought that although I didn't like getting into trouble, it really was more exciting doing things like that than being good. I knew I didn't want to start being bad again, but the more I thought about swearing and smoking and telling lies and going to places that were forbidden, the more I felt that these things were exciting, and that not doing them was dull and that I couldn't go on much longer without yielding to temptation.

I got to Garry Nab without finding a single thing, and I went round the Nab, and up the Cove, which was a favourite place for visitors and where I thought there was a better chance of finding something than anywhere else. I searched among the dead seaweed at high-water mark, keeping a sharp look-out for the miller's daughter, and I had just made up my mind that there was nothing when I found something raffled up with a piece of weed that looked like a fishing line, but when I looked closely, I saw it was a bit of a shrimp net, all torn and raffled. I pulled it out and looked at it closely, and I thought at once that it must have been the remains of the very shrimp net Charley had left on the scaur the day we had first met. It was no good, of course, yet I started trying to unraffle it, and as I did so I thought of that day, of the fight and of all the wicked but exciting things Charley and I had done together, and I wished like anything I was just seeing him now for the first time and that everything was beginning all over again. I felt as though I could just see him, and hear his voice, and I felt so sad I nearly started crying. And then suddenly I just felt wicked again. I felt that I *must* do something wicked. I thought of a certain word, which I knew was a wickeder word than bloody or damn or blast because it was disgusting as well as being a swear. I went on thinking about it, and it was just like something buzzing inside me, trying to get up through my throat and out of my mouth. And suddenly I said the word, just like a whisper at first, and then right out loudly. I threw the net away then. I looked all round me, for I felt frightened, as though someone might have been standing near and heard me, then I ran out of the Cove as far down the scaur as I could get, and then I said the word again and again, shouting it out, and I said every other swear word I knew, including God and Christ. I was frightened. I knew I'd been wicked again, but I didn't feel anything like so miserable as I had done before, when I was good, and I didn't feel so lonely. It was just as though I had met Charley again, and that we were starting off to Garry Wood, to have my first fighting lessons, and I began to think of something else I could do that was more wicked and exciting.

And it was then that I looked along the beach towards the village, and saw a small boy running along towards me and waving his hand. I didn't recognise him at first. And even when he got close up, and I saw his face and heard him shout my name, I could scarcely believe that it was true that it was Chicken himself, and I just stood staring at him, thinking that it must be a dream and that I'd soon wake up. He was dressed in the same clothes he'd gone away in, although they didn't seem quite so big for him, and he looked different in other ways for he was very clean, and yet when he spoke, it was just in the same voice and I knew very well that it wasn't a dream, yet I was so surprised I couldn't do anything but stare.

Before he got right up to me he started shouting:

"Hey, I've been looking everywhere for you. I went round to your house, only I daren't ask your mother, but I met a lad and he told me he'd seen you coming along the shore ... How are you getting on, eh? I've come back! I've come back!"

He came right up to me, but I still couldn't say a word; and I could feel my face getting quite hot.

"*By!* I am glad to see you," he went on, "I am glad to be back. It's champion being back after being in Leeds. Didn't you know I was coming back? Didn't you expect me?"

I said, "No," and I still hadn't got over my surprise, and yet I was beginning to feel happier than I'd done for weeks and weeks and that it was just wonderful to see Chicken again and hear his voice and feel that he was with me.

"Haven't you heard anything?" he went on.

I said, "No," and then he said, "Haven't you heard about Mother and Bob Walsh?"

I said, "No," again, and he went on quickly, like he always used to do.

"Eh – I thought you'd have heard about it. Mother's going to get married to Bob Walsh. That's what we've come back for. She didn't like being in Leeds, and I didn't either. She had too much work to do, and the preacher chap she worked for was always going for her and making her go to Chapel as well as cleaning it, and I had to go too, *and* to Sunday School. She said she'd rather be back at Bramblewick any day, and Bob wanted to marry her before she went, so at last she said she'd give up the job and go back. I don't think much of Bob Walsh, because he drinks just as much as Father did, but he never wants to hit you like Father did, and he told Mother he wouldn't drink so hard if she married him, and work harder and live in a proper house. I don't care, anyway. I'm glad to be back. I don't like living in a big town. Shops are all right, but if you haven't got any money to spend, you're not much better for seeing them. Bob Walsh is tight this afternoon. Did you see him? But he gave me a penny, and I bought some sweets. Would you like one?"

Chicken offered me a bag of sweets that had already got sticky and dirty, but I took one, and then he said:

"Where were you going when you saw me? Are you looking for things? Has anything washed up lately?"

I had at last recovered from my surprise at seeing Chicken although I could hardly believe what he had told me about his mother and Bob Walsh. Yet I knew it must be true, and that Chicken had come back to Bramblewick to live, and although I had felt just the same as I had always done about him talking too much and chewing sweets, I was so pleased I could have hugged him. But I thought straight away that I must never show him that I liked him as much as that, or he might start getting cheeky, and I began to think of all the things I had done since I had seen him last, particularly of how Charley had shown me how to fight, and of how I'd beaten Ginger. So I pretended I wasn't really a bit surprised that he'd come back, and I told him quite coolly that I was going on to Browe Beck and that if he liked he could come with me. We started to walk up towards the cliff, and I let him go on talking about Leeds and the Chapel where his mother had worked, and what he'd seen in the train coming home, and how glad he'd been when the train had come through High Batts tunnel, and he'd got his first sight of Bramblewick Bay again. He hadn't had any real adventures, of course. But I didn't mind listening to him. I was happy. And I thought that once I started telling him about mine I'd never stop.

THE END

Before you go ...

Thank you for reading this book. If you enjoyed it, please help other readers by recommending it and reviewing it online.

About the author

LEO WALMSLEY was born in Shipley, West Yorkshire, in 1892, and was brought up in Robin Hood's Bay on the North Yorkshire coast—the 'Bramblewick' of several of his novels.

After serving with distinction in the Royal Flying Corps in the Great War, where he was awarded the Military Cross, he determined to become a writer, beginning with boys' adventure stories.

He lived for a while in London before returning to Robin Hood's Bay in the late 1920s, then settled in Fowey, Cornwall and wrote *Three Fevers* (1932), the first of his 'Bramblewick' novels, followed by *Phantom Lobster, Foreigners,* and *Sally Lunn*.

In addition to over twenty books, he wrote 200 or so short stories and articles prior to his death in 1966.

Details of Leo's other books and further information can be found at

www.walmsleysoc.org